THE MURDER
OF KARLA PLANE

A Novel

PETER BEALE

Peter Beale
18 Rue de Montpensier
75001 PARIS, France
beale.publishing@gmail.com

Printed Worldwide
First Printing 2023
First Edition 2023

THE MURDER
OF KARLA PLANE

NEWPORT, RHODE ISLAND

7.50am, Tuesday, October 29, 1929

Weather: Partly cloudy, chilly, with a high/low of 49º/33ºF

It was cold outside. Huddled in front of the open fireplace of the Black Pearl Tavern on Thames Street, the Poben brothers were having breakfast before setting off to look for work.

"You see what it says here in the paper, Lake?"

"What's it say, Kale?"

Kale took a sip of coffee, cleared his throat, settled his spectacles on the thin ridge of his nose and set to.

"It says here, '*Murder Mansion on Bellevue,*'" Kale said, his voice a high treble curious in such a thickset man. "'*Newport, Sunday, October 27, 1929, this afternoon, residents of the fashionable Bellevue Avenue section of Newport joined hundreds of policemen, detectives, firemen and Boy Scouts in the hunt for the slayer of Mrs. Karla Plane, the wealthy widow of Sir Kobe Plane, deceased. She was shot and beaten to death yesterday morning in her home, Planetree House, No.6 Bellevue Court, adjacent to The Elms, by a man thought to be a maniac. Staff living in the Carriage House on the premises reportedly heard nothing.*'"

"Boy Scouts? To catch a maniac?" Lake said.

"Yeah," Kale said, still reading. '*Two negro women met a stranger with a bloodstained face on a lonely road…*'

"Then it ain't you, an' it sure as hell ain't me," Lake said.

1

"Listen, will ya?" Kale said. *'A lonely road crossing the woods in Morgan Park...'*

"That's miles away. How old's that paper?"

"I just finished tellin' ya. Couple of days. Why? Anyway, stop interrupting," Kale said and continued to read while sipping his coffee. *'The two negro women, Miss Jane Jackson and Miss Evelyn Wood, said the man's face was bloodied, and, after he tried to accost them and they got away, Miss Jackson said to her companion: "That man has been in a fight with a woman who clawed his face."'*

Kale sniffed. *'The story of their meeting with the man in the woods was the first real clue obtained by the police in their dragnet following the slayer's flight from the Plane mansion. Chief of Police Sermon Hazard, Sheriff Brenton, District Attorney William Clarke, several private detectives, and State troopers, immediately held a conference with the result that the woods were combed, but without avail.'*

Lake laughed. "What? They think this guy would be settin' there, waiting for the troops to show up?"

"Sush," said Kale, going on: *'during the hunt for the man in the woods several police bloodhounds and Alsatian search-and-rescue dogs lead the chase for the quarry. Despite approaching from different directions, they converged at a sandpile in the woods about 200 feet from the spot the two negro women said they met the strange man the night before.'*

"How's that possible if she was murdered in the morning?"

"He must have holed up, waited till dark."

"Says who?"

"Whynot just listen? *'While Policeman Thomas Brady of nearby Jamestown was beating among brush near Bailey's Beach where it meets Cliff Walk, he found shreds of a pair of trousers on a wire fence...'*"

Lake whopped so loud other diners looked up from their breakfast to frown at the brothers and the unseemly noise.

'...Detectives who examined the torn pieces of cloth said they tallied in colour with the trousers reported to have been worn by the men seen to enter Mrs. Plane's home about an hour and a half before her body was found in the dining room by the maid.'

"Men, plural? Next there'll be ghosts," Lake said. "They must invent this stuff to sell their paper."

"'*Earlier in the day,*' Kale continued over the interruption, '*detectives hunting for the slayer on the outskirts of the woods, detained an itinerant gardener, Johnathan Buck, 33 years old. Buck, well-known in the community, told conflicting stories about his whereabouts the previous Saturday and the reason for his presence in the woods. After he was questioned at intervals for approximately 8 hours, District Attorney Clarke ordered him held this evening as a material witness before Justice of the Peace, Mr. Henry Coddington.*'

"Buck, you say?" said Lake. "If that's our Buck, he was drunk as a skunk Saturday over at the White Horse. Surprised he didn't fall into the harbour."

Kale took off his glasses to glare at his brother. "Keep it up and I'll stop, and you won't know what comes next." He shook the paper straight, read forthrightly on. '*Buck said that on the day of the murder he was employed as usual by the Rector of Trinity Church, on Queen Anne Square, to tend to the parish gardens, but that he left the place at noon to keep an appointment with his sister, Mrs. Georgina Mahler, for dinner at her house in Brewer Street, where he remained until evening and then slept in the small shed at the bottom of her backyard. State troopers were immediately dispatched to question Mrs. Mahler and Mrs. Evelyn Paisley, caretaker at the church rectory.*

Mrs. Mahler, it was reported, told the detectives she had not seen her brother for several weeks, while Mrs. Paisley said that Buck did indeed appear at the rectory the previous Thursday, but remained there no later than 9 o'clock in the forenoon. When confronted with these denials of his story as to his whereabouts, Buck then repudiated part of his original statement.

When he was remanded in custody to the Newport Jail, Assistant District Attorney, Elmwood Easton, was heard to remark that the two negro women and Mrs. Patrick McCarthy and Mrs. Jacob Roberts, neighbours of Mrs. Plane, who saw a strange man enter the slain woman's home shortly before noon, could none of them identify Buck. Miss Jackson and Miss Wood in fact declared that the man they saw in the woods was at least 48 years old, tall, and thin, wearing a blue suit and blue cap, whereas Buck was a head shorter, had no scratch marks on his face and dressed like a tramp. Nonetheless Buck was denied bail and held over pending further enquiries.'

"Sonofabitch," Lake said.

'While the woods were being scoured for the murderer, Dr. W. Taylor Chambers and Dr. Arthur D. Barnes of Tufts University, Boston, performed an autopsy on the body of the slain woman, and announced, contrary to the belief of the officials investigating the murder, that Mrs. Plane had not been shot dead. They said that the deep wounds in her face and body had evidently been made with a stiletto-shaped file or an ice-pick, but that the woman had died from a fractured skull and a concussion of the brain. The autopsy also developed that the woman had been outraged by her slayer, and it is believed that the murderer stabbed her repeatedly with the stiletto before he used the bludgeon.'

"Outraged?" Lake said, leaving the word lying there.

Kale sniffed again, tweaked a long hair from his left nostril, and went on. *'When the police began their first search of the Plane mansion, after the maid, Miss Molly Malone, found the naked body in the dining room half hidden under rugs and gave the alarm, they sought evidence of theft as they assumed a burglary had been interrupted. "Not so," District Attorney Clarke said. In examining one of the rugs thrown over the body by the murderer a detective found a strand of hair. It was of a reddish colour and the detective was inclined to believe it was torn from the slayer's head in the struggle with his victim, but, DA Clarke said later, he believed the hair was blood-stained and had been torn from the head of Mrs. Plane. The District Attorney also said that Mr. Charles Ripley, the fingerprint expert of Cranston County, had obtained distinct fingerprints on a bureau in Mrs. Plane's room which he believed were those of the assassin. The fingerprints will be compared to those of Buck, the material witness in the investigation. DA Clarke said his investigation indicated that robbery was not the motive for the killing and that there was evidence that Mrs. Karla Plane fought desperately for her honour before her head was crushed in by the murderer. He added that the autopsy also revealed that her slayer struck her across the face with the bludgeon, as her right jaw was badly fractured.'*

"Bastard," Lake said.

+ + + +

4

PARIS / KARLA

1925

Karla is a waitress in a Parisian cafe, the Café de L'Époque. It was founded in 1826 and is nearly 100 years old.

It is also 17.30 on this fine Tuesday afternoon in May. She is late for setting up her station in the dining room. As she comes in the front door both the Maître D, Gaston, and the chef/owner, Monsieur Aubert, yell at her. Mentally she gives them the finger, goes into the ladies to change into her work clothes and comes out wearing the quintessential black, long-sleeved dress with white collar-and-cuffs and white pinafore of a French maid. Through the lace curtains in the windows the passersby on the Rue du Bouloi and the Passage Vero Dodat see her laying place settings for the evening rush hour traffic as the first customers arrive. Klara closes her eyes. Over the sounds of a bustling business, these are her thoughts, one by one:

Je suis serveuse dans un café Parisien.

I can say that in three other languages.

Because I have had three boyfriends.

One Italian: Sono una cameriera in un caffè parigino.

One English: I am a waitress in a Parisian Cafe.

One German: Ich bin Kellnerin in einem Pariser cafe.

But I am still single…and nearly 30!

A waitress in a cafe. Stupid.

Because I must be stupid…je dois être bête…

Despite my baccalauréat and degree in history from the Sorbonne.

5

And all that happened in the war.

AND…and nearly 30!!!

Thirty is a dangerous age, Karla!

She is still embedded in her thoughts as she approaches a table for four, where a bourgeois family, the Duponts, are out for dinner, a rare treat after years of deprivation. In Karla's imagination they look like hogs, two big pigs and two piglets.

M. Dupont says, "Mademoiselle?"

Karla ignores him.

M. Dupont says, "Pardon, Mademoiselle?"

Karla ignores him.

Mme. Dupont: "Mais elle est sourde ou quoi?" She snaps her fingers at Karla. "Nous n'avons pas de menus!

Karla ignores her.

Now the Maître D, coming up to Karla's elbow, says, "Arrête de rêver…"

Karla shakes her head, remembers where she is, stops dreaming, smiles at the Duponts.

The little piggies smile back.

She gives them their menus.

The restaurant fills up, waiters and waitresses hustle, a syncopated rush of food, busboys, wine being served, orders given, orders taken, checks, cash, checks, cash, turn the tables, relay places, knives, forks, glasses, food, checks, cash, as the evening becomes night, and drags on and on until finally - finally! - the restaurant empties, the last tables are cleared, the staff start to leave.

With the flick of her hand to the Chef locking up, Karla is last out.

She walks across the Rue des Bons Enfants into the Palais Royal, around the dark, cloistered galleries until she comes to a tiny door opening into an artist's studio above which is a mezzanine, 20m2, a bed, a bathroom, her home.

Up there Karla opens the taps on a free-standing, old-fashioned, white, claw-footed bathtub, and, while it fills, slowly undresses out of her waitress's uniform watched by an 18th century courtesan whose half-naked portrait hangs on the wall above the tub.

As Karla slides into the tub the warm water closes over her shoulders. She sighs and shuts her eyes. Away she goes on her dreams…

Of a gallant, young lad, handsome, an 18th century Milord Anglais. Who comes up her tiny staircase, smiles on seeing Karla in her bathtub, winks at the portrait, takes off his wig, unbuckles his sword, undresses, and glides into the warm water behind Karla. She leans back into his embrace. He fondles her breasts…Karla dreams while the water goes lukewarm, then cold.

Early the following morning, on the empty terrace of the cafe, M. Aubert, his chef's uniform unbuttoned, is at a table doing accounts. As a shadow goes across his ledger he looks up.

"Mon Dieu, Karla? What are you doing here at this hour?"

"Pardon, Monsieur Aubert. I am sorry to trouble you, but I am here to tender my resignation."

"Nonsense. Sit down, child. Tell me what is the problem? You sound like you have caught a cold."

"I would prefer to stand."

"I am an old man, Mademoiselle. You have been with me for what, ten years now? When I invite you to sit down, please sit down."

The voice is imperative. Karla sits. Looks at her hands. She shakes her head. A thought won't go away. 10 Years! Silence. She looks around. The tables are pristine, already laid in immaculate order waiting for the first customers to arrive.

"Do you know in all this time I haven't once sat here on your terrace." Karla knew she was being bold.

The Chef smiles. "Rules are made to be broken, n'est-ce pas? Now, have you had your breakfast?"

"Merci, non…"

"I thought not. There are fresh croissants on the bar. Please take one and make yourself a coffee. Come back and we will talk."

Croissant in one hand, café crème in the other, Karla returns to sit across from M. Aubert. Silence. Aubert writes in his ledger.

Karla is not sure how to resume the thread of their conversation but decides to make a confession. "I never thought at 20 I would still be here at 30…"

"Just as I never thought at 16 when I started here as a busboy, that I would one day own this place and still be here at 75." The old Chef nods, smiles. "Sometimes the paths we take are not obvious. So? What is the problem?"

"My life has no purpose."

"Being of service is an honourable métier, Mademoiselle. You are still young and, if I may be permitted the observation, very attractive. Perhaps you do not know how much joy you bring to this place by your presence?"

"Please, Monsieur!'

"I do not say it to flatter you. I only make the observation. But if you wish to resign, what will you do?"

"Honestly? I don't know. I always imagined I'd be happily married by now with a couple of kids in my own home."

"For that you would need a husband."

"Of course!"

"Strange you did not mention him?"

"I have not been very lucky in that department."

"With respect, is it down to luck or your lack of judgement in the attachments you make?"

"Monsieur!"

"Let me see…if memory serves, you met all your partners here. Customers of ours. You flirted with them - "

"They flirted with me!"

"A distinction without a difference. And like a badly blended dressing, too much oil, not enough vinegar, the hoped-for emulsion never takes place." The Chef chuckled at his own wit. Then pats her hand. "What did you see in that skinny German?"

"Markus? I knew him from before the war. He was a musician with wonderful hands…"

"He was a philanderer who conned every woman from here to the Louvre with no more money in his hat other than what he could sponge off you. That lasted two years?"

"Off and on."

"And when you finally kicked him out you traded him in for that car dealer, the Englishman. With a lot of different cars and no manners. Just because someone shows up in a second-hand Bentley…"

Karla laughs. "I was tired of walking and taking the metro…besides, I would never have seen Deauville if it wasn't for him."

"Isn't that where the gendarmes came to arrest him?"

"He escaped though…"

"And they arrested you instead!"

"And you had to bail me out!"

Like old friends, they are both laughing.

A Pause.

"So why do you want to leave?" M. Aubert said.

"I love it here, but…Monsieur Aubert, I have these dreams…there are things I want to do…and if I don't do them now…" (suddenly Karla is crying) …"I do not want to be 75 and know I never tried…you understand?"

"Yes. Yes, perhaps I do. This is what comes from your liaison with that Italian fellow, the anarchist. Change the world by destroying it, instead of giving thanks for our survival through…ah, here comes Madame, my wife. She will set you right."

Dressed In an exquisite turquoise cheongsam, a diminutive Vietnamese woman comes into view with a chow on a turquoise lead.

"Phuong," her husband says, "Karla wants to leave us. Please talk her out of it."

With no preliminaries and no hesitation, Phuong sits next to Karla, takes her hand, palm up, traces Karla's lifeline with the tip of her finger and says, "Have you chosen your death music?"

Taken aback, Karla says, "I have not given much thought to my death."

"It is why we are born," Phuong said. "Just as you did not know when you would be born, you do not know when you will die. But you can know the music you would like to hear when you go."

"You see?" said the Chef, and returned to his patiently waiting accounts.

+ + + +

BERLIN / 1054 KILOMETRES NNE of PARIS

Auf den Punkt gebracht

Markus was a silent child who grew into a singular, solitary man of habit whose best company was himself. His parents separated shortly after his birth in a garret on Stahlstrasse, just a stone's throw from Charlottenburg Palace. Appalled at what they had brought forth there was never a question of another child. Sibling less, on his second birthday, Marcus's mother vanished, leaving behind the memory of overlarge, soft breasts which tended to smother her infant son. Left holding the family bag, his father was furious on learning of her departure via the stammered explanation of the mother's maid who had helped Madam pack her valise and been assured Monsieur would pay her any wages due. What really made him angry was he had planned on doing the same thing to her. Such treachery! Duped by a wife he affectionately called 'mein süsser kleiner Dummkopf.'

Markus' recollection of life back then was that of a ping-pong ball passed from parent -to-uncle-to-aunt-on-and-on in houses and flats of ever diminishing importance, to all intents and purposes an orphan. Even the various nannies, governesses and tutors, hired at no little expense, would refer to him as 'where's thingy' when they forgot which corner they had dumped him in.

Out in his pram one day being pushed along the Ku'damm by Nanny Ursula, an exceedingly stout woman from Pomerania given to window shopping, he observed this worthy suddenly stop, bend over, and pick up a

11

small coin whose bright shiny face was greeted with, 'Ach, was haben wir hier?' After examining it she showed it to him before carefully cleaning it and putting it away in her purse. 'The beginning of every great fortune is just such a small coin,' she said. It was one of the few lessons from his childhood to prove profitable. As he grew, wherever he went, he made a habit of carefully scanning the pavement as he walked and noting in the diary he kept the exact place he chanced to find a coin in the street. Two pfennigs outside the Opera House on Bismarckstrasse, he wrote. Or half-a-crown three steps down the entrance to the Underground at Ealing Common. Or 20 centimes in front of Juvenile's on Rue Richelieu. Being frugal, the coins were never used, but kept in a succession of packed glass jars that accumulated and now had their own locked armoire in his office.

Older, he invented another habit. Whenever he ate in a restaurant, which was most days since he had an aversion to cooking for himself, he habitually paid and tipped himself the exact amount of the bill and tip he gave the waiter.. If, by way of example, after dining at Scott's in Mayfair, the bill was £12 and he left a £2 tip, then on returning home to Hans Place, before retiring to bed, he would place an order with his broker to buy £14 of stock in a conservative, dividend-paying, Utility - be it water, gas, electricity, whatever - which dividends were then used to buy more shares in the future.

Thus, by the simple expedient of keeping his eyes open and maintaining a healthy appetite, over the years he became rich. Filthy rich. None of which he felt inclined to explain to Herr Dr. Minor when he was summoned to meet him.

Markus was unaware of the fact that on the same day the meeting was to take place his name was mentioned in the 1st Arrondissement of Paris, in fact exactly at the moment he was being ushered, with considerable ceremony, into the first-floor conference room of Deutsche Bank located at 5 Alexanderplatz on the corner of Bernhard-Weiss Strasse. For the occasion he was using an alias, Herr Kenneth Opalbe, as engraved in italics on the business card he now handed to Herr Dr. Heinz Minor, a senior director of the bank in a department which would come to be called Wealth Management. Dr. Minor handed off the card to an underling while inviting

Herr Opalbe to be seated at the head of the impressive mahogany table, fully five metres long, shining in layers of immaculate veneer.

"We have not met before, Herr Opalbe," said Dr. Minor, taking the opposite seat.

"Is that a problem?" said Markus.

"On the contrary, it is a pleasure!" Slightly flustered, Dr. Minor adjusted the red silk handkerchief peeking out of the breast pocket of his impeccable pinstriped, pale-grey mohair suit as he studied his client. "We make it a central point to personally meet and get acquainted with our distinguished clientele."

"Provided they have a large enough account parked in the vaults downstairs," said Markus.

The banker permitted himself a thin smile. "You may jest, Herr Opalbe, but these have been difficult times in our industry. Very difficult. The war…"

"The war?"

"Reparations. The Allies don't just blame Germany but demand financial restitution for the whole thing, as if we alone are responsible, to the tune of 132 billion gold marks. As the premier bank in Germany, we are heavily involved. They know we cannot remotely pay such a sum and must borrow from the Americans. In theory the Treaty of Versailles was supposed to pay for damage to the civilian economy of all parties, including rebuilding Germany. In practice they lend us the money so we can repay back to them interest on what they claim for a debt they conjured out of thin air."

"In what way is this germane to the letter I received from you calling for this meeting today? I hope I am not overdrawn?" Markus laughed, the laugh of a man living large, certain of his good fortune and substantial bank balance, whose chauffeur-driven Maybach limousine was parked outside the bank, with a lively young lady reclining in the backseat smoking a cigarette in a long ivory holder.

Notwithstanding all his training in the highest echelons of commerce, something about Herr Opalbe's smug contentment began to get under Dr. Minor's skin. The man wore clothes evidently bought in a thrift shop yet had the most expensive motor car made in Germany waiting for him downstairs. His shoes were a disgrace, and his stockings did not match. For a rich man he was thin where he should have been fat. And, most annoying, they needed him but he, it was evident, did not need them. Glancing down at notes he had made at the Berlin headquarters of the Bank on the Kurfürstendamm, Minor felt at a loss.

He had met with his senior colleagues to strategize an appropriate method of obtaining the investment secrets of this individual in front of him. None could fathom how a young, non-professional, basically unknown in the financial community, could have amassed such a huge portfolio of stock, principally public utilities all over Europe and America, worth an immense fortune in cash before, during and after the war. Such a sum would greatly enhance the tightly stretched capital of the bank. What could persuade the owner of this treasure to make such an investment? Ask any competent strategist and he would tell you, attack is the best defence, so the good Herr Doktor cleared his throat and said, "As concerned custodians of the well-being of our clients we feel it our duty to draw attention to any aberration we see in the market. In our view it is substantially overpriced."

"Indeed," Markus said, neither statement, nor query, although he did raise his eyebrows a fraction.

"A well-balanced portfolio will eliminate some risk in such a market."

"Some?" This, with a question mark.

"The Authorities have asked us to identify certain accounts…"

"Which 'Authority'? Hitler's lot or the Weimar? Is this because you think I'm a Jew? Auf den Punkt gebracht, Herr Minor. Cut to the chase, please."

Dr. Minor felt his cheeks redden. He was not accustomed to being addressed in such a tone. "It is not that at all," he said. "They are desperately looking for money to further their expansion. Specifically, large amounts whose provenance cannot be adequately explained. There are suggestions of irregularities. Of our complicity in facilitating certain transactions. We suspect they will next send in inspectors and forensic accountants with the aim of closing those accounts they deem suspicious and confiscating their funds."

"Provenance? Irregularities? Complicity? Was meinen sie, Herr Minor?"

"Please do not be alarmed, Sir. We raise these issues to make you aware of what hyperinflation and frothy over-speculation may do to the most well managed portfolio. Our suggestion is that you consider an investment in the capital of our bank as a safeguard."

'Really? I'm not sure I see the connection. Here I was thinking we were all making out like bandits in the Roaring Twenties," said Markus.

"Only in America," Dr. Minor said.

"Then it's simple," Markus said. "Move my account to New York."

+ + + +

NEWPORT, RHODE ISLAND, IN THE
BLACK PEARL

9.23 am, Tuesday, October 29, 1929

'*District Attorney William Clarke said that although the furniture in nearly every room of the house was overturned, and desks, closets and other places in which Mrs. Plane could have secreted valuables had been ripped open, many things which a thief would be inclined to take had not been disturbed. However, during their search of the house, the detectives had found a tin trunk, untouched, under the bed in Mrs. Plane's room, which contained a rope of pearls, a pearl bracelet, two diamond rings, two ruby rings, a necklace of matched emeralds, $28 in bills and thousands of share certificates in stuffed manila envelopes, the values of which were still to be ascertained. Another envelope Mrs. Plane had left on the telephone table in the hall contained $7, also untouched. In conclusion, pending further enquiries, Attorney Clarke said the investigation indicated that robbery was not the motive for the killing.*'

"There are more holes in his theory than in Swiss cheese," said Lake.

"An' I'm out of coffee," said Kale. "All this readin's dried up my throat." He held out his cup to his brother.

"You think I'm a waiter?" Lake said.

"C'mon, Lake. I'm doin' the work here. Be a sport."

Grumbling, Lake went to the coffee urn where it was placed next to the cash counter. While filling his brother's cup he noticed the cashier bent over to listen to a radio on the shelf behind him. The cashier was frowning. Glancing at Lake he said, "You heard this?"

16

"What?" Lake said.

The cashier turned up the volume.

'...*Hundreds of billions were wiped off Wall Street this morning when the market opened to panic selling as the toxic cocktail of recession and rising inflation revealed in Monday's news from the Federal Authorities, spooked investors. This is the worst...*' for a moment the reporter seemed to choke '...*I've never seen anything like it in all my life and I've been in the market for thirty years. It's already got a name, Black Tuesday. Margin investors are all but wiped out as the banks call in their obligations. Even they are under threat as the falling value of loans cannot be refinanced in the total absence of third-party debt. Right now, there is no sector in positive territory. There are no buyers. The most valuable blue-chip stocks are in free fall. Everyone is selling. Selling, selling, selling. More than 13 billion shares...14 billion as I speak... Just when we thought there was no end to how high or how fast stocks could climb during these boom times, it's about to come to an end...15 billion...16 billion...it's over! It's over, I say, it's over! Nance Rogers for NBC News.*'

The cashier turned down the volume. Stared at Lake as if Lake had the answer.

Lake said, "You got any shares?"

'No."

"What're you worried about then? The coffee's cold."

+   +   +   +

NEWPORT COUNTY COURTHOUSE, RHODE ISLAND

Wednesday, October 30, 1929 - The Day after the End of the World

When kept waiting, Sheriff Brenton, a patient man with a penchant for words, liked to make word games on his police-issued notepad.

'Take thou
From without
And you have wit.'

Beneath which, more prosaically, he wrote:

PLANE MURDER
Suspects:
1 - A maniac? (Conjecture)
2 - An unknown man in the woods? (two reliable witnesses)
3 - A man seen entering the victim's premises at noon? (ditto)
4 - Men seen, by whom, 1hr30mins entering house before maid gave alarm (time at which Malone (maid) found the body?)
Possibilities:
1 - An unknown maniac seen entering the victim's premises?
2 - An unknown maniac seen in the woods?
3 - The man in the woods is unknown to the victim?

4 - The victim knew the man who entered the premises?

5 - The victim scratched her assailant's face? (see 2 above)

6 - 2 & 3 cannot be the same man (witnesses' descriptions)

7 - Coincidence - Two unrelated events?

8 - Do not forget 'torn trousers'

Motivation:

1 - If not robbery? What was he searching for?

2 - Rape? How? Why? Time Frame?

3 - Shares? What value today?

Modus:

1 - Gun? Calibre? Who's?

2 - Why shoot, if she's dead?

And beneath that list he wrote:

BUCK - material witness? in custody

1 - is not a maniac

2 - matches neither description of the witnesses

3 - Has no scratch marks on his face

4 - is not unknown

5 - trousers whole (but could have changed)

He was about to write 6 when he was called into the presence of District Attorney William Clarke, whose name, in italics, was painted in fine calligraphy on the frosted glass door to his office. ***District Attorney William Clark***. Sheriff Brown could not help but notice the letter '*e*' missing from District Attorney Clarke's name. He thought it best not to mention it, sat down where directed and opened his notepad. And started another list:

CLARKE meeting, Newport HQ, 10/30/29

Present: D.A Clarke

A.D.A E. Easton

C.O.P. S. Hazard

P.C. T. Brady

And almost as an afterthought…. Brenton.

DA Clarke's corner office on the 2nd floor of the Courthouse overlooking Washington Square provided it's occupant more than ample room for a large walnut desk behind which he sat in a cushioned oak swivel armchair facing an array of uncomfortable ladderback chairs where the assembled company sat at a slightly lower elevation (Clarke, on ascending to his position in the judiciary, ordered the County's carpenters to take three inches off the legs of each chair). Strewn across his desk were the morning editions of most of the major national newspapers.

The headlines screamed in the largest font the printers had. '**HUGE SELLING WAVE CREATES NEAR-PANIC AS STOCKS COLLAPSE**' (Washington Post), '**MARGIN ACCOUNT DUMPING BRINGS STOCK CRASH**' (The Boston Globe) '**STOCKS COLLAPSE - AVALANCHE OF SELLING SWAMPS WALL STREET**' (NY Times), '**STOCK CRASH GREATEST IN HISTORY**' (The Indianapolis Times), '**SELLING FRENZY MAKES NEW DRAMA IN MARKET**' (The Halifax Chronicle), '**DOW DIVES IN PANIC ON W.STREET**' (The Philadelphia Inquirer), **WALL STREET CRASH! Black Thursday in America** (London Herald). **STOCKS DIVE AMID FRENZY - BILLIONS GO IN LIMBO** (The Los Angeles Times) **WALL STREET'S BLACKEST HOURS** (The Times). And the best of them, '**WALL ST. LAYS AN EGG**' (Variety)

Leaning forward, fists clenched on his desktop, the District Attorney said, "You would think it was the End of the World." He picked up the Post and read it out loud. "'In a matter of hours two hundred and forty issues lost fifteen billion, five hundred and ninety-four million, eight hundred and eighteen thousand, eight hundred and ninety-four dollars.'" Pause. He shook his head. "And to think our request for two thousand dollars for repairs was turned down by the State Assembly." Another pause. "Let us pray."

To no one who knew him would this have been a surprise. Clarke was a Quaker, descended from a long line of Quakers. On the wall above the door to his chambers was painted in illuminated letters a foot high Simplicity, Peace, Integrity, Community, Equality, Stewardship - the core principles of the Society of Friends.

"Let us pray," he said, folding his hands, closing his eyes and bowing his head. "Lord, give us of thy wisdom in this hour of need. Amen"

When he opened his eyes again, he found PC Thomas Brady staring at him, mouth ajar. Brady had never been invited to such a high-level conference. At his station in Jamestown the only prayer, unspoken, was that the Sergeant didn't catch you at whatever it was you should not have been doing.

"Yes, young man," the DA said to him, "we invoke God's help in all our endeavours." And pivoting to the small task force assembled in front of him, despite his upbringing, he felt a surge of very un-Quaker like anger that the greed and hubris of a handful of men could threaten the very welfare of the Nation. He made $4800 a year and guessed the Sheriff, with overtime, would be lucky to see $3000. It was all downhill from there, Brady probably pulling in less than $1300. They were all married with kids, but for the Sheriff, who was a widower, and Brady, who was too young. Standing up, he took off his jacket, rolled up his sleeves and said, "Right, men. We've work to do. Are we all here?"

"Coddington, called in sick," the Assistant DA said.

"As usual. No matter. Life goes on. Five days in, where are we in the Plane affair? Sermon?"

"The place is secure. We have patrolmen on duty day and night. But we have a problem," Sermon Hazard said. As Police Chief it was not up to him to criticise his boss. Years of experience had taught him how to pass the buck, so he said,

"Sheriff?"

Slumped on his chair, Sheriff Brenton sat up. He was an old hand. He knew how the game was played. He fished in his jacket pocket for where he had stashed his notes, flipped to the right page, said, "I made a list. I'll get a copy out to each of you. Bottom line, we may be looking for two guys. A murderer and a robber."

Silence. The men looked at each other.

"Please elaborate," the DA said.

"Okay," said Brenton. "The last probable sighting of the dame - (off a frown from the DA) - Sorry, victim, is a little before noon on Saturday, the

26th. A man is seen to enter her house, witnessed by McCarthy and Roberts, her neighbours. Nobody sees him leave so we have no clue when he left, but we know he did because he was not on the premises when the maid gave the alarm later that afternoon"

"At what time?"

"Unknown." The Sheriff shrugged. "Make a note, Brady. Cross-check the maid's estimation with when her call was booked in at the station."

"In Newport?" Brady said.

"No. In Kalamazoo…Christ! They train you guys, or what?"

"Easy Sheriff. He's only a lad," the DA said.

Brenton rolled his eyes. "While you're at it," he said to Brady, "ask McCarthy and Roberts if they actually saw Mrs. Plane let the man in. It could have been the maid. Or the butler if she had one? In fact, find out who was on staff there and exactly where they were Saturday and Sunday."

"Good point," the DA said.

"That's a cul-de-sac, you know," Sermon Hazard suddenly interjected. "Back in the day I used to be a cop on the beat down there. Bellevue Court is short, can't be more than four, five houses with a dead end when you get to the old Van Hals place at the bottom. Been empty for years."

"Check it out," the Sheriff said to Brady. "While you're at it check every hotel and boarding house. Get the names of any new guests over the past week, no, two weeks. Ignore regulars for the moment."

"Where're you headed?" the DA said.

"Just a hunch," the Sheriff said. "This guy, an' maybe the other guy if there is one, the one in the woods, must be living somewhere. Newport's on an island. We're in October, nearly November, it's windy, cold as shit, an' raining most of the time. Nobody's camped out if they can help it."

"Good point," the DA said again. "What about these men who supposedly entered the house an hour and a half before the maid found the body?"

"There's some confusion about that. A couple of papers put it out, but it smells. My guess is that like all good reporters trying to get one-up on the opposition what we have here is a little embroidery. There are no verified witnesses. As the Chief just pointed out it's a short dead end. How could a group of men walk down Bellevue Avenue to Bellevue Court without being seen? Leave alone walk into the house?"

"So, what's the problem?" the DA said.

"Problem is I think you will have to release Buck," said the Sheriff. "No way he could have done it."

+ + + +

PARIS / KARLA

1918

Karla was baptised Karla with the letter 'K' over the parish priest's objection that it wasn't French and should be spelled with the letter 'C'.

"I am a socialist," her father said. "It is in honour of Marx."

Her father and two brothers were among the 1,300,000 French army casualties in World War 1. She was a student living in Paris when the war started and she learned of each successive death by the arrival of a postcard from her mother, still living in her hometown, Briançon, in the Alps, on the border with Italy. The cards were lined up in a sad row stuck in the bottom of a picture frame with a photograph showing her family in sepia sitting on the ramparts of the fortified town. Louis, Mother, Father, Herself, Henri.

The cards, written with the same steel nib pen her mother had used since she was a schoolgirl, in the same careful script she had been taught, all said the same thing:

> *'Ma Chère Fille, Je suis désolé de t'apprendre le mort de ton Papa, le 24.12.1914.*
>
> *'Ma Chère Fille, Je suis désolé de t'apprendre le mort de ton frère, Henri, le 10.10.1915*
>
> *'Ma Chère Fille, Je suis désolé de t'apprendre le mort de ton frère, Louis, le 2.6.1917'*

They were all signed *'Maman'*.

Nothing else. No details of where and when. No expressions of grief. No tears. Just the facts.

'My.Dear.Daughter.I.am.sorry.to.tell.you.of.the.death.of....'

Karla had read and re-read the cards so many times they were dog-eared. But no matter how often she did, the words never changed. The outcome was the same. And she sometimes wondered where 1.299,999 families had put 1.299,999 postcards.

Karla was 22 when the war ended. She never told her mother what she did during the war.

+   +   +   +

NEWPORT, RHODE ISLAND

Wednesday, October 30, 1929 - In which the Sheriff gives instructions

"**S**trike down all evil!"

With these words the DA ended the meeting and swept the newspapers from his desktop into a wastepaper basket. "God's speed, gentlemen."

Dismissed, the task force rolled out of his office, down the stairs, into a cold, damp squib of a day, an amalgamation of wood smoke hanging in the humid air from countless fires burning autumn leaves under heavy clouds coming in from the Atlantic already beading water on the parked cars and threatening black ice on the roads that night. Before driving off, Sheriff Brenton took Police Constable Brady aside.

"Listen up, Brady," he said. "We're the only two working stiffs on this deal. They're here for the show to pick up whatever kudos they can," waving a hand as the others drove off. "I want you to start with one thought. At a given moment a woman is slain in her own home by someone. This someone, man, or woman, is out there. Alive. At this point we know nothing about this person. Nothing, despite what you heard upstairs just now. Got that? But we do know the victim. And by knowing everything, every little thing, about the victim, we may learn who killed her." The Sheriff sniffed the cold air. Tried to light a cigarette. Failed. "If we're lucky."

He opened the door to his car, a relatively new Ford Victoria. "You came on your bike?" Off Brady's nod. "Guessed as much. Get in here before you freeze your ass off." Then, once they were settled, sitting side by side on the front bench seat, the Sheriff said, "You're an intelligent man, Brady.

In your mind I want you to latch onto that. Use that intelligence. Someone alive, right now, today, deliberately took the life of another human being. This can only be possible if at a given time and place the trajectory of two lives crossed. Two, individual, singular, people met for a reason we do not know."

Pause, while the Sheriff fixed himself a light, inhaled a deep breath, held it, then offered his pack to the young policeman. "Smoke?"

Brady shook his head.

"Good man. Today is Wednesday. We've already got a cold trail. Five days ago, Saturday morning, Mrs. Plane, was alive, going about her business and at a certain point someone finds the opportunity and has the motive to kill her. Focus on that. Make a picture in your head of a wealthy widow in a large house. How many servants does she have? What is her normal Saturday morning routine? Was there anything that departed from that usual routine? Who were her friends? How often did she see them? Did she see them on Saturday mornings? What did they do together? Was she expecting anyone over for lunch? If yes, who? If not, did she habitually dine by herself? Or in company? Which raises the question, with whom did she socialise? This may all appear simplistic to you, but the answers permit us to inform ourselves of the woman's habits. By assembling a maximum of detail, we may, we must, become Mrs. Plane in thought and deed. I want you to know her better than you know your own mother. Same for the house. So, focus. Every detail is important. Every scrap of information. At what time did she habitually wake up? Did she bathe in the morning? Were her clothes laid out? If yes, who laid them out? Or did she choose to dress herself? Make a diagram of the house.

Picture it. Does she come down for breakfast or is it brought up to her in her bedroom? If it is, who brings it up? If not, does she go down for breakfast in her dressing gown or already dressed for the day? What was her usual mood in the morning? Staff usually know. They can even tell if their employer slept well or badly. What did she have for breakfast? Did she have a good appetite? Was she left or right-handed? Where did she habitually have her meals? Was she kind? Generous? Strict? Rude? Happy? Afraid?"

The Sheriff wound down the driver's window, flicked the butt of his cigarette out into the drizzle, lit up another. "Family. Who are they? Have they been informed of Mrs. Plane's death? You know The Reading Room here in Newport?"

"No."

"Gentlemen's Club on Bellevue, corner of Church. I'm a member. I've arranged a suite for us to use. Discreet. You report to me there, not at the station. I'll fix it with Jamestown." Then the Sheriff added almost as an afterthought, "They say she was wealthy. Vanderbilt wealthy or just rich? Who'd she bank with? Find out. Find out who managed her money? Provenance? Find out what she inherited when her husband croaked. There must've been a will. Probate. Also, any debts? Mortgages? Creditors? With all those share certificates under her bed she must have had a broker. Find out." Pause. "Which begs an interesting question?"

"Are they worth anything today?" said Brady.

+   +   +   +

THAT MORNING IN NEWPORT

Karla woke up with a splitting headache as the maid drew back the curtains.

"Bonjour, Madame," the maid said as she had been taught to say.

"Oh, hello Molly. What's it like outside?" Karla struggled to sit up. She always slept naked, so she pulled a sheet over her breasts, plumped the pillows into a comfortable shape behind her head, settled into them, and groaned. "Mon Dieu, my head! Please pour the coffee. I don't think I can manage."

Molly put the bamboo bed tray she was carrying across Karla's lap where she lay. From the silver coffee pot on it she poured out a full cup for her mistress, careful not to spill a drop. "It's like being home in Ireland out there," she said. "Pissin' down."

Karla laughed. She and the maid were of the same age and she often thought that if it were not for luck their positions could have been reversed, she the maid, serving Molly in bed. "Too much white wine. I couldn't stop. Drank the whole bottle myself," she said to explain her headache. "Don't know why. I should know by now, 'stick to red.'" She squinted at what was on the breakfast tray. Scrambled eggs, crispy bacon, toast, butter, orange marmalade, honey, freshly baked croissants, a basket of fruit. She shook her head. "Not for me. You eat it, Molly."

"I've had me porridge, thank you." Molly said.

At 6 this morning, it being Sarah's day off. Sarah was the Housekeeper, a stickler for rules. If she could be up and working at dawn, so could her stand-in. A long list of chores of what had to be done was left in the pantry, with a timetable appended.

- 6am Item: Bedrooms 10. Strip. Air sheets and pillowcases. Remake beds. Dust. 50 minutes

- 6.50 Item: Clothes to laundry. Instruct the new laundry maid on the correct amount of bleach to use on whites and starch in collars.

- 7am Item: Scullery. Count the silverware for cleaning. Watch Jimmy. The boy's light fingered.

- 7.15 Item: B'fast - Make sure Cook beats the eggs properly. Mrs. P. dislikes them when they are too runny. No juice. Just fruit - must be fresh!

- 7.30 Item: Coal delivery. Have Jimmy go down and open. Tell the man the invoice has been paid. Make certain he cleans up after his delivery.

- 8am. Item: B'fast to Mrs.P; draw her bath; open curtains and windows (weather permitting); ask what she would like to be put out to wear; iron where needed; strip bed when she leaves her bedroom; new sheets, pillowcases, towels, etcetera... and so on throughout the day.

As each item was done Molly would tick it off on the list and move to the next task. She knew the routine by heart; didn't need an old list. Sometimes she wondered if the housekeeper didn't make lists for the sake of making lists, as a way of commemorating all she did for the household and making sure they knew it.

"You have a note," Molly said. It was there, standing on edge, a pale beige envelope between the silver sugar bowl and the delicate silver milk jug.

"Not another invitation I hope," said Karla.

Every man in Newport, married or not, having a molecule of red blood in his veins lusted after Karla. How to snare her was the question? Particularly now old man Plane was safely in his coffin. Witness the innumerable invitations she received to every function, dinner, ball, outing, regatta, yachting party, all of which received the same polite reply: *Thank*

you for your invitation, but Mrs. Kobe Plane must regretfully decline to attend.'
Apparently, the bloods at Bailey's Beach had a handicap going for the one
who finally got to bed Karla.

"No. It was under the front door. Jimmy found it when he went to
brush the steps."

"Well, it can wait. I'm not in the mood. I'm going to soak in my
bathtub for the longest time and not think." Karla yawned, stretched, slid
out from under the tray, and carrying her coffee, went into the bathroom.

It must have been at least 40 minutes later, when Molly was putting
all the new clean sheets and pillowcases back on the bed, that Karla finished
bathing and came out of the bathroom in all her naked, nubile glory. Molly
could not help herself. She literally gasped. "How can you still be single?"
she said.

To which Karla said, "I have not had much luck with men."

And winked. Then went into her dressing room.

+   +   +   +

"What do you mean, she winked?" said Police Constable Thomas
Brady. He was conducting the interview in the library to which he had been
shown by the maid when she opened the front door to him when he
knocked.

"She winked. You know, like this." And Molly winked at him.

Brady felt himself blushing. There were so many new things
happening. For a start he had never been called an intelligent man.
Somehow it grounded him. Gave confidence to a boy intrinsically shy. Who
had grown into a young man unsure of his own worth. It was something of
a miracle he graduated from the Police Academy, and yet, here he was, in
charge of making enquiries in an important case. Why had Sheriff Brenton
appointed him when there were so many policemen and detectives better
qualified? No idea.

He had set out early in the morning from The Reading Room with
instructions from the Sheriff to familiarise himself with the surroundings of
Bellevue Avenue and Bellevue Court before his appointment at Planetree
House at 10 AM. Just the names of the so-called summer cottages and their

occupants made you dizzy. De La Salle, The Elms, Marble House, The Breakers, The Vanderbilt Mansion, Belcourt, Rough Point, Rosecliff, Chateau-sur-Mer, Kingscote. With winter approaching most were now closed. But even closed you could look through the fences and imagine a way of life as far removed from that of everyman as that of an elephant to an ant. Just a recitation of the figures boggled the mind.

Imagine instructing your architect, as Cornelius Vanderbilt II had done, to replace a burned down wooden shack called 'The Breakers' with a 'cottage' measuring 125,000 square feet, more than two times the size of the White House in Washington. Set in 13 acres overlooking the Atlantic Ocean. With 70 rooms. A ballroom four times bigger than the Brady family home in Jamestown. Its own electricity powered by a coal-fired generator kept operating year-round by servants shovelling coal in a bunker 24/7 in three eight-hour shifts. With stables a half mile west of the house in which 12 grooms and stable boys tended 28 horses in 28 stalls in a U-shaped building 100 feet long and 150 feet deep where they lived directly above in dormitories under the supervision of the head coachman with his own five-room apartment. Even closed there were 18 permanent gardeners. More than 50 staff all told. 150 in season from May to September.

Or ordering 500,000 cubic feet of marble, as Cornelius's brother William had, to build Marble House, a modest 'cottage' of 50 rooms and 36 servants, at a cost of $11 million Gold-dollars which Thomas calculated would take him 687 years to earn on his policeman's salary.

That Planetree House, as befitting its name, had only 10 bedrooms was almost comical.

"Did she have many guests?" Thomas asked.

"No," said Molly. "Apart from her lawyer, none. Ever."

"Then why make up the 10 bedrooms?"

"It's the way Mr. Plane ordered it. Just in case, he used to say."

"Every day?"

"Yes."

"Even after he died, she carried on with that?"

"Yes." Pause. "And now she's dead." Molly could feel tears coming and looked away.

"I am sorry," Thomas said and busied himself making notes in his pad. When he looked up Molly had composed herself.

"Miss Malone..." he said.

"Molly, or Malone," she said. "Nobody calls me Miss Malone."

"Sorry, Molly." Even as he said it, he couldn't help himself, he started to smile.

"Sorry, Molly," she mimicked him, smiling back.

"Solly, Morry!" they both said in unison. Burst out laughing. And, just like that, fell in love.

+ + + +

They thrashed it out, of course. Molly was not one for giving herself up without a thorough understanding of where this was headed and with whom. By the time, weeks later, they were holding hands on Bowen's Wharf gazing at the yachts and fishing smacks, dreaming the turgid dreams of young lovers, she had set the course as precisely as the Commodore of the New York Yacht Club would set his for the forthcoming America's Cup the next year between Sir Thomas Lipton's 'J' Class 'Shamrock V' and Harold Vanderbilt's 'Enterprise'.

It goes to show, that two people unaware of each other in the morning could by evening set out on the oldest calling in the world, the family business. For better or worse, Molly's terms were no hanky-panky until they were married with the approval of their parents; had a house in which to raise at least three kids; tithed to St. Joseph's Holy Catholic Church in Providence, designed by an Irishman, Patrick C. Keely, God bless him; and made plans to visit the Olde Country. None of which figured in Constable Brady's first report to the Sheriff.

+ + + +

NOW

Is the present culmination of all that went
Before
and the start of all that will come
Hereafter
Subtracting fore and after gives
Be Here
Which raises the question:
Where?
The reverse of now is
Won
Which raises the question:
What?
Now and Won contain
Own
Both in
The Past
The Present
and
The Future
The Answer to both
What?
and Where?

+ + + +

THE READING ROOM, NEWPORT

The Secretary was staring at the text pinned to the bulletin board when the Sheriff came in. "This you?" he said, pointing at the offending article.

'Yes," Brenton said.

"What does it mean?"

"I'm not sure."

"Well, it has to mean something or you must take it down."

"I'll keep it in mind."

"Wretched business about Plane's wife. What a thing to happen here."

"Tragic."

"Will you be long, do you think?"

"Long?"

"Sorting it out. The Members are asking questions, you know. You've got the culprit, right?"

"As a matter of fact, no, we don't."

"It's not what it says in the papers."

"No comment," the Sheriff said.

"That's all you guys say," the Secretary said.

"Yes. Now, If you will excuse me, I must get on."

"Not before you sign this. People might think I wrote it, God forbid."

The Sheriff signed his name, '*Brenton*'.

"That's better," the Secretary said. "Gives it more of a cachet. Extraordinary, isn't it how much more authentic it looks when signed."

+ + + +

The note was unsigned. Glued to it, cut-out letters from a newspaper containing five words and an exclamation mark.

'Wait till I get you!'

It had been torn into tiny pieces and crushed into a ball.

"Where did you find it?" The Sheriff said.

"The maid gave it to me," PC Brady said.

"Where did she find it?"

"In the wastebasket in the parlour."

"Who put it back together?"

"I did."

"Show me where it was found."

On a large table the two men bent over the careful plan Brady had made of all three floors of Planetree House and its basement. It was a classical layout. On the ground floor the Great Hall, the reception rooms, music room, dining room, library, office, parlour, billiard room, doors leading from one to the other, with an enclosed glass terrace along the west facade; on the first floor, reached by a grand staircase that branched left and right from a mezzanine, two two-bedroom suites with attendant bathrooms. On the floor above, six bedrooms sharing one bathroom, one shower-room and a separate toilet. With his finger Brady traced the way from Mrs. Plane's bedroom on the first floor down to the parlour on the ground floor adjacent to the glazed veranda looking out over gardens which were themselves overlooked by the vast fenced lawn of The Elms across the street.

"Why would she leave it where it could be found?" the Sheriff said, as much to himself as to Brady.

"Maybe…"

"Go on, say it."

"She had no idea what might happen. No reason to think someone would look in the wastebasket."

"To tear it up like this she was either angry or scared. Or both. Did the maid say?"

"She didn't see her open the note. It was on the breakfast tray and gone when the maid took the tray downstairs. She only thought to look for it after she found the body."

"So. Let's think this through. A note is hand-delivered under the front door by an unknown party sometime that night or in the early morning. It is found by Jimmy, the boot-boy, when he goes to brush the front steps. Time?"

"Sometime after 6 but before 7 when he had to be in the scullery."

"Okay. He gives the note to the maid, who puts it on the tray which she takes upstairs at 8 o'clock. The breakfast is untouched but for the coffee when Mrs. Plane gets out of bed to go into her bathroom. She emerges 40 minutes later, gets dressed and in the interim the maid takes the breakfast tray downstairs minus the note. So, at some point between getting out of bed, at say 8.15, and 9 o'clock when she goes into her dressing room, she takes the note from the tray unseen by the maid. There is then a gap of time in which the maid is downstairs and Mrs. Plane upstairs when she opens and reads the note. Less than 3 hours later her body is found downstairs and the torn, crunched up, note, is in the wastebasket. Three hours? Where was the maid in those three hours?" The Sheriff scratched his nose. Looked at a grandfather clock as if it could give him the answer. "Where was Jimmy? The cook? Other staff? Who else was there during that time? Because let us not forget, someone inside opened the front door to someone outside before noon. If any of the staff opened the door, they would have seen who came in. Since none claim to have done so, the assumption is Mrs. Plane herself opened the door. How can that be?"

The Sheriff was pacing across the requisitioned suite, touching objects as he went, a vase, a lampshade, the back of a chair, as if navigating through the shoals of his own thoughts. "She had servants to open doors. It follows that it was deliberate. *She* opened the door to whoever it was that knocked. Because of the note she received? Because she did not want a servant to witness who came to visit her? But servants move haphazardly, going about their business in such a large house. Ergo, there were no servants. *She* had ordered them out. Yes. That must be it." With his nicotine-stained forefinger he tapped the floor plan. "Brady, draw up a schedule from 9 to noon. I want you to locate as precisely as possible the exact location of all the servants when they were told to leave the house and the exact time when they left. Also, find out if they were told when to be back. Get hold of those two women, the neighbours…?"

"Mrs. Patrick McCarthy and Mrs. Jacob Roberts," Brady said.

"Yes. Good man. Those two; question them closely about the man they claim they saw 'shortly before noon.' What do they mean by 'shortly'? 5 minutes before? 10? Half-an-hour? It can't be longer because otherwise they would have said shortly after 11. We know the maid called the station to report finding the body half-hidden under some rugs at a time certain after 12 noon, which time must be logged at the station. Have you verified that yet?"

"I'll ask Molly?"

"Molly?"

"The maid." Brady blushed.

"I see," said the Sheriff, frowning at his protégé. "Remember what I said? Focus. Do not get distracted. This is murder. A murder that we can now say with reasonable certainty occurred between 11.30 and 12.30, max 12.45, Saturday morning. So, the servants are out of the house by 11.30. The doorbell rings - say, 5 minutes later - 11.35. It takes Mrs. Plane 2 or 3 minutes to get to the front door to admit someone. Say, 11.40. Do they talk? Where do they go? When does the fight start? We know it ends in the dining room where she is killed and half-hidden under a rug. Why bother? Or maybe her assailant was disturbed? Yet still finds time to rip the place apart? Looking for what? Before, during or after he killed her? And then he gets away unseen. Through the front door or another? How many are there? So, all this happens in somewhere around forty-five minutes, soup to nuts. Is that possible? Which begs the question, how long does it take to assault and violate a woman furiously defending herself and then bludgeon her to death?"

"And shoot," Brady said.

"Yes. And shoot. How come nobody reported hearing a gunshot?" said the Sheriff.

+   +   +   +

NEWPORT, RHODE ISLAND

The Black Pearl, 7.30.am, Tuesday, November 5, 1929

"We're no longer on the front page, Lake."

"You're a sick man, Kale. I don't want to hear about it. Let me eat my breakfast."

"Listen up," said Kale. *'Sir Kobe Plane, the victim's husband, died of a heart attack in New York City on his return from Europe three years ago, purportedly leaving the whole of his estate to his widow, who was his second wife. The Plane family, originally from Chestnut Hill, Boston, was one of the oldest on: Aquidneck Island, and the house in which his widow was slain had been occupied by the family for more than forty years. Plane was knighted for services to the Crown by Queen Victoria at the turn of the century.'*

"She's dead," said Lake.

"What's that?" said Kale.

"The Queen. She's dead. All you care to read about are people who are dead. I am not listening to another word."

"Yeah? Well get this. It says *'There were eighteen rooms in the house and the detectives when they began their investigation of the murder were surprised to find that although Mrs. Plane had been the sole occupant of the house since the death of her husband, every one of the ten bedrooms in the house was luxuriously furnished, with fresh linen placed on each bed. According to neighbours, Mrs. Plane was 33 years old, attractive, with a very becoming wardrobe. While it was known her husband had left her in comfortable circumstances, she did not entertain at her home. She enjoyed the friendship of all her neighbours, but it had been common gossip among them that she had*

39

never invited any of them to visit her. The discovery, therefore, that she kept the ten bedrooms ready for occupancy was the source of much comment.'"

"They must have hated her," said Lake.

"Who?"

"The nosey neighbours. Bet they were jealous as hell, her being rich and good-looking and all."

"Yeah? I thought you weren't listening. It goes on *'District Attorney Clarke said he was particularly anxious to question Mrs. Jacob Roberts, one of the two women who claim to have seen a man entering the premises sometime before noon on that fateful day, but that she was too hysterical to be questioned. Reportedly she had a telephone conversation with Mrs. Plane less than an hour before the murder was discovered and it was not clear whether the man who called on her was in the house at the time of the telephone call as reference was made to a Mr. Pal Konbee, or Konbee Pal, or Paul, she was not sure, but she was certain Mrs. Plane told her the man was in the automobile business in Providence, come to sell her a new car. Detectives and State Troopers, aided by the Providence police, have made a thorough canvas of Providence for a man engaged in the motor trade with a name sounding like Konbee, but without avail. 'I believe,' said DA Clarke, 'the man gave a fictitious name to Mrs. Plane under the pretext of wanting to sell her a car in order to gain access to her home.'*

When asked to characterise the profile of someone who could commit such a violent crime, the DA said, 'No comment.'"

+ + + +

A B&B in MIDDLETOWN, RHODE ISLAND

Friday, October 18,1929

The man signed 'P. Kobeen' in the entry register for the 6-room B&B on Oliphant Lane in Middletown, declined breakfast in the morning, paid for three nights, took his key and walked up the creaky wooden staircase to the room on the first floor as directed by Mrs. Penelope Mason, owner, manager, caretaker, housemaid, cook, laundress, general handyman of her establishment since her husband absconded with their few savings and the neighbour's wife at the end of the Great War, 10 years ago. Good riddance. But she kept his portrait on the wall behind her desk in the parlour which served as the reception area for her guests. The picture, now faded to a pale sepia, showed a farmer, his thumbs hooked into the top of dungarees, in a field, with two cows over his left shoulder and a spotted dog at his feet. It reminded her of the rural life, fast disappearing, of her childhood and upbringing on the island in this very same gingerbread house, her haven, to which she was forever chained by the obligations of her business.

Being of a sunny disposition, she never complained, even if it meant no holidays, or travel. Instead, ever the gracious hostess quick to offer a drink, she lived to entertain and in entertaining she vicariously lived the lives of her guests as they regaled her with their myriad doings, children, jobs, traffic, taxes, graft, the daily folderol of well-lived lives. That someone should walk into her place, grab a key, and disappear upstairs without so much as a howdeedo was upsetting. More than that, disquieting.

From where she sat, through the window in the centre of the front door, she could see the car he had come in. A grey-and-white, 1929 Hudson 7 Roadster. Much too grand for a small B&B. With out-of-state plates what's more. Black on yellow. New York. Empire State. You developed a nose in her line of business, and this guy smelled.

+ + + +

TWO COUSINS CAUGHT IN THE MAELSTROM

"I didn't know you were hysterical, Helen?"

"Me? Don't be ridiculous!" Mrs. Jacob Roberts was having her hair done in the private salon of the National Tennis Club at 19 Memorial Boulevard, on the grounds of The Newport Casino.

"It says so here in The Globe."

From where she was sitting in the adjoining barber's chair, Mrs. Patrick McCarthy, leaned over to show her cousin the offending adjective.

"Piffle! I am probably the most rational woman left in America. How many times have I told you, you must not believe what you read, Daisy."

"You think Willie Clarke would make that up?"

"No. He's just miffed because we didn't invite him to our end-of-summer party. Jacob can't stand the man." She turned in her chair to look at the barber hovering over her, comb, and scissors aloft. "You didn't hear me say that Freddie."

"No, Madam." Frederick had been the barber in the Club for so long nobody knew his last name. As a matter of policy, he really did not listen to his customers, particularly two wealthy women who assumed they had the privilege of using the Men's Barbershop simply because their husbands sat on the Board of the Court Tennis Association. That he knew how to coif women came from his mother, a parsimonious woman of French descent from the Auvergne, a region known for the calculated cunning of its inhabitants. Against the wishes of her husband, a roofer, she encouraged her

43

boy when he said he wanted to be a hairdresser. "More money in women, mon petit Freddo," she would say and apprenticed him to an Italian coiffeuse she knew in Providence. All of them dead and buried now, a distant memory stored in his balding head, as he snipped a straying curl from the fringe Mrs. Roberts thought was a la mode and made her look younger.

"Forget Clarke," she said to her reflection in the long horizontal mirror she was sharing with Daisy. "Have you spoken to Patrick about what's happening in the city?"

"Yes. He said not to worry."

"They always say that when the ship's going down. They think we're idiots. I told Jacob he could do whatever he wanted with his own shares, but under no circumstances did he have permission to touch what Daddy left me."

"I wish I could say the same thing," Daisy made a face in the mirror. "I sink or swim with Patrick. He has unlimited liability if it all goes belly-up."

As young girls, after graduation from Smith in the Class of 1903, they had both been on the Grand Tour in Europe when they met their respective husbands at a private masked ball to commemorate the Carnival of Venice. Jacob Roberts was a banker, descended from a family of Jewish bankers in Amsterdam. His friend, Patrick McCarthy, was a high net worth 'Name' with Lloyd's of London and ran two insurance syndicates from their New York office. Like the girls, the two had graduated from the same school, Harvard, and in the same year, 1881. They rowed on the Varsity 8 and were double-skull finalists at Henley. It was a running joke that the girls were born the same year their husbands graduated. And an even better one that If it hadn't been for their accents behind the masks they would never have met. Serendipity, working its magic, had seated them at a cosmopolitan table of guests speaking half the languages of Europe, and the four Americans were relieved to hear a familiar tongue they could understand. In short order they wooed and, upon returning to America, married. The Roberts in what would become the Central Synagogue, on the corner of 55th and Lexington, and the McCarthys, in St. Patrick's Cathedral, on 5th Avenue. They honeymooned together in the Florida Keys and had adjacent

10-room apartments facing Central Park on West 72nd Street in The Dakota Building. Then followed the obligatory children, two to each family, kindergarten, school, college, and out-the-door to make their way in the wide, wide world. Leaving behind a vacuum. Empty nest; empty nesters. Where they differed was in the chosen occupations of the men.

"Weird to think we could lose everything," Daisy said.

"Don't be silly," said Helen.

+ + + +

JACOB IN MANHATTAN

Jacob Roberts, 68 years old, is eating oysters at his usual table in The Viceroy Hotel, 32-stories, newly built on the corner of 59th and Park. White-haired, tanned, slim in his charcoal-grey, three-piece business suit, he epitomises his trade. Money-Equals-Power. More money, more power.

His bank has financed the construction of the building in which he sits and holds the first mortgage. Despite the convulsions on Wall Street in the past few days he feels comfortable. Unlike many, his Bank will survive. For a simple reason.

Risk aversion.

On Black Tuesday, he had been summoned to 33 Liberty Street, headquarters of the New York Fed, along with the senior partners of Chase, Mellon, JPMorgan, Goldman Sachs, most of the major banks, for some arm-twisting. To stem the tide, they were told. Man up. Buy. Support the Market.

When asked his opinion by the Governor, George L. Harrison, Jacob stood before his colleagues and said, "If King Canute could not stem the tide, what you are asking us to do is impossible. This tidal wave of selling must by its very nature subside when there is nothing left to sell. The Market will take its course, gentlemen." Pause. "As you know, we are a conservative institution, not a gambling house. As a policy, we have always chosen the preservation of capital over the supposed potential for a higher-than-average-return in high-risk investments. We prefer certainty over uncertainty. We do not lend money to investors to buy overvalued stock.

Nor do we lend to them on margin." A distinct rumble of malaise in his listeners. "All of you in this room have been aware for at least the past two years that the market has been overbought, with inflated valuations due to excessively bullish expectations." Sniff. "Then ask yourselves this, how many defaulting loans do you have on your books?"

"So, you would have us do nothing?" Governor Harrison said. "Is that your recommendation?"

"For what it's worth, I would order the Stock Exchange closed."

Sipping a dry Chablis between each oyster, he knows he has not made many friends by being so candid. Little does he care. Better to be honest. And sit on cash.

He hasn't told Helen he has sold his and her stocks when he saw the Market heading south. Nor will he tell her he would apply young Getty's formula 'Buy when everyone is selling and hold on until everyone is buying.' But only when the Market bottoms. Simple, really.

If he is honest, he doesn't tell Helen much of anything anymore. They weren't exactly estranged so much as grown apart; the twenty-year gap in ages perhaps? Separate bedrooms now, not that it mattered. Sex was never that important. Though he feels the odd twinge whenever Daisy shows up. Maybe he's married the wrong girl?

Adrift in his own thoughts, as the waiter takes the empty oyster platter away and brings the veal cutlets he ordered, Jacob sees a 1929 Duesenberg Model J Convertible Coupe, in a two-tone, pale yellow-on-midnight blue colour scheme, drive past the hotel, its 7-litre, double-overhead cam, supercharged Straight-8 engine, growling. Despite the weather, the driver is in shirtsleeves with a striped cap on his head. The car is out of sight down Park Avenue before Jacob realises it was Patrick driving.

+ + + +

PATRICK ON CENTRAL PARK WEST

The Duesey swings under the porte-cochère, the driver steps out, gives the keys to the doorman, says 'Roberts, Apartment 444' and then he's gone. The doorman of The Dakota tags the keys, 444, and when he gets a break, parks the car in one of the two spaces reserved for 444 in the garage on 77th Street and Amsterdam. As he does, the garage keeper comes out from his office and shouts, 'Wrong slot! That's 445's.'

"Not what the guy said," the doorman says.

"You tellin' me my business?" the garage keeper says. "That's Mr. McCarthy 's car. 445. You the newbie on the door?"

The doorman nods. The garage keeper taps his forefinger to his brow.

"Get smart, kid. Get smart. What did he look like, this guy gave you the keys?"

"I dunno," the doorman says. "Older guy, sixties, maybe seventy? Long grey hair, one of them caps jockeys wear. In a hell of a hurry the way he took off down the street."

"No shit," the garage keeper says. Thinks, that's McCarthy? What the hell's goin' on?

+ + + +

INTERROGATION IN THE MURDER
MANSION / 1

PC Brady was thorough. Once the body had been removed to the morgue and the dining room sealed off, a photographic inventory was made of every room that had been disturbed, with every item thrown, smashed, ripped, upended, in close-focus detail. The rooms were then put back in order, the books on the shelves and the beds remade. Then he made a list. On the list was a series of questions and, depending on the answers, a series of follow-up questions. He chose to conduct his interviews in the library with views over the croquet court laid out to the west of the house, where the hoops of a long-abandoned game lay partially hidden. A 6-hand mahogany reading table covered in patinated pale-green leather, standing on an immense Persian rug, bisected the huge room. Four of the chairs had been set aside against the floor-to-ceiling bookshelves; the two remaining chairs faced each other. Thomas took the chair facing the view, notepad in front of him. And began:

"Please state your name."

"Sarah Lister."

"Occupation?"

"Housekeeper."

"Address?"

"Here. I have a room above the carriage house. All the staff do except Jimmy, the boot boy."

"How many live-in staff are there?

"Five, including myself.

"Who has keys to the house?"

"To the front door? Nobody but Mrs. Plane and myself. The staff were not allowed to use the front door. They use the door to the pantry leading to the kitchen below stairs."

"How long have you been employed here?"

"Seventeen years.

"So you knew the family well?"

"Intimately."

"You were here fourteen years before the arrival of Mrs. Plane?"

"The second Mrs. Plane, yes. I was with the first for eight years before she died."

"Were you on good terms?"

"With the first, yes, better than with the second."

"Where were you on Saturday, October 26, 1929.

"It was my day off. I left, as usual, Friday evening to catch the bus to Providence to visit my mother in her home. She's not well."

"And you returned…?"

"Sunday evening, like always."

"When did you learn Mrs. Plane had been assaulted?"

"When I got back. It was terrible. Who could believe…"

"We are not here to speculate. As the housekeeper, what was the nature of your work?"

"I ran the house and its maintenance, including the grounds. Hired the staff. Paid the bills. I care for the well-being of my employers."

"By yourself?"

"Yes. After the death of Sir Kobe, Mrs. Plane dismissed his butler and I assumed some of his duties."

"This would be…?"

"Three years ago last August."

"1926." Thomas made a note. "Cause of death?"

"A heart attack, the doctor said. In his sleep. In his apartment in New York."

"Let me see if I have the dates right. You arrived in 1912. The first Mrs. Plane died eight years later, in 1920. How old was she?"

"Fifty-seven."

"Six years later, Mr. Plane died in 1926. The same year he married the second Mrs. Plane?"

"Yes. They married in January. In the French Alps. In winter. Somewhere Mrs. Plane's mother lives."

"So they were married for just seven months?"

"Yes. More like eight months."

"Did you know Mrs. Plane before she married?"

"No. Sir Kobe met her on one of his frequent trips abroad. She didn't want to marry him when they first met, you know. I believe it took him at least a year to persuade her."

"What was the objection?"

"Well, everything. She's French, he's American. She's a waitress, he's a wealthy businessman. She lives in Paris, he lives here. She's thirty, he's seventy-three!"

"Despite all that they marry. I can see the attraction for her, he's rich. What was the attraction for him?"

"Are you kidding? Look behind you!" Sarah pointed. In the middle of the far wall, in an elaborate gilt frame, surrounded by leather bound books, was a life-sized portrait by Pyotr Alexis Belanopek of a naked nymph in a bosky dale wearing nothing more than a pearl necklace and an artfully draped pink gossamer veil, which did not so much hide her modesty as accentuate what was hidden.

Thomas gaped.

"Yes," Sarah said. "She was stunning. Absolutely stunning. Sir Kobe commissioned that portrait before they were married."

"I know nothing about pictures," Thomas said. "I thought it was some old masterpiece when I first came in here."

"And now you know why he wanted to marry her."

"Were you surprised he remarried?"
"That is not for me to say."

+   +   +   +

THE READING ROOM, NEWPORT -
that evening

The Sheriff was blunt when Brady showed him a copy of the transcript.

"It is not because you are new at this that you must be slipshod. Did you get the mother's address in Providence? No. How then can you verify Lister stayed with her? When she says she returned Sunday, exactly when, and exactly who told her of the assault? Did you ask? No. If you don't ask, how can you corroborate what she said with what someone else tells you? Did you get the doctor's name? No. You blithely accept he told Lister it was a heart attack. Heart attacks may be common, but they don't usually happen without cause. We need to see a death certificate and talk to this doctor. And find out who handled the probate." Then, jabbing the transcript, "Look at this: Lister volunteers 'she didn't want to marry him.' How does she know? You didn't ask. Is this part of being 'intimate' with the family? You don't know because you didn't ask. And when she speculates 'I believe it took him at least a year' you accept that as gospel? And then you start fishing 'what was the attraction for him?' and we end up with Lister conducting the interview 'are you kidding?'"

Thomas hung his head.

"Then you fail to ask her if she knew whether a gun was kept in the house, and, most confounding, this gap of three years between the death of Plane and the murder of his wife. The beguiling widow, who admits to having been a waitress, lives in that house for three years? With ten beds made up? And you don't question that? Ask yourself, is she there the whole time on her own? Scarcely credible. Then who visits her?"

Thomas was about to say that Molly had said nobody but thought better of it and said nothing.

"Stop looking like a schoolboy. You're a cop. Buck up, man!" Vexed, the Sheriff stood up from behind his desk, stretched, glanced out of the first-floor window of his suite down onto Bellevue Avenue in the dusk, with the streetlights coming on showing swirls of dead leaves scurrying before a strengthening wind. "Be a gale by morning," he said. "Enough for now. You eaten? No? Let's go. Any case, sun's down, time for a drink."

And as they went down the stairs to the Club dining room, he threw over his shoulder, "Remember what I said about details? You'll have to get Lister back to fill in the blanks. Pain in the ass, but that's what we do."

+ + + +

JARDIN DES TUILERIES, PARIS

May 1925

"Il est beaucoup, beaucoup trop vieux!" Karla said.

"Oui, mais il est gentil et surtout riche !" Phuong said, ever practical.

"I don't care how kind or rich he is, I'm not going to marry someone who could be my grandfather. Imagine going to bed with all that flabby flesh, not to mention bad breath which could choke a pig." Karla was steaming. She was sitting on one of the green metal benches next to the pond with a view through the gates onto the Place de la Concorde.

Phuong seated next to her, watched her chow chase a pigeon. They had chosen a time to go for a walk between lunch and dinner when Karla had her break, taken off her waitress's costume, and put on a light linen dress with buttons from hem to neck, a pale sandy-pink colour which contrasted with the black-and-beige geometric pattern on the silk dress worn by Phuong. Both carried sunshades to protect their complexions from the Indian summer baking Paris.

"Do not get into a temper, Karla," Phuong said, carefully picking her words. "It's not as if he were married. Il est seul, pauvre homme. Think. You say you want to change your life? This is your chance."

"But I don't love him."

"Love? Be serious. What's that got to do with anything. Voyons. Imagine how it will be to live in America? To have servants? Beautiful clothes? Your own motor car? Jewels, perhaps? I could come and visit you. It would be fun."

"I am not for sale," Karla said.

"Who said you were? The man is besotted by you. Ever since he commissioned that painting by Belano Whatshisname."

+   +   +   +

It started with the arrival of Spring. One day Karla came down the stairs from the tiny mezzanine apartment she occupied to find an overweight gentleman in conversation with her landlord in the organised chaos of his paint-splashed studio. Space had been made in the stacks of unsold canvases and the two men were bent over a portfolio of drawings open on the floor.

"Ah, Mademoiselle Karla herself!" Belanopek said. "May I introduce Monsieur Plane from America. He is greatly taken by the drawings I made of you."

Karla put out her hand. "Bonjour, Monsieur," she said.

The portly Monsieur Plane was plainly dumbstruck. He just stared at her. Didn't even shake hands. Just stared. Long black hair to her waist. The poise of a dancer. Dark green eyes. Upturned lips set to smile. Taller than him. A vision giving lie to art.

The long silence that followed was broken by the artist, stroking a fledgling beard, glancing at the two of them, raising his eyebrows in appreciation of the unfailing aim of Cupid's arrow and saying, "Monsieur Plane, may I present to you the greatest beauty in all of France!" An exaggeration perhaps but spoken with the sincerity of someone who loved his subject.

After that Monsieur Plane was always in and out of the studio in the hope of seeing Karla. Inevitably he followed her to work and soon became a regular at the Café de L'Époque, much to the delight and profit of M. Aubert. And it was Aubert who first planted the seed for the commission by adroitly slipping the subject into the conversation he had with this wealthy patron over cognac and a Davidoff at the end of every meal. It happened the evening Plane said he had to return to the States on business.

"Mademoiselle will miss you," the Chef said.

56

"And I, her!" cried out the gallant Knight. "I will be back, fear not, as soon as they can turn the damn ship around. Please tell her that in private." A deep puff on his cigar. "My only regret is not being able to take her with me. Turned down flat. Do you know I even tried to persuade Belanopek to part with one of those sketches he made of her. Not a chance. She made him promise to never sell one of them."

"Oh, la, my friend. That is not how you must proceed. Non, non. A word in confidence…"

+ + + +

"Your husband put him up to it," Karla said, to which Phuong just smiled and called to her dog.

Karla frowned, and a moment later, cottoned on. "Oh, I see. It was you!"

"Ma petite Karla, how do you think I got Aubert? We poor women must have our little tricks, n'est-ce pas? Be prepared to compromise, or we end up comme des vieilles poules. You surely don't want that? I told Aubert, Karla is 30. From here it is all downhill for her. You do not want her to be an old maid. He understood. And look what's happened. A poor young artist makes some money, his model gets a fee, and a jovial American widow has a masterpiece to hang on his wall to remind him of what is missing in his life. You! He is a great collector. He will invite you to the Expo. You must go."

+ + + +

FALL RIVER, MASSACHUSETTS

Tuesday, 22 October 1929

When he finally saw the clapped-out, clapboard B&B on 2nd Street, half hidden by overhanging tree branches, set well back from the road, he thought it perfect. He parked the Hudson where it could not be easily seen and walked up the wooden steps of the dilapidated cottage built in 1873 - as a faded sign above the door attested - crossed a wide veranda and entered a gloomy hall. No carpet on the floor in front of an unattended reception desk, upon which lay an open register, an ink pot, a steel nib pen, and a round-domed bell.

Behind the desk, a key rack. Every key in its place. No guests? Even better. He rang the bell on the desk. Waited. Rang again.

"Comin," a voice croaks from up the stairs. "Keep your pants on, ringin' that damn bell like that." Thump of a heavy door being closed. Shuffle of slippered feet. "No one nighters," the voice calls down. "Can't see you. Come to the foot of the stairs."

He did as instructed. Looked up. Saw an ancient crone in pyjamas and a patchwork robe, her grey, greasy locks under a sleeping bonnet that seemingly predated the house, round granny glasses on, through which she peered down at him.

"Well?" she says.

"Three nights?" he said.

She nods. "Sign the register. Take the first key top left. Room's down the hall. Lights out at 10. Breakfast at 7. Put $2.85 each morning in the cash box on the shelf under the desk. Got that?" Nods again. Turns.

Shuffles out of sight. Pause. A door opens. Then… the croaking voice… "I am not to be disturbed." Thunk. A door closes.

Perfect.

He signs the register. *B.O.Palkeen.*

Outside it begins to drizzle.

+   +   +   +

A TEMPORARY UNEMPLOYMENT OFFICE, 221 THAMES STREET, NEWPORT

10.45 AM

Standing stoically silent in the slanting rain the men wait to be called into what was once a haberdashery. Nobody's hiring. Neither in the fishing industry, nor construction, not even in the Naval Yard while a Subcommittee of Congress debates the Navy Department's Appropriation Bill. All around Narragansett Bay, in all the yards, of all the villages, there is little commercial activity. It is as if, after the debacle of Black Tuesday, the frenetic fluctuations of values on Wall Street have everybody waiting for a second shoe to drop.

"We've been here two hours, Kale. Nothin's goin' to change. I'm soaked. Let's get the hell out," Lake said.

"I'm down to five bucks," Kale said.

"Freezin' your nuts off standing here's not goin' to get you more. If there's no work, there's no work. Let's go."

Dropping out of line, turning up their coat collars, they made their way for a good half mile north along Thames Street to Marlborough, where they turned right, to the corner of Farewell, and the welcome warmth of the barroom in the White Horse Tavern. They had scarcely closed the door behind them when it opened again to admit Johnathan Buck, in rags as usual, drenched to the skin.

"Christ, Buckee, I thought you were locked up?" Kale said.

"Bastards let me out," Buck said. "Just my luck. Thought for a moment there I had three square meals and a roof over my head to last me through the winter. Nope! Not even compensation for wrongful arrest, the bastards."

The three men join a scrum around the fireplace, a commonwealth of the poor. Most are fishermen. Rude men in a trade where life is cheap. Those with money buy drinks for those without, knowing it will be turn-and-turn-about with the ebb and tide of each individual's fortune.

Clothes steaming as they dry, the lads cram into a booth, where, by chance, a previous patron has left that day's copy of The Newport Mercury. Pounced on by Kale.

"Here we go," said Lake.

"Ready?" Kale said, adjusting his spectacles. "Let's see, Page One: 'Council Favours Plan - Orders Commission to Study Problem of Teachers' Retirement Fund.' Nah. I don't think so. 'Exemption for new Hotel in Jamestown considered by Board of Trade.' Good luck with that. 'Unity Club to present 'Much Ado About Nothing' by William Shakes…'"

"Who reads this crap?" Buck interrupted.

"Kale," Lake said.

"Cut it out," Kale said, turning a page. "Ah, here we are, Page Three: '*A witness comes forward. Mr. Jason Appleby, of Bonniecrest, walking his dog past the long-unoccupied Van Hals mansion at the bottom of the cul de sac that is Bellevue Court, reported a break-in to the police. On his walk, he said, he saw that the usually padlocked front gate was open and ventured into the unkempt grounds. A window leading to the kitchen in the rear of the house was broken and the kitchen door to the back yard ajar. Entering the house Mr. Appleby reported calling out and, receiving no reply, proceeded to look further. In the hallway beyond the kitchen, spread on the floor, were two women's capes. One of the capes was a black broadcloth and the other was of a brown-coloured Scotch cloth, he said. It looked as if someone had slept on them. Given the proximity to Planetree House, Mr. Appleby regarded it as his civic duty to report the matter to the police. Upon investigation the detectives also found several burned matches, a candlestick and cigarette butts, and a man's footprints tracked in the thick dust which lay throughout the empty house upstairs and downstairs. Assistant District Attorney Easton allowed it was possible that the slayer of Mrs. Plane slept in the house on the night before the murder.*

'It would have been easy for the slayer to observe Mrs. Plane's home from the windows on the second floor of the Van Hals Mansion,' Mr. Easton said. He cautioned, however, that it was premature to assume the two capes belonged to the victim.'"

+ + + +

THE NEW YORK YACHT CLUB

37 WEST 44TH STREET, NEW YORK

At the stroke of noon, in the pouring rain, Jacob Roberts strode under the Beaux-Arts limestone facade of what he regarded as his Club on Clubhouse Row, between the Harvard Club at No. 27, the Penn Club at No. 30, and the Princeton Club at No. 15. Although a graduate of Harvard he preferred the menu at the New York Yacht Club, and this is where he had asked Patrick to meet him. He gave his umbrella, hat, and overcoat to the attendant at the door and went up to the dining room on the first floor to find Patrick already seated in one of the bay windows overlooking the street, with what looked to be a half-empty bottle of Claret.

"Got an early start, I see," said Jacob, sitting down, spreading one of the Club's vast monogrammed linen napkins over his knees.

"So would you if you'd been through what I've been through."

"That bad?"

"Disastrous. Under our liability every kind of obligation and guarantee has been called. There's nowhere to hide. I'll be down to my undies by the time this ends."

"Hence the Duesey in my parking space?"

"Yes. You don't mind, do you, Jacob? I couldn't bear losing her."

"No problem." He nodded at a nearby table where the Astor brothers and cousins were dining. "You're not alone. Look at them."

Grim faced, Vincent, William, John Jacob, and Waldorf Astor, were seated at a table presided by Jack Morgan Jr., of the eponymous bank, and Alfred Sloan, Chairman and CEO of General Motors, whose shares had suffered a catastrophic loss, falling from $73 a share to $8 in a single day, October 29.

"I bet I know what Morgan's telling them," Jacob said. "If you don't have to, don't sell."

"I'm told four-fifths of Rockefeller's fortune has vanished," Patrick said.

"Says who? You think JD's out on a margin call? It's all those working stiffs, the tens of thousands of men he employs, suckered into buying shares they couldn't afford. They are, or will be, crushed. The old man will do what he's always done, pick up the bits for pennies. Talk about unintended consequences," Jacob warmed to a subject on which few men were better informed. "When the Supreme Court busted up Standard Oil back in 1911 to dismantle his control of ninety percent of the Nation's petroleum industry, they never imagined that the thirty-odd companies they created would make him richer than he's ever been. The parts were worth more than the whole, particularly now the parts have become Chevron, Exxon, Mobil, BP, and Marathon. His stock has doubled because of the split."

"You're trying to console me, right?" Patrick said.

It was the way he said it that stopped Jacob.

"What have you done, Patrick?"

"What you always told me not to do."

For a long moment Jacob studied his friend. "You've been borrowing money to buy stock? On margin?"

Patrick nodded.

"Christ in Heaven, man. Are you out of your mind?" Despite himself, Jacob said it loudly.

"Shh, please keep your voice down," Patrick said, looking at the other diners to see if they were listening.

"How much do you owe?"

"Too much. Daisy will kill me."

"Don't tell me....?"

Misery written in his very posture; Patrick nodded. "I had to use the apartment as collateral. They've called it."

For a moment Jacob's face hardened, his eyes became bleak, a vulture circling the kill. Then, with an effort, he remembered. This was his friend.

"Who has the paper?" he said.

Patrick blinked, then looked across to the Astor table.

"Morgan?"

Patrick nodded.

"I'll talk to Jack."

"Daisy…"

"Not a word to the girls! Helen is the world's biggest gossip. Just as well they're up to their ears in that murder."

"I don't know how to thank you, Jacob," Patrick said.

"Don't. Just stop blubbing. Act like a man. Can we order lunch now?"

"You think I should resign from Lloyds?"

"No, you moron. Sell that car and buy the shares. You'll never see GM at eight bucks again in your lifetime!"

+ + + +

THE READING ROOM, NEWPORT

The Sheriff sat doodling while waiting for the Chief of Police.

A life is on file
An ile in each
And if also
I think.
Try fie,
The elf said.
Tar and art are like me
Said the rat.
And God is dog
Spelled backwards.

He signed *Brenton*, took it downstairs and was pinning it to the bulletin board when the Secretary came alongside to read what he had written.

"You're a strange man Sheriff," he said. "I don't get this one any more than the last one. You want to tell me what it means?"

"More fun if I don't," the Sheriff said.

"Well, wish I had time to fool around the way you fellows seem to," the Secretary said.

"I've got work to do. Good day."

When the Sheriff got back up to his suite, he found Sermon Hazard seated in his chair studying a transparent envelope in which the killer's note was safeguarded.

"Hi, Chief," the Sheriff said. "How'd you sneak in?"

"Behind your back while you were talking to that Secretary."

The Police Chief was not a member of The Reading Room and would normally have to be signed in by a member to be admitted. Some part of him resented this, but another part acknowledged he didn't belong in what he thought was an elitist establishment and the Sheriff did. Rank aside, the two of them, over the course of lengthy careers working in tandem, accepted their respective roles and played their hand as dealt.

"Nosey bastard, never puts up a nickel for the force," the Chief said as he tapped the note. "Enough said, where are we on this?"

"If I'm honest," the Sheriff said, "we're stuck. Bits and pieces, but nothing hard. Remember I asked Brady to check the hotels and boarding houses? Well, a week before the murder, on the 19th, a guy checked into a B&B in Middletown for three nights. Signed the register Kobeen. Came and went. Never said a word. The Manageress described him as 'a skinny guy looking fishy'."

"So?"

"Mrs. Jacob Roberts in her phone conversation with Mrs. Plane recalls Mrs. Plane saying she was visited by a Pal or Paul Konbee."

"Yeah? Maybe she misheard."

"Could also be coincidence. We're checking. Same with Appleby. He was obviously trespassing when he went into the Van Hals place, but he did the right thing by reporting it. None of the neighbours have identified the two capes as belonging to Mrs. Plane, but someone was in there for sure. For when or how long we don't know. Maybe a tramp? Maybe the killer? Again, we don't know." The Sheriff pulled up a chair and sat down facing his boss.

"Another thing, Chief. We haven't found any of the murder weapons. Neither the pick or stiletto or knife or gun, not even the iron bar, if that's what was used, to bash her head in. Incredible. As if he needed to kill her in many different ways. Or to make sure she was dead. And then covering her with a rug before carting off all the implements he used? I don't get it. This is a ferocious attack, Sermon. On the one hand murderous rage, slaughtering a defenceless woman, tearing the house apart searching for something, and on the other a meticulous clean-up. In all my years I've never seen anything like it."

"You think it's a man now?"

"I can't prove it and I try to keep an open mind, but, yes, I think it is a man. I can't imagine a woman doing so much damage."

"One person? You said probably two, at that meeting with Clarke."

"I know. Maybe I'm wrong. But how do you tie in the house being ransacked with the murder? Did it happen before or after? And don't forget she was raped. How could one person do all that in such a short timeframe? Plus take off without being seen or heard and without leaving a single clue behind?"

"What about the fingerprint?"

"Good luck with that."

"You're forgetting the tin trunk."

"Yeah? What are we going to call that? A negative clue? As if this isn't complicated enough." The Sheriff shook his head. "What happened to those share certificates?"

"The DA impounded them. He's still waiting on a valuation."

"They won't be worth shit way things are going on Wall Street."

"Out of my league, Brenton. Out of yours, too. Reason I came over was this here note of yours."

Chief Hazard picked up the transparent envelope again to peer at the note inside. Five words. *'Wait till I get you!'*

"There's a clue here but I can't puzzle it out. Does he mean something that's happened or something that's going to happen?"

"The 'I'll get you' is a threat. 'Wait' implies a prior condition, something she's done. Or hasn't done."

"So, whoever sent this already knew Mrs. Plane, right?"

"You're on to something, Chief. Let's write it out." Suiting action to words, in his careful hand, the Sheriff wrote in his pad:

- Mrs Plane does something (*Wait*)
- (*Wait*) is something important or dramatic in her or their past (*!*) Done when?
- It affects the assassin when he learns of it – motive? Enough to kill?
- The killer is known to Mrs. Plane (*I'll* get *you*)?
- *AND knows where she lives* (Note delivered by hand to her address)

Both men studied what the Sheriff had written and what the note said.

"What if she didn't know who sent it?"

"She knew. They must have met or at least spoken before. Maybe several times. The note is an ultimate threat."

"If she knew him, why has he bothered to make his message anonymous out of cut-up newsprint?"

"Beats me. Maybe that's why the note is torn into so many tiny pieces, balled up and thrown away? Perhaps she was angry? And maybe afraid."

"If she was afraid, why did she let him in?"

"We don't know."

"How could he be sure no servants would be there?"

"It's possible if he had the house under surveillance. He could have seen the staff come and go and know how many there were in at any one time. Don't forget that phone call."

"We have no proof the guy was there when it was made."

"Right. We don't know."

"That's a lot of 'don't know,'" the Chief said.

"Here's another," the Sheriff said. "We don't really know it was somebody from the outside. It could have been somebody on the inside. My fear is time. The longer this takes the colder the trail."

"You know what the DA told me? 'Get it wrapped by Christmas. I don't want this dragging on into an election year.'"

"I hope you told him to go fuck himself," the Sheriff said.

+ + + +

PETER BEALE

INTERROGATION IN THE MURDER MANSION / 2

"Your name, please?"

"Marjorie Bassett, sir."

"Occupation?"

'I am the cook"

"Address?"

"Here, sir. I have rooms above the carriage house."

"Rooms?"

"My husband was the general handyman here before the war. We have a flat of three adjoining rooms."

"He has retired?"

"No sir. He is an invalid. Gassed in the trenches. He spent five years in the hospital in Fort McHenry, Maryland, and when that was closed in 1923, Mr. Plane had him admitted for permanent nursing care to Newport Hospital where I can visit him."

"I see. I am sorry."

"Not as sorry as I am. He suffers so much it were better that he died in the field."

"Would you like a moment…?"

"No, I am fine, sir."

"Good. So…How long have you been employed here?

"I have been with the family thirty-nine years, all told."

"Since 1890?"

"Yes. I was eighteen then. Came here as the scullery maid. Mrs. Plane insisted Old Cook taught me on the job."

"Old Cook?"

"Mrs. Lawrence, she was. Nobody called her that. Been dead with the flu in '19."

"And you succeeded her?"

"No. Long before that. She retired in 1900 when I took over."

"Then you were already here when Mrs. Lister was appointed housekeeper."

"Yes."

"How would you describe your relationship with her?"

"Cordial...Until the arrival of the second Mrs. Plane."

"Yes?"

"She, Mrs. Lister, tried to have me replaced. Thought somebody younger would better suit, seeing as Mrs. Plane was French."

"And...?"

"Karla, I mean, Mrs. Plane, would have none of it. Insisted I show her how to cook all the things Mr. Plane liked. Came right into the kitchen, apron on, ready to learn. She was a quick study too, no airs or anything, she having been a waitress for years and years in Paris. She showed me how they did things there. Truth be told, I probably learned more from her than she did from me."

"Were you surprised Mr. Plane remarried?"

"No. The surprise, if there was one, is it took him so long. His first wife had been dead for nigh on ten years. He was a great catch, a very jolly man, rich too, with an eye for the ladies. It was a tragedy he died so soon after they married. He worshipped her, you know. Took her everywhere with him across the country to show her all he owned."

"How did she take his death?"

"How did she...?"

"Yes."

"I cannot say for certain. But my impression was...I find it difficult to put in words...it was as if fate would not let her be happy. No. Not exactly that. It was...They were happy together for those few months. I could tell. Standing shoulder to shoulder in the kitchen you sense how the other feels. She was a joy to be with, but...it was as if there was a shadow somewhere in her past."

"She spoke of this with you?"

"No. It was more what she didn't say. To answer your question, when he died, she was not distraught so much as resigned. Like in the war, you hope nothing bad will happen to your man, but in your heart, you are resigned to the fact that something will."

"And after his death how did she manage?"

"Manage? You mean the probate and not finding the will?

"I don't understand?"

"Mr. Plane left her everything in a new will he made when they married. When he died the will couldn't be found and the Judge decided that until it was, a man from New York would be appointed executor to manage the estate. Still does in fact. Pays our wages. Paid her an allowance, if you can believe it, bloody nerve."

"Well, she lived here for another three years. With ten beds made up. Was she on her own the whole time?"

"Yes. Her lawyer would occasionally stay over, but other than him," the cook shrugged.

"What? No family? No friends call on her? No man or men?"

"There is only her mother, who lives, or lived - I don't know if she is still alive - in some remote town in the French Alps. As for friends, she had none here, just acquaintances. People she met with her husband when they came back after their honeymoon. And men? Many tried. She didn't give them the time of day. She was going to go back to France once she sold the house, you know."

"In those three years did she ever leave Newport?"

"The first year, no. She almost never went out. Maybe the odd walk in the evening when she was less likely to be seen."

"And the next two years?"

"She went skiing."

"Skiing?"

"She was brought up on skis. She went to the 1928 Winter Olympics in St. Moritz, Switzerland."

"With whom?"

'I don't know. I know she went because I saw the labels on her luggage when she came back."

"How long was she gone?"

"Most of the winter. Two months maybe, including the boat trips there and back."

"Okay. Now, where were you on Saturday, October 26, 1929?"

"In the kitchen as usual."

"All day?"

"No."

"Can you be more specific?"

"I always start early, baking bread about 6 in the morning. Mrs. Plane took her breakfast in her room at 8 as usual. I made coffee, extra strong, and scrambled eggs and sorted the fresh fruit she liked. Molly, one of the maids, took the tray up to her and brought it back down untouched about an hour later. 'She only wanted coffee,' she said. Around 10 Mrs. Plane announced all staff would have a half-day holiday and asked us to be off the premises by 11."

"Was that usual?"

"Getting a half-day off, yes. Being told to clear off, most certainly not. Don't forget we live here - at least we do for now. She gave no explanation, just a very polite instruction. It must have taken me all of an hour to clean up the kitchen, change my clothes, gather a few things I thought I might need and leave."

"Where did you go?"

"It was windy and cold, so the beaches were out for a picnic. We all finally ended up in front of the fire in Jimmy's mother's house."

"All?"

"Myself, the maids, Molly, and Lucy, and of course, Jimmy. Meg, the scullery-girl went off to see her guy down at the docks."

"And Sarah Lister?"

"She left Friday evening to see her Ma. Did it every weekend. Back on Sunday.

"Did you see anyone lurking about the house when you left?"

"No."

"And when you returned?"

"Neither."

"At what time did you return?"

"We had till 6 in the evening, in time to make dinner for Mrs. Plane. It was already getting dark by then, so we came back early, without Jimmy, about 4.30."

"When did you learn Mrs. Plane had been assaulted?"

"As soon as we came in and saw the house was upside down; then Molly found blood trails leading into the dining room. It was terrible what was hidden under those rugs. That poor woman. Lucy and I got sick while Molly called the police."

"In the days before Saturday, October 26, did you notice anything unusual in the behaviour of Mrs. Plane?"

"No."

"Any unusual visitors?"

"No."

"Phone calls?"

"None in front of me.

"Mail? Packages?"

"No. Nothing."

"Was there a gun kept in the house?"

"A gun? No. Unless you mean Mr. Plane's old pistol in the mudroom?"

'The mudroom?"

"Through there, the other side of the pantry," Mrs. Bassett pointed to a small door. "It's where you take off coats and boots when it's wet and muddy outside."

"Thank you, Mrs. Bassett."

+ + + +

"Better," the Sheriff said to Brady. "Was the gun there?"

From the expression on Brady's face, he knew the answer.

"Christ in heaven, Brady, you didn't look?"

"No gun was reported found anywhere in the house when it was first searched after the murder," Brady said. "Anyway, she said it wasn't there."

"You should still have looked to confirm the exact location where she said the pistol was kept. But at least you've confirmed what we thought that she ordered the staff out. If it hasn't already been done, verify the time the maid called the station and who took the call. And you've made three important discoveries. One is to our timeline, with the maid finding the body shortly after 4.30pm not 12.30. That gives the killer at least five hours instead of 45 minutes. Changes a lot of things. Second, we learn she wanted to sell the house, so perhaps she spoke to an agent? Probably local. Find out who specialises in the sale of these estates? Third, she went to Europe. Ostensibly to ski. You know anything about skiing, Brady?"

"No, sir."

"You slide about on snow with long bits of wood attached to your feet." Sniff. "Is that all she did? Seems unlikely. As if this wasn't complicated enough, we now have an international element. I'll talk to the DA. See if we can get some cooperation from across the pond. While we're at it, check to see if Mrs. Plane's mother is still alive. She would be next of kin if she is. Which brings up the subject, did Mrs. Plane leave a will? Has one been found?"

"Not to my knowledge, sir. And not according to Mrs. Bassett."

"Has anyone thought to look?"

"I do not know."

"Right, then. Find out about this lawyer? Probably the same firm her husband used since she had no contacts over here independent of him. Find out if, in the three years since the death of Mr. Plane, his widow drew up a will. At the same time have a thorough search made of the premises in the event she wrote a holographic will. Because if there is no will and she died intestate, her estate will be decided in probate. Right? Who's next?"

"The chambermaid, Lucy Watson."

"Okay. Cross-check and cross-reference everything. Good man. On your way down please post this on the bulletin board by the Secretary's office."

+ + + +

DYLAN ON THE JOB

Loud new boots
　　Sideways lie
　　Swallowing unhappily
In a smoke-filled room.
On the drink he climbs the stairs (each had a different voice) to the
Safe island of his bed, his story burned up
Conducted by a wind, unfamiliar to hisself…
And there saw the stranger boots
And the bright blonde girl who
with them came
looking out from the covers of his bed…smoking a cigarette in…
(His bed!)
You asked me up and here I am she says…waving the fag.
From the girl to the boots to the door
He hazards a look
Shakes his head
Nor, never I did, he says.
And sees the pile of clothes she left for him to see.
So? Smiles at the girl
(thanks his god)
Undresses with care
Climbs on board
And…
Nearly there…

Quite falls fast
Asleep !

Brenton

THE READING ROOM, NEWPORT

"**R**abelaisian," the Secretary said, beaming, when next he chanced to meet the Sheriff on his way out of the Gents. "I think I'm beginning to get the hang of what you're up to. I am the first to admit I am no critic, but your latest is a truly noble effort. Nothing wishy-washy. A bit bawdy, am I wrong? I like the racy tone, splendid stuff. Rabelaisian!" Repeating the word seemed to inflate the man, so he said it for a third time.

"Rabelaisian!"

"Thank you," the Sheriff said.

"I have one question," the Secretary said.

"And that is..?"

"Who is Dylan?"

"A Welshman. Thomas is the name."

"Can't say I've heard of him."

"A young Welsh poet. It's written in his honour."

"Well?" The Secretary was flummoxed. "Welsh, you say? And a poet? I doubt we have many of them as members."

"Aie, 'tis a pity," said the Sheriff. "Duty calls. I must be off. Come on, Brady."

"Rabelaisian!" The Secretary called after them.

+ + + +

"What does he mean?" PC Brady said, when they were alone walking down Bellevue toward Washington Square for a meeting with the District Attorney.

"I don't think he knows who François Rabelais was," the Sheriff said. And the way he said it shut off Brady's next question.

"When we get to our meeting, say nothing about your discoveries," the Sheriff continued. "It is always smart to keep your mouth shut. Let others voice their opinions and only voice yours if asked directly. The idea is to come away from one of these gabfests without speaking. Take your cue from me."

Once arrived and shown into the District Attorney's office the Sheriff's strategy disintegrated with the DA's first question.

"What have you got for us, Sheriff?" William Clarke said. "We're under the gun here. The French Ambassador in Washington is asking questions. It appears Mrs. Plane was someone other than the simple waitress Sir Kobe married. Apparently, she was a heroine in the Great War and France demands an answer as to how and why she was slain."

+ + + +

SORBONNE, PARIS - KARLA

Monday, August 3,1914

'Sie sind alles verrückt!'

For the rest of her life Karla would remember exactly where she was when she heard Germany had declared war on France. In the Polidor, founded in 1845, on the corner of Rue Monsieur Le Prince and Rue Racine. She was sitting at a table by herself reading Le Petit Journal recounting in every salacious detail the murder trial of Henriette Caillaux, who shot a man her husband should have shot to 'protect the honor of her family' when, above the babel of normal conversation in the restaurant, a voice exclaimed "Ça y est! C'est la guerre!"

Then a mushroom of excited comments made reading impossible. Karla left, to walk up the hill, past l'Odeon, to the Rue de Vaugirard, to join a growing crowd in front of the Palais du Luxembourg where a special session of the Senate was in progress. Every deputy, entering or leaving, was bombarded with questions. Every answer was inadequate. It seemed totally ridiculous that the assassination of an obscure Archduke and his wife by some lunatic student in the Balkans more than a month previously could lead to a world at war.

"Sie sind alles verrückt!"

The words, in German, were spoken by a thin man, almost a boy, standing in the crowd next to her. "They are all crazy!" He wasn't talking to her. The words went out over the heads of the crowd to mingle with the shouted cries of others. Perhaps the boy-man was saying it to himself. Karla found herself staring at him, a young German, here, in the middle of Paris. Next to her. As he turned to stare at her.

Their eyes locked.

"Markus," the man said.

Without another word, he took her elbow and escorted her out of the mob. For some reason she didn't struggle. They got to the top of the Rue de Tournon before she said, "Karla."

"I know who you are," the man said. "You are the history student in her first year at the Sorbonne. Every fellow is in love with you."

"Don't be silly."

"I am not, 'silly.' I observe. It is what I do best." He still held her elbow, and he now guided her into a small bar on the corner of the Rue Saint-Sulpice. "We'll be safe here," he said, and added "Look, there is a coin." And bent and picked it up, rubbing it between thumb and forefinger, before putting it in his trouser pocket.

"You are a strange man, Monsieur," Karla said

"With that accent, you are not Parisian," he said. "Where are you from?"

"Why should I tell you?"

"We have to trust each other. To trust you must know. Without trust we cannot collaborate. So, I will start. I am from Berlin. I am a postgraduate student specialising in Franco-German military history. If there is one thing I have learned it is this: Never trust the Generals, never believe the politicians and every historian writes fiction. You have a father?"

"Yes."

"Brothers?"

"Yes…?"

"Your father and brothers will be called up. What will you do?"

"Do?"

"Yes. Think. Yesterday I was just another foreign student studying in Paris. Today I am a German. An enemy of France. Your enemy. Who determines this? What forces me, or you, to accept being categorised in this way?"

From a passing waiter he ordered a small carafe of red wine and some cheese.

"I cannot drink without eating, and I cannot think without drinking," he said. When the wine arrived and was poured he touched the rim of his glass to hers, locked eyes and said, "Salud, Amor y Pesetas"

Having sipped, he put his glass down and said, "It is like this. I am two years ahead of you. As an enemy alien I will be expelled from France, and I will not be able to complete my doctorate next year. I am determined to refuse to fight and to do whatever I can to frustrate the madmen in my country. I will obtain information which I will pass to you. Your task will be to identify those in command in France who can be trusted to best use this information. You will never reveal who gives you this information, nor how you get it."

"You cannot be serious?"

"But I am, Mademoiselle, I am."

"We will be spies!"

"No! We will be two students of goodwill, determined to prevent the destruction of our world."

"Why me?"

"I told you. I must choose someone to trust."

"But you don't know me."

"No. And you don't know me. What is there to know when we have so little time? It is better like this. Neither can betray the other. Yes? Let us begin. Where are you from?"

"The Alps"

"That is like saying the desert. Please be specific. Where in the Alps?"

"A small town, Briançon, on the Italian border."

"Who knows you are here in Paris?"

"The school authorities, my parents and brothers, a few friends." She shrugged.

"How do you manage?"

"Manage? You mean money? I have a bourse."

"You are like me then. Poor. A poor student trying to get by on a scholarship. Where do you live?"

"In the 14th."

"So do I. Rue Campagne Perrier."

"Then we are neighbours. I have a room in the Passage d'Enfer."

"Chez La Vieille?"

"Yes."

"Yet I've never seen you in our neighbourhood?"

"Maybe because I come and go by Boulevard Raspail."

"You are segregated, right? To protect her pensionnaires, la vieille won't allow cohabitation? No matter. We are free in my building. You can visit me. We have little time and much to discuss. When the men are called up they will close the university. You will be sent home unless you find a job."

"Doing what?"

"That is the question." He poured more wine into his glass which was empty; Karla, after the first sip, had not touched her's again.

"I have it. With your looks you will be a model. I have many artist friends. They will pay you, not much, but more than your bourse. Enough to afford a room and to eat."

"No."

"No? What no?"

"No. I will not do it. I do not know you. I want no part of this."

Which is when two pretty girls came into the cafe. Looked around. Saw them. Simultaneously called out "Markus!" and rushed over to fall into his arms. Karla found herself a spectator at what seemed to be the beginning of a public orgy. Finally, when all the kissing and fondling was done, Markus straightened his clothes and said, "This is Denise and this is Florence."

"We are his lovers," Denise said

"Two of the many," Florence said.

They giggled.

"You know he is a musician?" Denise said.

"A piano player," Florence said.

"When he plays the piano for you, you will understand," Denise said.

They finished the wine and got up to leave.

"Salut!" they said in chorus, giggling again.

"Salut, Flo! Salut Denise!" Markus said.

When they had gone, into the silence they left behind, Karla couldn't help herself, she said, "Okay. I will do it."

+ + + +

He was right about having little time. A notice posted that same day, in the main entrance hall of the Sorbonne on Rue Victor Cousin in the 5th Arrondissement, advised all German, Austro-Hungarian, Serbian, Russian and Turkish students they had one week to evacuate France or they would be forcibly expelled or incarcerated in camps. The Russians protested. They were allies of France. To no avail.

"You see," Markus said, "the bureaucratic mind. Nothing can change a decision that has been made. It is the same in the military. Their vaunted objectivity and pragmatism mask their inflexibility; always on the lookout for simple solutions to complex problems; they will doom us all if we don't fight back."

Karla learned more history in the week they had together, holed up in the shambles Marcus called his crib, than she would glean in a semester at the university. In between a seemingly endless rotation of girlfriends attending to his Priapic appetite, where he would ask her to leave or wait outside his door while he 'got on with it', he indoctrinated her in what he called the 'reverse engineering of history.'

"Forget the Middle Ages. Forget Charlemagne. Forget William the Conqueror of Normandy. Forget all the Louis from I through XVIII and above all forget that arch war criminal, Napoleon. You French are besotted by La Gloire. You justify defeat by raising triumphal monuments to your dead heroes and chopping off the heads of any that stand in the way of your beliefs. Liberté, Fraternité, Egalité, my arse. This so-called republic is a joke. A farce. Your President Poincaré, has gone off on holiday believing this 'petite guerre' will fade away after his not-so-secret rendezvous with the

Russians in Saint Petersburg, while the great unwashed are distracted by the murder trial of Henriette Caillaux."

Karla felt herself blushing.

"As I sit here," Markus said, propped against unwashed pillows in the disorder of stained sheets and the sweet-sick smell of sex, "the Russians are mobilising, but France is holding its breath waiting for a verdict. The English think they will be home by Christmas. And we? What do we learn at the Sorbonne? Langlois and Seignibos would have us believe in 'the implementation of documents' as if we were librarians filing books in alphabetical order. We are taught not to judge. Not to interpret the past. There must be a complete separation between the historian and history. The historical fact exists and must not be distorted or interpreted through the prism of contemporary thought, fashion, or belief. I have to take a piss."

Naked he got out of bed, crossed the room to the toilet, left the door ajar, pissed loudly into the toilet bowl, flushed the toilet, hawked to clear his throat, spat, flushed the toilet, scratched his crotch, put on an un-ironed shirt, and, hopping from one foot to the other, a pair of filthy, striped cotton trousers with a button missing from the fly, recrossed the room to sit on a bench in front of the only clean object in the place, an antique upright Bösendorfer piano, removed the green felt cover protecting the ivory keys, placed his fingers on them ready to play, and said:

"Febvre and Bloch have a more holistic view. History is to be viewed in time and space, considering the facts of society as a whole. What use is this now? I will tell you. It is not what our dear professors would have us believe. We, as historians, know something. We know what has been done in the past and who did it. We also know they cannot change because fundamentally they have never changed. Thus, we know what they will do in any given circumstance and by reverse engineering we can anticipate their every move. Karla, my dear, you could beat Lasker, the Chess Champion himself, if you knew which piece he would next move. The one certainty, if we survive, is that we will each remember what happened in a different way"

+   +   +   +

His fingers move. He plays. Beethoven. '*Für Elise.*' From the first five repeating notes, alternating E and D-sharp, she instantly recognises the melody and can feel the goosebumps on her arms.

He stops. Gestures with his left hand. "Sit here next to me," he says.

+   +   +   +

INTERROGATION IN THE MURDER MANSION / 3

Mrs. Jacob Roberts was shown into the library by Molly. She did not immediately sit where invited but surveyed the room from the door. Against all four walls, intimidating rows of leather-bound books rose from floor to ceiling in serried ranks of parchment yellow, Bordeaux red, biblical black, clerical grey, pontifical purple, olive green and five different shades of blue. By their aged patina and wear it was obvious they had been well read, and by their lustre, well-loved. They had been replaced with care. No one seeing them now could imagine the disorder in which they had been found strewn across the floor.

Mrs. Roberts, having never opened a book since her graduation from Smith, was unimpressed. She came from a generation of emancipated women free from any restraints other than those invisible mores imposed by Society: catch your man, raise a couple of kids, breathe a sigh of relief when they leave the parental home, enjoy what life has to offer, make sure you got yours. To which one should add curiosity. In her case blended with a hefty dose of jealousy and envy. At random she pulled a book from one of the shelves, glanced at the title, '*OVID: Ars Amatoria*', saw it was written in a language she did not recognise and put it back. Pulled out another, '*TACITUS: Ab excessu divi Augusti*'. Put it back. Pulled out a third, '*ERASMUS: Μωρίας Εγκώμιον*', put it back, sniffed, ignored Thomas waiting to interview her, walked to the French doors looking out over the garden, assessed the view and proximity to The Elms, and ended up in front of Belanopek's full-length nude of Klara. That the picture was a masterpiece was immaterial. For her it was an affront. Who could be so vulgar as to display his wife in this way?

"I demand this picture be taken down or covered up," she said. "No decent person should be made to look at it." While noting every detail which she would embellish when recounting to Daisy what she saw on this, her first visit, inside the Plane Mansion.

"Please be seated," Thomas said.

"Only if you move my chair so that I don't have to look at *that*!"

With the chair positioned to her satisfaction, Mrs. Roberts smoothed the skirt of her fawn-coloured, linen Paul Poiret dress under her bottom and sat down.

"Yes?" she said.

"State your name, please."

"How absurd. You know who I am."

"Madam, there are certain formalities…"

"Formalities?" Mrs. Roberts wrinkled her nose as if detecting a bad smell. "How tedious. Put down Mrs. Jacob Roberts."

"First name?"

"Helen."

"Address?"

"You know that as well."

"Address?"

"God in heaven. Number 2, Bellevue Court. Two doors to the left of this house. On the corner of Bellevue Avenue."

"Thank you. Occupation?"

"Occupation? You think I work? I am the wife of Jacob Roberts, the banker!"

Pause. Thomas was about to react but, just in time, remembered the Sheriff's word: focus. He took a deep breath. From a folder in front of him he took a sheet of paper.

"On the evening of Saturday, October 26," he said, "you made a statement to the police that you and your cousin, Mrs. Patrick McCarthy, saw a man enter Planetree House, and I quote, 'shortly before noon'. Correct?"

"Yes."

"Could you be more precise as to the time."

"The Trinity Clock struck twelve shortly afterwards. That's how we knew the time."

"How far were you from the man you say you saw?"

"From the front of my house to here."

"Could you be more precise?"

"You mean in feet? Don't be ridiculous. Measure it yourself."

"But you saw the man clearly?"

"Not really."

"Oh?"

"Daisy and I had been shopping. We came around the corner from Bellevue, our man opened the front door to help with the packages and I, or maybe it was Daisy, spotted someone going in the gate here and said 'Who can that be?' It was very brief. A glimpse, as I told the police."

"Could you be more precise?"

"How do you mean?"

"Tall, short. Fat, thin. Young, old. Any detail you may remember?"

"I'm sorry. As I said, it was just a glimpse."

"You say your man opened the front door? Could he have seen this person?"

"Jason?"

"Jason?"

"Our butler. He needs glasses to see his feet."

"But you are certain it was this house the man entered?"

"This is getting tedious. Go to the front door. Look to your left. And judge for yourself. Unless you are blind you will see the entrance to my house and if you can see the entrance to my house from here then you can see the entrance to this house from there. Clear?"

Thomas blushed. To hide his confusion, he pretended to consult his notes, then he said:

"When you saw, glimpsed, this man, did you perhaps also see who let him in?"

"No."

"You then telephoned Mrs. Plane?"

"Yes."

"How long after you glimpsed the man?"

"I don't know. Ten minutes, perhaps. Daisy went upstairs to freshen up and put away her packages. I spoke to Cook about lunch. So ten, maybe fifteen minutes."

"Do you recall your conversation?"

"I had heard she wanted to sell her house. My cousin is looking for a property to buy. I thought it opportune to call and ask the price."

"How did Mrs. Plane reply?"

"She was noncommittal. Something about not yet having made up her mind to sell, and I sensed she was reluctant to discuss the matter, so I said 'I'm sorry, if you are busy I will call back at a more convenient moment.'"

"In your police statement you mention a car dealer?"

"Yes. She said something about a man who came to sell her a car. Peculiar, to say the least."

"You gave his name as Pal or Paul Konbee. Is that correct?"

"It's what I heard. She obviously wanted to end the conversation. Anyway, Kondee, Tondee, Ponbee, what does it matter?"

"And then you hung up?"

"Yes."

"Did you connect this Kondee, or whatever his correct name might be, with the man you saw entering the house?"

"Why can't you say 'this' house? We are in 'this' house, not 'the' house."

"Mrs. Roberts…"

"You police always try to make a mystery out of everything. The murder happened here, in this house, not some abstract 'the'."

"Mrs. Roberts, please answer the question."

"Of course, I thought there was a connection. Why do you think I called her?"

Pause. As best he could Thomas tried to digest this information, then he said:

"That will be all for now. Thank you for your time, Mrs. Roberts. Please ask your cousin, Mrs. Patrick McCarthy, when would it be convenient to interview her?"

"Daisy? She left for New York."

+ + + +

APARTMENT 445, THE DAKOTA
BUILDING, NYC

I t was their habit. After sex, talk.

They were like tumescent teenagers, aroused by absence. Daisy had hardly walked into the apartment when she was tearing off her clothes and trying to help Patrick off with his. No need for foreplay. The anticipation was such that she was wetting her pants before the train from Providence reached Grand Central. It was like this from the moment they met all those years ago in Venice. Fired up, like a well-lubricated machine whose moving parts would accelerate from idle to flat out and back to idle, husband and wife shifted through the automatic gears of familiar passion until, sated, they lay in a happily dazed and sweaty embrace on their pillows and Daisy said, "One day you'll give me a heart attack."

"That's my line," Patrick said.

"Honestly, I don't know how you do it, Pat?"

"Look in the mirror."

Daisy had no need. Even after two children she had the natural build of a honed athlete. It was not fair. All the mothers she knew, pear-shaped, apple-shaped, strudel-waisted, hated her. And she didn't care. She had Patrick. Patrick with heart problems and kidney stones and the enormous stress under which he lived.

Patrick said, "Helen called. She wants you to call her back. Something about that murder and the man you saw."

"She saw. I didn't see anybody. Anyway, never mind her. With all that's happened, I want to know are we alright? With the mortgage? And you?"

"Yes, thanks to Jacob."

"Meaning?"

"He's saved us. We can keep this." He waved his hand to encompass their apartment, and all it contained, the art, the silverware, the rugs, her jewellery, his stamp collection, the kernel of their privileged world. "He bought the paper from Morgan. Even got a discount, believe it or not."

"And the firm?"

"So-so. We'll take a hit, but London won't let us down."

"Oh, Patrick…"

"I know. I shouldn't have gambled. Buying on margin is a mug's game. I'm sorry. I even had to let the car go."

"Your Duesey? Oh, Patrick…" Daisy knew how much he loved the car.

"Jacob bought it. Or maybe I should say he swapped it for shares in General Motors."

"What!"

"Don't get mad. They're dirt cheap right now. In two- or three-years Jacob thinks the stock will climb back up and we could buy five cars if we want. But…"

"No house in Newport." It was a statement, not a question.

"Not for now, Daisy, no. I'm so sorry. And there's one other thing - not a word to Helen. Jacob is adamant. He regards her as a dangerous gossip."

"He used those words?"

"Yes."

"I can't believe it. I know she talks, but dangerous?" Daisy sat up in bed to look down at her husband. "How can she be dangerous?"

"These are tricky times. The wrong word in certain ears can be easily misinterpreted. Confidence is so fragile; Jacob does not want it known what he's done for us. Nobody must know."

"Jack knows."

"Morgan? Yes, he does. He also knows how to keep his mouth shut if he ever wants to deal with Jacob's bank again. They swap paper all the time, you know, so something small like this will not be noticed in the shuffle. But shine a light on it? God forbid."

"I don't understand."

"Okay. Imagine Helen opens her big mouth at a private little dinner party with some close friends. One of them happens to be the wife of a banker who is a competitor of Morgan or Robert's or both. The wife says to hubby when she gets home 'Guess what? Helen Roberts has told me in confidence that her husband has made a deal with Jack Morgan to buy the mortgage they hold as collateral on loans they have made to Patrick McCarthy for him to speculate and buy shares on margin, which shares have lost most of their value, and require him to liquidate his positions or front more money to keep his investments, money which he doesn't have. The banker thanks his wife and next day has a quiet lunch at his club with a member of the Fed. 'What's all this I hear about Morgan and Roberts doing a deal to bail out McCarthy?' The next thing a reporter for the Financial Times, quoting a 'source', questions the propriety of two publicly traded banks colluding in such a deal with the deposits of their clients in such perilous times. We, Daisy, you, and I, would be ruined. Jack and Jacob would be grilled and, if not shot by a firing squad, politely asked to resign from holding any fiduciary position in any publicly traded company." All said quietly, without once raising his head from the pillows. Then he put a finger to his lips. "Got that? Not a word. Understood?"

Daisy nodded. She didn't say she was frightened. But she was. Her intuition told her, as sure as a bat pinging radar, that Helen would find out via the kind of bio-acoustic echolocation all scandals generated. As if reading her thoughts, Patrick said: "Blame me if it comes up. Say I prefer the Hamptons to Newport."

+ + + +

Later, when Daisy returned Helen's call, all Helen could talk about was Karla's portrait in the library. "Believe me, there's not a detail missing. She must have been posing there for weeks, completely naked, while this artist nobody's ever heard of painted her down to the finest curl in her pubes! God! And try to picture this, she's smiling! You know that demure kind of Mona Lisa smile, with her arms reaching up behind her head to make her breasts taut, standing against a beech tree in a kind of glade with sunlight coming through the branches behind her, lighting up her black hair hanging to her waist?"

"It sounds magical."

"It's a picture. It doesn't make a noise."

"Not the picture. You. The way you describe it makes it magical."

"Well, it's not. It's rude. Imagine if everyone who came into your home could see you hanging there stark naked."

Daisy could feel herself smiling at the thought.

"And you can stop smiling," Helen said from 180 miles away. "I know what you're thinking."

"Why not if it was done by Boldini, or Sargent, if he was still alive."

"Really, Daisy!"

"I can see myself as Madame X. And what about Conny Vanderbilt's picture we saw at her house in London?"

"At least she has her clothes on."

"I think it would be fun. Tell me the truth, is she lovely?"

"The truth? During my interview, that little policeman had to sit with his back to the picture because he couldn't take his eyes off her. By the way, he wants to talk to you when you return here. He wants to ask about what you saw?"

Silence.

"Daisy? Daisy, are you there?"

"Yes, Helen."

"For a moment I thought we were cut off. I was saying…"

"I heard you. You know I saw nothing, Helen."

"The man…"

"What man? The man you glimpsed. You say you saw him. I did not. We said these very words at the time. You said, who was that? I said, who?

You said, didn't you see a man just now, going into Plane's house? And I said, no. I was bending down picking up my packages, not looking down the street, so how could I have seen him? I don't know what you've told the police, but that's what I'm going to say."

Silence.

+   +   +   +

IN THE BLACK PEARL

"We're screwed, Lake," Kale said. He was reading the small ads on the second last page of the Reporter. "There's not a single job offer, just guys looking for work. Listen to this. 'Desperate Family man, four children, former manager of restaurant chain, will trade work for rent. Any work considered.' And this. 'Skilled plumber. Will work for food.' There are dozens of them. What are we going to do?"

"I say we take off for Providence. Must be more opportunities there," Lake said.

"More competition too." Kale said. "Nah. Let's hang tight. We're locals here. We know how things work. 'Sides we've got the boat."

They were sleeping on one of the boats moored off Bowen's Wharf for the winter. The owner of the boat lived in Chicago; happily ignorant his boat was now a hostel. If the boat was kept immaculate the Harbour Master could see no harm in the arrangement. Plus, the boys were cheap security on the Wharf at night and good for a drink whenever they had money. That they made a bit of change renting a berth to the odd desperate navy cadet out with a date but unable to afford a motel room was nobody's business. Live and let live. They could see their boat from where they were perched on barstools in the Back Bar of the Tavern.

Kale turned to the last page. "Jesus H. Christ," he said. "Get this. The World's population will surpass 2 billion next year, despite a daily death toll of…Take a guess? What d'you think the average daily death toll is?"

"You really are sick," said Lake. "All you read about is death. Morbid. You're morbid, you know."

"A report from the U.S. Census Bureau, says 40,000 people die per day in the World. By way of comparison, the U.S. has a population of 121,770,000, an annual death rate of 11.2% per 1000 population, which equates to…"

"Harry," Lake said to the barman, " do me a favour, throw this guy out."

Harry the barman ignored the request. The Poben brothers were better entertainment than any serial on the radio.

Kale said, "I'll be darned. Here's one for you, Lake. Bottom of the last page. *'A Cold Trail. Mr. Justin R. Roche, of Leroy Avenue, Newport, who is in the real estate business, told District Attorney William Clarke that two days before the killing of Mrs. Plane, she called on him at his office and told him that she desired to dispose of her home, because she was becoming uneasy about the loneliness of the isolated section of the street in which she lived and was intent on returning to her native country, France. DA Clarke said there will be no funeral for Mrs. Plane in Newport as her body will be repatriated by the French Authorities on instruction from their Embassy in Washington. A private commemorative service for friends of the deceased will be announced at a future date. DA Clarke had no further comment.'*

"So, the bastard gets away with it?" said Lake.

+ + + +

BRISTOL, RHODE ISLAND

Sunday, October 27, 1929

A s soon as he came in the door, he knew he had made a mistake. Perhaps he was tired. He saw the sign on Main Street outside an 18th century clapboard townhouse. Parked, in a convenient spot, directly in front of the steps leading to the front door. And was greeted at the reception desk by a friendly teenager, agog to show his knowledge.

"That's a Hudson 7, right? Wow! Don't see many like that in these parts. Is that the Model R? Inline six? 92 horsepower?" He came around the desk. "Mind if I take a close look? You just go on ahead; sign the register."

He signed: *P. Blake.* No point making it easy.

The kid came back grinning. "Briggs body, boy. Musta cost a ton. One day maybe I'll have one." He went behind the desk. Glanced at the register. "How many nights will you be stayin' with us, Mr. Blake?"

He was about to say three, again, but caught himself. Don't leave a pattern. "Just the one," he said.

"One night," the kid repeated, writing it down in his register. "We have a great room open. First floor, front. Quiet after 6, when they roll up the sidewalks. You can watch your car from up there. Be sure I don't steal it. Ha, ha!"

The kid was right. He could see the damn car parked right under his window. If you're going to steal a car, steal something anonymous, a Ford, a black Ford, you stupid fool. He could never resist temptation. That was his problem. He'd have to ditch the car.

Hope nobody questioned the kid. Be crazy to have come so far and lose it all because of a nosey kid.

+ + + +

THE CHELSEA HOTEL, W. 23rd Street, NYC

True to his nature, upon arrival in New York, Markus did what he always did, he walked. He walked the city. Since it was set on a strict grid of streets and avenues with only Broadway to diagonally disrupt the pattern, after a few hours he was comfortably at home with the notion of Uptown, Downtown and Midtown, where a frenetic construction boom seemed underway between the transportation hubs of Grand Central Station at 42nd and Park, and Penn Central at West 31st and 7th Avenue. On billboards erected to announce the birth of each new skyscraper were the names of the architects and developers responsible. Markus noted they were almost without exception the names of foreigners. Immigrants. Like himself. Abraham Lefcourt, born in England, Herman Bergdorf, from Alsace, Adam Gimbel, from Bavaria, Benjamin Winter, a German, Frederick Brown, from Austria, Rosario Candela, an Italian, Gaetan Ajello, from Sicily, Emery Roth, born in Slovakia. If they could do it, so could he.

He registered as Kenneth Opalbe when he arrived at the Chelsea Hotel, recommended by a fellow passenger after an uneventful voyage across the Atlantic. Being in First Class, he disembarked in Manhattan avoiding the indignities of Ellis Island, the entry port for all immigrants in steerage, where they were deloused before submitting to medical tests for any signs of contagious disease.

And it was as Kenneth Opalbe that he presented himself at the headquarters of JPMorgan & Company, 23 Wall Street, the correspondent bank for Deutsche Bank, where he was received by a senior director with the respect that a few million dollars in bearer shares and bonds always commands. After opening an account and depositing his bonds and shares in a security box in the bank's vaults, he asked three questions.

One: Could the bank arrange for him to meet some of the influential names he had gleaned from the billboards? They could.

Two: Could the bank organise the necessary funding of such mortgages as might be required to finance the acquisition and development of the future real estate projects he had in mind? They could.

Three: What would be the loan to value ratio for such acquisitions?

"In today's market, seventy-five percent," the director said. "Subject to our appraisal."

"And with maximum leverage?"

"Maximum leverage?" the director said

"Yes."

"Ninety percent," the director said, adding, "reserved, of course, for our long-term, well-established clients." There was something about this brash young German that unsettled him. Apparently, he didn't have an office, but worked out of his hotel, the Chelsea of all places.

"Just so. The ten percent balance would be their equity?"

"Correct."

"Which you will lend me against the value of the bonds and shares I have deposited with you."

It wasn't a question. It was a statement.

"I -" the director began.

"Or would you rather I move my account to the Bank of New York?"

Thus armed, with the credibility of the Morgan name, Herr Opalbe became a player in the snakes and ladders of the property game as played on the island of Manhattan. The never-ending boom in building seemed to stretch forever into the future. In two short years he was the proud owner of three developments nearing completion, a twenty-seven-story office building on the corner of 61st and Madison, a magnificent block of apartments in Midtown and a hotel on Central Park South. The Gods seemed to smile on him.

It was in New York that the Roaring Twenties roared loudest, with the Dow Jones Industrial Average increasing six-fold, everybody and his aunt making a mint pursuing money, money, money, amid an ever-changing skyline of giant buildings propping up the sky. The balloon of optimism expanded on the shrill advice of a fledgling industry of brokers touting margin accounts which enabled Mom and Pop to purchase corporate equities with borrowed funds and use the stocks they bought for collateral on their loans. An avalanche of borrowed money fuelled stocks to higher and higher prices.

+ + + +

Markus was in the habit of reading the newspaper over breakfast in the Chelsea dining room. On September 5, 1929, he read an article headlined 'SKATING ON THIN ICE,' in which the reporter covering the Annual National Business Conference quoted the economist, Roger Babson, saying 'sooner or later a crash is coming, and it may be terrific.' It was the chance juxtaposition of the headline and the word 'crash' that for a moment made Markus feel in his gut the first crack in his confidence, as if the words were aimed directly at him. Refusing the waiter's offer of more coffee, Markus went to his room. He knew what he had to do. Bail.

Just as it had in the war, his instinct for self-preservation allowed for no illusory hope or wishful thinking. The buildings were 100% mortgaged to the hilt. Unfinished, they could not yet generate any income. If things went south, the bank would foreclose, and he would lose all his equity. Act now before it occurs to them.

Over the following days he was a frequent visitor at 23 Wall Street, ostensibly to bring the bank the latest draw requests and projected finishing schedules on his three projects. He was meticulous in going through each line item, matching both his copy and the bank's, against the reports and drawings of the architects. At the end of each meeting, he made a habit of going down to the vaults to check his safety deposit box. It was a simple matter to substitute the shares and bonds with that day's newspaper, carried in his briefcase.

+ + + +

At the beginning of October, after two years in residence, the receptionist at the Chelsea Hotel was asked to prepare Herr Opalbe's account.

"We are sorry to see you leave, Herr Opalbe," she said.

"My visa," he said. "Time for me to go back to Europe."

+ + + +

"That's what he said," she told the private detective employed by the bank to track down defaulting debtors after he had given her a Lincoln to open her mouth. "Didn't even leave a forwarding address."

"Has anything arrived for him since he left?"

"No. No mail." She hesitated. "There was a woman who called for him several times some days ago."

"Did she leave a number to call back?"

"No."

"Anything else?"

"No. He paid in cash, got into his motorcar and left."

"His motorcar? I thought you said he left for Europe?"

"Maybe he took it on the boat?"

"What kind of car?"

"I don't know. Sporty looking, in two tones. Ask the doorman."

It cost another Lincoln.

"A Hudson," the doorman said.

+ + + +

IN WHICH THE SHERIFF LEARNS
FROM THE COOK

Sheriff Brenton let himself into Planetree House early in the morning. He had not been able to sleep and rather than toss and turn in The Reading Room he got up while it was still dark, shaved and showered, and came down a deserted Bellevue Avenue without seeing a soul. Entering the mansion, he could hear sounds from the kitchen in the basement. Not having breakfast, he went down the servants' staircase to investigate. The consoling smell of baking bread came up the stairs to greet him.

"Good morning," he said to the cook when he saw her standing in front of her stove, flouring up to her elbows.

"Morning, Sheriff,' Cook said.

"How do you know who I am?" he said.

"Your young feller said he had to report to the Sheriff. You look the part with that badge and all on your vest." She chuckled. "Let me guess - you haven't had breakfast? Do you mind the kitchen table? Thought not. Sit yourself down. Give me two shakes and its eggs and bacon with a pot of coffee and, if you can be patient, fresh bread. We've honey and marmalade if that's to your taste."

Being a patient man, the Sheriff took off his jacket, hung it on the back of a well-worn kitchen chair, and, while waiting, took the opportunity to inspect the mudroom, then sat down, stretched his legs and was rewarded with an excellent start to his day. Over his second pot of coffee, to his silent amusement, he found himself being grilled by an expert.

"Like I told your deputy, the pistol's not there," Cook said, with a nod in the direction of the mudroom as she cleared the table. "From what I hear, you're at a dead end, Sheriff."

"How's that?" the Sheriff said.

"We all, that's those of us that live here, got a registered letter from the District Attorney's office advising us we could still live here pending the Probate Court's decision on what will happen to Mrs. Plane's inheritance. It's the 10th of November. She's been dead these past two weeks. They've released that man Buck and arrested no one else. You are conducting interrogations upstairs. You cannot explain the violence used to kill Mrs. Plane; leave alone why she was shot with a gun you cannot find."

The Sheriff nodded.

"Put a line through the dots, you're at a dead end. May I ask you, how long have we got?"

"How long?"

"To stay here? While they do this probate business."

"Well, let's see. Some probate estates can be wrapped up in as little as a few months. Probate in Rhode Island usually takes that long. The value of the estate must be established. Next-of-kin identified and informed; and if none, such other beneficiaries, if any, informed. Tax returns filed, both State and Federal, which are due every year after the estate owner's passing. Given she was a foreigner and the large, complex nature of her estate, inherited at the death of her husband, the entire process could take much longer. Much, much longer," the Sheriff repeated. "I'm not an expert, but I imagine you can count on at least six months."

"And we? What are we supposed to do in the meanwhile? How do we live? With her death, who pays our wages?" Cook stopped what she was doing.

"The Executor. In that you are caring for an important asset of the estate, he will recognise that and recompense you appropriately."

"Can he do that?"

"Absolutely. He's the Court's appointee to settle the estate and will have full powers over any asset of the estate, including any monies found, any rents collectable, or any dividends received. He is also responsible to maintain the value of the estate. You will all be paid whatever you are currently paid until the appointee decides otherwise."

"So, we carry on?"

"Exactly as if she were still alive."

"What if someone wants to leave?"

"They are free to do so. But with no claim on the estate."

"Not even for those with long tenure?"

"If there is a signed contract it will be honoured. As are all debts and obligations."

"Contract? Whoever signed a contract to work in a place like this? We come with the furniture. We work for wages, Sheriff. A number the housekeeper writes down in her little black book when she takes you on, and which you sign for each month when your wages are paid. Tenure is an understanding that you will be compensated for the years you put in looking after the family. What else can you look forward to in your old age?"

"Unfortunately, the appointee will not honour an 'understanding'," the Sheriff said.

For a long moment the cook stood still.

Finally, she said, "Lead us not into temptation."

And off the Sheriff's look of incomprehension, she added, "Have you any idea how many books there are up in the library? Or what they are worth? Did you know Mr. Plane was a polyglot and could read every one of his books in the language in which it was written? Mr. Plane's old butler once calculated there were over 14,000 rare books in that collection. Every volume is worth more than my yearly salary. Think on it, Sheriff Brenton, when you go back upstairs."

+ + + +

Upstairs, the Sheriff wanders from room to room. He is unsatisfied with himself, his thoughts, a jammed mess of contradictions. As dawn breaks, he enters the library. Without switching on the lights, he perambulates around the shelves, the fingertips of his right hand lightly caressing the leather-bound spines of the books. Haphazardly, he takes one down. Goes over to a window where there is more light. The book is bound in calfskin, dyed light blue. Embossed on the front cover is a shield, quartered, with six golden crowns and two lions rampant. The title says 'Kristina' and under that 'A Play by August Strindberg'. It is a first edition, published in 1901. Inscribed on the frontispiece is an inscription in Swedish *'Till min gode van, Kobe'* and the initials, *'AS'*. The Sheriff pulls a chair over to the window, sits down, opens the book. Pinned to each page is an English translation written in an immaculate copperplate script with hardly any corrections. The Sheriff reads. As he reads, he makes notes in his police notebook. He is so engrossed in the hardly credible story that he does not hear Thomas Brady come in. Brady is about to say something, thinks better of it, withdraws. The Sheriff does not notice. Never looks up. Reads on. Trinity Church clock strikes noon, and he has nearly reached the end, when he has the distinct impression someone is watching him.

Broad daylight in the room, the Sheriff stands, stretches, makes a half-turn away from the window, walks across to the facing wall to confront the portrait of Karla, mistress of Planetree House. She is taller than he is. Her eyes look down into his. A half smile plays on her face. I know what you're thinking, the smile seems to say.

It was you watching me, the Sheriff thinks. Smiles back at the picture. Who are you Karla Plane? Tell me something. What happened here?

+ + + +

KARLA PLANE, WIDOW

Out of patriotism, Karla sailed from New York to Le Havre on the French Line's new transatlantic ship, *SS L'Ile de France,* the first major ocean liner built after World War 1, weighing 43,000 tons, with a top speed of 23.5 knots, carrying 1486 passengers, 1200 crew and a glorious Streamline Moderne Art Deco interior by Pierre Patout. She had met Patout in 1925 while being wined-and-dined by Sir Kobe Plane during multiple attempts at seduction on excursions to the Exposition Internationale des Arts Decoratifs et Industriels Modernes held in Paris from April to October, visited by 16 million people in those few months. It was her first introduction to La Haute Société. Coached by Phuong, prodded by Phuong, lectured by Phuong, dressed by Phuong, Karla the waitress metamorphosed into Karla the courtesan. She led Sir Kobe a merry dance. To every invitation she said 'maybe'. To every proposal 'perhaps'. It wasn't until the Gala des Galas, on June 16, in the Grand Palais, where 300 dancers from all the Paris ballet companies, dressed in white tutus, performed the *Ballet de Ballets,* that she gave way and agreed to a wedding the following year, provided the ceremony was held in the Alps with her aged mother in attendance. Eight months later she was a widow.

As she told Phuong, it was not fair.

+   +   +   +

Phuong came to meet her when she disembarked at Le Havre and the two women shared a private first-class compartment in the train to Paris. As soon as they were seated, Phuong took Karla's hand and said: "Raconte-moi tout."

"How can I tell you everything when I don't know where to begin?" Karla said, tearing up.

"Start by not crying. You are not a child; don't behave like one." The reprimand was swift. "Look at you! Anyone would think you are the first person to lose her husband. The man's been dead a year or more. You were never in love with him. Why on earth are you still dressed in black?"

"You don't like this?" Karla wore a long-sleeved black silk blouse buttoned at the wrist by black pearls, a matching waistcoat, a slim black mohair skirt cut on the bias at mid-calf, a black astrakhan coat with facings in black mink, black silk gloves to her elbows, with a black pearl bracelet on her left wrist and a black silk bow tying her long black hair.

"Très chic, as if you are going to a Dracula party. Surely you didn't wear that on the boat?"

"I didn't wear much of anything. I stayed in my cabin most of the time if you must know. The weather coming across was awful, with people getting sick all over the place."

"At this time of the year what can you expect? Why didn't you wait till summer?"

"My mother."

"Quoi?"

"She's not doing so well. I thought I'd invite her to the Olympics."

Phuong said nothing, just looked at her in astonishment.

"She loves the idea," Karla said. "I only hope she's well enough to go. You should come too, Phuong. It's only a couple of weeks. It will be fun."

"What would I say to Aubert? He's getting old; I couldn't possibly leave him for so long. He still goes every day to the restaurant, insists on it, even though we have a new chef."

"You're so lucky."

"What do you mean?"

"You have each other. It's not fair."

"Don't you start crying again. What's fairness got to do with anything? Face it, life's not fair. Instead of moaning you should thank me. If I hadn't insisted, you would never have married Plane and today you would not be a rich young widow with all life's opportunities in front of you. So, tell me what it was like?"

"You mean America or death?"

"Everything. Tell me everything."

Which Karla did. Starting from moving out of her minuscule apartment in France to an 18-room Mansion in America, from working for a daily wage to having her own limitless bank account, from being a servant to having servants, from endlessly darning her few clothes to entire wardrobes full of the latest fashions, from the familiarity of Paris to the strangeness of a seaport, from being responsible for no one but herself to having a husband to look after, who was selfish enough to die on his own of a heart attack while on a business trip to New York leaving her abandoned in a strange town with no friends and a huge house with ten bedrooms and a funeral to arrange and search for the will giving her his entire estate which she never asked for which she told the executor from New York whom she didn't trust any more than all the thieving lawyers and crooked accountants intent on suing her because she married Plane and saying no to all the men trying to seduce her while she spent a year learning what it was like to be rich and finally deciding to travel and what better excuse than the Olympics for a mountain girl? When Karla finally paused to take a breath, 4 hours and 20 minutes after they had started their journey, the train was entering the Gare St.Lazare in Paris. She was staying at the Crillon. Waiting there for her arrival was a letter from her mother. In her familiar schoolgirl script, it said:

'Ma Chère Fille, Je suis désolé, mais je ne suis pas en état de voyager. Amuse-toi bien aux Jeux. Affectueusement, ta Maman.'

+ + + +

ST. MORITZ, BADRUTT'S PALACE HOTEL

Saturday, February 11, 1928

Wilfredo, the concierge, is her new friend. Also guide, protector and chaperon. She arrived, alone, before the Games opened and by the generosity of her tips to the hotel staff, she now has one of the best of the coveted 37 suites. There are officials and athletes from 25 National Olympic Committees all over the town, and in and out of the hotel day and night. The concierge knows all the names and has an opinion on the chances of every athlete. "You see that young girl over there by the piano?" he says. "She's an ice skater from Norway. 15 years old. Her name is Sonja Henie. She is incredible. Nobody will beat her." He sees the French delegation. "Ma pauvre, Dame," he consoles Karla, "your countrymen are not serious. The only medal they will win is for drinking wine."

He also offers advice on the multiple invitations she receives to every function, ball, and party in town. How he knows this, since the invitations arrive in sealed envelopes, is part of the mystique of his trade.

"Madam," he bows and on a silver salver offers her an envelope sealed with red wax, embossed with the arms of Hanover. Before she has opened it, he shakes his head, the movement almost imperceptible. Leans forward. "C'est un ours, Madam," he says in whispered confidence, "he is a bear. Ungebildet. Incolto. Uncultured."

Without qualm she accepts these multi-lingual qualifications and, unopened, the invitation ends, like so many others, in the wastebasket beneath the Concierge's desk.

In his frock coat, grey vest, starched shirt, sporting a silver and black striped tie, Wilfredo is to Badrutt's what an Archbishop is to a cathedral, the personification of authority. Omniscient. Omnipresent. There to give absolution, sing praise, and distil benedictions. Ever mindful that he has this beautiful woman - una creatura meravigliosa, as he describes her to his Italian wife - under his roof, in his care. When the day comes that the invitation bears the Coat of Arms of the House of Windsor, he takes it upon himself to personally go to the fifth floor suite overlooking the lake to deliver the missive to Karla. With his blessing.

The invitation, on ivory parchment, read '*HRH Edward, The Prince of Wales, requests the pleasure and company of Mrs. Karla Plane, to the Opening Ceremony of the Winter Olympic Games, St. Moritz, Switzerland, February 11, 1928.*'

"It was hand-delivered by Lord B, his Equerry," Wilfredo says. "He wanted to bring it up here to your apartment, but I told him that was not necessary, I would handle the matter personally. There is however a delicate problem. This!" As if by magic he offers Karla a second invitation. "It arrived a few seconds after that." A nod to the Royal effort.

The second invitation, on cream bond, read '*Le Baron Pierre de Coubertin, au nom de La Comité Olympique, a l'occasion de la Cérémonie d'Ouverture des Jeux Olympiques d'Hiver, au Stade Olympique, St. Moritz, à l'honneur d'inviter Mme. Karla Plane d'y participer au sein de l'Équipe Français.*'

"I see what you mean by delicate," Karla says.

"It is difficult," the Concierge allows. "On the one hand your countrymen, plus le Baron, the father of the Olympics; on the other, a Prince. Alors? What is to be done?"

"What?"

"A pirouette: you refuse them both. With thanks. You have unfortunately already accepted a previous invitation."

"I have?"

Wilfredo plays his ace. "You are the personal guest of Herr Badrutt, the owner of this hotel. His sleigh will take you from the front door to his private loge in the Tribune Olympique. Everyone will understand. Etiquette will have been observed. Mission accomplie!"

"Does Herr Badrutt already know this?"

"Madame! Am I not the concierge? Me ne occupo io." Wilfredo bows. "I will take care of it."

+   +   +   +

On the great day, as so often happens when mortals make plans without consulting Mother Nature, a blizzard blows through the Engadine Valley, dumping 2 metres of snow on St. Moritz in as many hours. At the Olympic Stadium - which designation includes a frozen lake for skating, curling and ice hockey, a 500-metre oval for horse racing and skijoring and the start-finish line for the men's long distance ski races - the flag poles of the 25 competing nations bend and flex like so many masts, their flags flapping and snapping with a rare violence, each gust of wind making them sound like firecrackers. The Grandstand was anything but grand, made of unpainted boards, knocked up for the occasion, that offered little protection to the viewing public. Not that they care. They are there in their thousands, under every kind of hat, cap, bonnet, beret, toque and leather helmet, smothered in furs, swaddled in blankets, coated, sweatered, gloved and scarfed, a gathered multitude braving the elements with schnapps, samovars of tea and, for the young and energetic, snowball fights behind snow forts built on all the approach roads to the Stadium.

Brought up in the Alps, Karla takes to the conditions as to the manner born. She was always an early riser. One look out of her window that morning and, over a long-sleeved silk chemise, on went unfashionable woollen long-johns, black woollen jodhpurs, thick woollen stockings, a thin black cashmere sweater, a thick, white cable-stitch fisherman's cardigan, a very long black silk scarf bound around and around her neck, and an ankle-length silver fox coat, with matching toque and hand muffler. Her studded handmade black leather boots came halfway up her calves. When she stepped out of the lift on the ground floor of the hotel it was as if the Tzarina herself had arrived from Moscow.

Wilfredo glides out from behind his desk to greet her and usher her across the hall to the front door and the waiting horse-drawn sleigh, scarcely visible in the snow-blown blizzard. Hans Badrutt, his son Hansjurg, and his second wife, Helen, the concierge explains, have gone on ahead and she will meet them in their private Loge. He makes a great fuss of handing her into the sleigh and tucking her up under thick beaver blankets and for a moment Karla thinks he's going to jump in. Then the coachman cracks his whip and she's off in the to-and-fro, creak-and-jostle, of the sleigh's runners slipping from one groove to another as they traverse the ice-bound streets in swirls of blinding snow, dodging other sleighs overcrowded with fans traversing the white valley of the Engadine, the bent boughs of trees shedding snow and ice crystals from every twig down onto them.

Bundled up in the sleigh, Karla has an insight. She misses Newport! Extraordinary thought. She must tell Phuong.

+   +   +   +

"La pauvre," Phuong tells Monsieur Aubert. "She's all alone. We must persuade her to sell that place in America and come back here where she has friends."

+   +   +   +

117

INTERROGATION IN THE MURDER MANSION / 4

"Please state your name."

"Lu..Lu..Lucy Watson."

"Don't be nervous, Lucy. I'm just going to ask you a few questions."

"I'm not nervous. I'm a little bit frightened if you want to know. What if he comes back?"

"He won't. We are in charge, the grounds are patrolled, so you have nothing to fear."

"Easy for you to say. You're not here at night. I hear things, soon as it's dark."

"I'm sure it's not easy. You must be a brave girl. Yes? So, let's start. Occupation?"

"Housemaid."

"Address?"

"I live in the Carriage House here."

"Age?"

"Twenty-two."

"For how long have you been employed?"

"Three years."

"Oh? So you were engaged after Mr. Plane married?"

"Yes sir. Mrs. Lister, the Housekeeper, wanted somebody younger seeing as Mrs. Plane was in her thirties."

"Very good, Lucy. Now I want you to think back. Where were you on Saturday, October 26, 1929?"

"Saturdays Molly and I always start early because it's Sarah's, I mean Mrs. Lister's day off. There's a list of things we have to do, so usually we split the work between us. If Molly does the breakfast, I start on the bedrooms, changing the sheets and things the way they like. It's what we were doing that day."

"Was there anything different that Saturday morning?"

"Different? In our work?"

"No. You were given a half-day off work were you not?"

"Yes."

"Where were you when you learned you would get a half-day off?"

"In the laundry room with Meg, showing her the ropes, seeing as she was new to the job. Molly came in and said we were off and had to be out of the house by 11."

"Was any reason given?"

"Reason? House staff are not given reasons. They're told what to do."

"I see. Were you surprised?"

"Not really. I was pleased if you want to know. Half-day's a treat, not that the weather helped, cold an' drizzly when it wasn't bucketing down."

"At what time did you leave?"

"11 as instructed."

"All of you?"

"Oh yes. Cook was upset, it being her home for so many years."

"By which door did you leave?"

"The pantry door, like always."

"Did you lock the door?"

"Not in the daytime, no, seein' as we're in and out all the time. It was only locked at night."

"Who locked it at night?"

"Whoever was last out, usually Mrs. Lister."

"Who took the key with her?"

"Well, no. There's a place we put the key if for some reason somebody has to go back inside. It's kinda hidden if you don't know where to look. I can show you where."

"Who knows of this?"

"The staff."

"There's just the one key?"

"Oh no. The Planes had a key. They sometimes had a snack at night in the kitchen and liked to stroll about in the garden when the weather was fine, so they'd go through the pantry instead of all the way to the front door."

"And where was their key kept?"

"In the key box."

"Key box?"

"It's hanging on the wall with all the other keys in the little corridor between the kitchen and the pantry downstairs. I can show you."

"How many keys are there?"

"Must be dozens, for all the bedrooms and all the cupboards, the wine cellar, the storage rooms, cloakrooms and bathrooms, even keys for some boxes up in the attic."

"You mean everything is kept locked?"

"Oh no, everything is kept open. That's why all the keys are kept in the key box in case it is decided to lock something up and you need to find a key."

"I see. So…you all leave by 11 that Saturday morning. At what time did you return?"

"We came back early around 4.30 even though we had till 6."

"Can you describe what happened when you got back?

"We…I…saw…"

"Yes? What did you see?"

"Do I have to say?"

"Yes. Be as accurate as you can."

"It's too horrible…it will make me sick again…ohh…"

(*At this juncture the witness ran to an open window in the library and vomited into the garden. When she regained her composure, the interrogation continued.*)

"Are you sure you want to continue?"

"Yes. Sorry. I'm okay now."

"I asked you to describe what happened when you came back to the house that afternoon."

"When we got back there was just Molly and me went in. Jimmy had stayed behind with his Ma who had given us luncheon, Meg was down the docks with her guy, Marjorie, that's Mrs. Bassett, the cook, went up to her rooms to lie down. Soon's we came in the pantry door we could see something terrible had happened. All the cupboard doors were open, everything on the shelves was thrown on the floor. I think we both cried out, then Molly said Lucy run and fetch Cook. Which I did quick as I could. The three of us then went through the kitchen, up the stairs, which is where Molly said Oh my God! Blood! It was everywhere! Molly shouted Karla! Karla! as we ran into the dining room where you could see all this blood and her leg sticking out from under some rugs. I…"

"Yes?"

"I don't want to say what we saw when Molly pulled back the rugs. Marjorie and I got sick. We had to go outside. Then Molly called the police station. That's all. Can I go now? I might throw up again."

"Thank you, Lucy. You have been very brave. I just have one last question. In the days before that Saturday did you see any strangers around the house?"

"No."

"Thank you. As you leave, please ask Jimmy to come in.

+   +   +   +

INTERROGATION IN THE MURDER MANSION / 5

"Your name please."

"Jimmy."

"Jimmy what?

"Just Jimmy. That's what I'm called. Jimmy.

"What's your mother's name, Jimmy?"

"Ma."

"When the postman brings her a letter, what's on the envelope?"

"We don't get many letters."

"When you do, whose name is written on the envelope."

"Ma's."

"Are you trying to be funny, Jimmy?"

"No."

"Okay. You call your mother Ma. What do other people call her?"

"Mrs. Piggott."

"Thank you, Jimmy Piggott!

"Where do you live?"

"With my Ma."

"The address?"

"Down by St. Mary's, on William Street.

"How old are you?"

"Eleven."

"You sound English?"

"My Ma and me, yes. From Guilford, in Surrey."

"How long have you lived here?"

"All my life."

"Oh, so you were born here. Did your parents immigrate?"

"Before the war, yes."

"Where is your father now?"

"Dead."

"I'm sorry. When…"

"In the war. He was serving on the *Britannia* when she was torpedoed."

"I'm sorry."

"My Ma says don't be sad or sorry. Be proud of your dad. He signed up when many didn't. Went back to do his duty. He was a hero, you know."

"Yes. Yes, he was. Now, how long have you worked here?"

"A long time. Years."

"Can you remember how old you were when you started?"

"About eight."

"And what do you do?"

"Whatever needs doing."

"Which is?"

"All the things Mrs. Lister tells me to do. Sweep the steps. Polish the boots. Polish the silver. Rake the driveway. Help the gardeners. Burn the leaves. Get up on the roof. Clear the gutters. Wash the windows. Lots of things. I'm her new handyman, she says."

"Don't you go to school?"

"Sometimes. It's better I'm here. We need the money, see. Ma's pension's not much."

"I see. Now I'm going to ask you some questions…"

"About the murder?"

"Yes."

"I saw him, you know."

"You saw whom?"

"The man that did it. Saw him through that little window down in the coal bunker. I told old Mr. Jason, ``Blimey, I said, who's that?'"

"Mr. Jason? The Roberts' butler? What was he doing here?"

"Not here. He walks their dog up on the Avenue. We often stop for a chat, find out what's going on. Sunday, he asked me what was all the fuss, with the cops and all? I told him I only found out when I came to work that morning. That there had been a terrible murder and Mrs. Plane was killed. And that I saw this man leave the house Saturday morning."

"Alright Jimmy. Take me through, step by step, exactly what you saw."

"About 9 o'clock..."

"Saturday morning?"

"Yes. That Saturday morning, 9 o'clock, the gate bell chimes. I know it's the coalman, cause that's when he comes. I'm helping Cook in the kitchen clearing up after breakfast and she says off you go and I take the key for the coal bunker from the box, go down through the wine cellar, along the corridor, past the storage rooms and the boiler room to where there's this little metal door into the bunker which I open with my key. Then, from the inside, with the same key, I open the door out of the bunker into the yard so the coalman can make his delivery. When he's done and we clean up, he leaves, I mean, he left, and from the inside I locked the bunker door to the yard. Crossing the bunker, which now has a great pile of coal in the middle, you have to sort of skirt the wall, which is when I looked out of the little window."

"Where's this window?"

"When you're in the bunker you're partly underground. The window's up near the ceiling. From outside the window's at ground level. It doesn't open or anything. It's there to let the light in. It's easier to show you than explain."

"Later. Now, as exactly as you can, what did you see?"

"The back of a man, bent forward, walking away from me, across the yard into the orchard that backs onto the property next door."

"The Van Hals place?"

"Yes. It's like a jungle. All overgrown an' spooky. Even us kids don't like to go in there."

"What did this man look like? Be as accurate as you can."

"I couldn't see much from where I was down the bunker. I'm looking up through a dirty windowpane thinking who's that bloke and he's already gone. Funny view of his legs and backside. Couldn't see his head the way he was bent."

"That's all? Was he tall, fat, thin, young, old?"

"You tell me to be accurate. Now you want me to guess?"

"Not guess. Sometimes you get an impression."

"He moved pretty quick, and his trousers looked smart."

"Smart?"

"You said an impression. They looked smart, ironed, not like a tramp. Like they'd been made by a tailor, with turnups."

"Colour?"

"Dark, with those thin stripes"

"You mean pinstripes?"

"Yes."

"A quick man in tailored pinstripe trousers. At a guess, young or old?"

"Neither. More like you."

"Like me? What's that, middle-aged? Now, was he carrying anything?"

"No. Not that I could see."

"What did you do?"

"I went back across the bunker, opened the door into the yard to see where he had gone but didn't see him anywhere. Then I locked up again and then we all had to leave."

"This was at 11?"

"Yes."

"When did you last see Mrs. Plane?"

"I didn't, not that morning. She was upstairs. I don't go there much if there's not something to do. I heard her though, talking to Molly. Telling her to be sure to get back by 6."

"You didn't think to say you had seen a man leaving the house?"

"I did so. I told my Ma."

"When?"

"After supper when we were saying our prayers, before going to bed."

"Thank you, Jimmy. That will be all."

+   +   +   +

TIL MIN GODE VAN, AS

And lo!
Riddarholm, the Church of Stockholm,
With a procession come to crown the Queen
Now eighteen, on her formal accession to the Throne.
Bow down!
Bow down!
The Queen! Kristina!
Voices in the Congregation:
'Tis she! Our Queen!
Daughter of good stuff…
Nay! Gustavus…what?
You would have me laugh?
'Twas Gustavus Adolphus, our King
Now dead, alas!
With no rightful heir that he must make a daughter King -
Mighty Adolphus laid low
In battle
Valiantly fought these past 30 years
Now ended
By this daughter who preaches peace to our enemies - at a
Price - a tidy sum
Some say 5 million riksdaller
But hard to find in the public purse…
Best whisper it

Sent by her to her Jew in Amsterdam
So 'tis said.
Aye…poor lass…
Your father slain before your eyes
At Lütsen
And you just six years old…
On the battlefield…
With that old watchdog, Count Oxenstierna,
Hovering at your back,
The Regent,
Ever ready to seize your Throne.
Bow down!
Bow down!

Brenton

+   +   +   +

THE READING ROOM, NEWPORT

W hen next they met in front of the bulletin board the Secretary said to the Sheriff, "I am perhaps presumptuous in offering you advice? Has it occurred to you that you should give up the law and become a man of letters?"

"Sometimes."

"Good stuff," the Secretary reads. "Fascinating. What does the dedication mean?"

"In Swedish it says, 'To my good friend.'"

"I see. I had no idea you spoke Swedish."

"I don't. I copied it from a book."

"And the 'AS'?"

"August Strindberg. The man who wrote the book. A play, actually."

"I've never heard of him."

"He's famous in Europe."

"When did all this happen?"

"In the 16th century. Gustafus had no male heir, so he made his daughter King."

"Never heard of her."

"A pity. She was quite extraordinary. At 11 she spoke 8 languages. At 18 she astounded the new British Ambassador, Bulstrode Whitlocke, by quoting Shakespeare. At 28 she abdicated the throne of Sweden, changed from Protestant to Catholic, and went to live in Rome on and off for 25 years, seducing every Pope and Cardinal she met. When she died half the town turned out for her funeral and burial in the Vatican."

"Wouldn't happen here."

"No. Nothing much does."

+ + + +

"What's happening?" The Chief of Police said.

"Not much," the Sheriff said. "If you don't count Jimmy seeing a man who could be the one we're looking for."

"Description?"

"Very vague unfortunately. He was seen going away from the kid who was down in the coal bunker." The Sheriff sniffed. Then detailed what was in the transcript. "I've put out a bulletin. One more unknown man being sought for questioning."

"Maybe they're all the same guy?"

"Maybe."

"Well, I've got news for you, Brenton. The DA called about probate and about those shares. Can you believe the probate on Plane's death three years ago has still not been resolved. His executor is an appointee of his bank in New York, a guy named Baxter. He says he has an obligation to maintain the estate in whatever jurisdiction the assets may lie. The assets are in several States across the country; monies held in different banks, shares, bonds, loans, commercial property, houses, art works, rare books, motor cars, sailing boats, you name it. The total value is enormous. He's engaged accountants and lawyers in all the relevant States. He confirmed Plane had written a new will after the death of his first wife thirteen years ago. Prior to her death she had been his principal beneficiary, but under the new will half of his estate was bequeathed to his butler who had served him for some thirty years and the other half to various charities, as he had no children and was estranged from his family. This will was in turn revoked when he married his second wife three years ago. He drew up a new will leaving the entirety of his estate to his new wife and confirmed Baxter as his executor. Got all that?"

The Sheriff shrugged his shoulders, nodded, and said, "I reckon."

"Okay. Now it gets complicated, and I can't say I understand all the bells and whistles. Baxter says the biggest problem is that they cannot find the original signed copy of this latest will. Without it the probate Judge will not allow him to wind up the estate but has ordered it kept in administration and confirmed him as Executor. The beneficiaries, if any, must wait. Adding to his problems he says the beneficiaries of the revoked will have filed numerous petitions in the relevant States essentially contending that, will or no will, the new wife deliberately ensnared a besotted old man, forty years her senior, into a marriage conditional on her being his sole heir." The Chief paused for thought. "Forty years! What gets into these guys? No wonder he dropped dead."

The Sheriff looked at his Chief thinking what's this got to do with murder?

"Baxter says it's a nightmare," the Chief said. "Just because Plane died in New York doesn't mean a determination on all this is made there. For the last three years, out of estate funds, he has been paying the costs of the mansion in Newport while also supporting the widow in the lifestyle to which she was accustomed. If she has now died intestate with no next of kin and no will is found who gets what could take decades, murdered widow or not. Add to that the bearer shares. Know what bearer shares are?"

"Vaguely. Whoever's got them, owns them. Something like that."

"Nearly. They are shares in an equity that is entirely owned by the holder of the physical stock certificate which bears no name. It's not registered anywhere. You give them to me, they're mine. I give 'em to you, they're yours. Someone gave Karla Plane a fortune. No brokers we can check. No clearing house. No bank."

"Surely someone issued them?"

"Of course. But the issuer has no inkling as to the identity of the buyer, leave alone knowing who now possesses their shares. Hence the name, bearer."

"Logically they belonged to her husband, right? Unless she went out and bought them herself in the three years since his death?"

"Impossible."

"I agree. She probably never bought a share of any kind in her life. Her husband would be the only person she knew with the means to buy the shares. I mean who else could there be? And if there was someone else, why would they give them to her?"

For a long moment both men stopped to think.

Then the Chief of Police said: "Something else. All the shares are for public utilities."

"So?" the Sheriff said.

"They are one of the very few sections of the Market that has not tanked. Those shares are worth millions."

"So, the guy who holds the paper is a millionaire?"

Pause. Then, simultaneously, both men said, "Shit!"

+   +   +   +

They called the District Attorney's office. The man was busy. Please call back. After ten minutes, they did. This time the telephone was answered by Assistant District Attorney, Elmwood Easton. The DA was tied up. What was the problem? The bearer shares. Silence. The bearer shares? Who has them? Silence.

Then the Chief of Police said, "Mr. Easton, Sermon Hazard here. We asked you a question. Your silence is not an answer."

"How did you know?" Easton said.

"Know what?"

"That the shares have gone missing?"

+   +   +   +

IN A MODEL T FORD

The black, second-hand Model T was probably the slowest getaway car in the history of crime the driver thought, driving north from Newport to Fall River, then south on the Lower Boston Post Road from Providence through Westerly and Mystic to Groton, on to New London and finally Madison, in Connecticut, a distance of 106 miles, covered in 2 hours and 50 minutes. Slow but anonymous. Supposedly there were 15 million black Model Ts that Ford had built and sold around the world, so much part of the landscape they were virtually invisible. Just like him. A thin non-descript figure getting out of his car, coat collar up, fedora on, carrying a couple of folders, into the rundown inn set back from the road, where he had booked the previous evening for two nights.

Going into his room, skirting the bed, he set the folders down on the desk, drew closed the curtained window which overlooked the backyard, took off his hat and coat to reveal a policeman's uniform: long-sleeved dark grey battledress buttoned to the throat, no tie, epaulettes, leather bandolier running left shoulder to right hip, where it was attached to a stout leather belt carrying a holster, dark grey jodhpurs to match the battledress, with yellow braiding on the seams, knee-high laced leather boots. On the left breast of the battledress, above the buttoned pocket, a generic patrolman's badge bearing the legend *Newport, R.I.* above the city seal, and below that *Police*.

In an alcove to the left of the bed was a washbasin on a stand, with a pitcher of water next to it. Hung on the wall above the basin was a small round mirror into which he now smiled as he carefully removed a thin moustache glued to his upper lip, prior to discarding his uniform.

In his underwear he returned to sit at the desk, rubbed his hands together, then, quite carefully, pulled the folders toward him, set them side by side, before opening first one, checking the contents, and then the other, likewise. When he sat back he smiled again. But this time his smile was grim as a thought surfaced. Was it a crime to take back what was his? Or was it a crime to withhold information?

+ + + +

THE BACK BAR OF THE BLACK PEARL

"Here's a rum one, Lake," Kale said. "Listen to this: *'An imposter disguised as a policeman is being sought by the Newport Police Department. Last seen at 4.44pm, Friday, November 15, 1929, leaving the grounds of the Courthouse on Washington Square, the man is described as being of medium height, clean shaved but for a thin moustache, carrying one or more folders. Any information from anyone who may have seen this man should be communicated to the nearest Police Department. All information will be held in the strictest confidence.*

Asked what the importance of the folders was, District Attorney William Clarke said 'No comment.' Asked what was in the folders, DA Clarke said 'No comment.'"

"As he wiped the egg from his face," Lake said.

+ + + +

IN THE DA'S OFFICE, NEWPORT

"Okay," the DA said, a sour look on his face. The usual task force, Hazard, Coddington, Easton, Brenton, Brady, assembled in front of him, sat silent, faces blank. "What have we got? In a nutshell, not much of anything. Three days ago, a guy comes in here dressed as a policeman. Asks the clerk at the door for directions to the evidence room. He goes there. Asks the officer in charge for any bagged documents on the Plane case. Asked for his credentials, he shows his badge, signs the log, takes the folders, walks out." The DA snaps his fingers. "Just like that. No questions asked." Pause. "Comments?"

Silence.

"Gentlemen, I need not tell you how embarrassing this is, but I, you, the Department, all of us collectively, have got egg over every goddamn face in this ROOM!" Shouting the last word so loudly his secretary opened the door to inquire if there was a problem. When she retired under a scowl from her boss, the DA pointed at the Chief of Police, "Sermon?"

"As you know, the Sheriff and I were in the Reading Room when we heard the folders had gone missing. No point in finger pointing, if they're gone, they're gone. We can have an inquiry at a later date. Before coming over here the Sheriff made some notes. Sheriff?"

Sheriff Brenton opened his notepad. On the first page he had written:

> The I looking in the mirror
> Does not see me looking back
> Eye to eye

He could feel Henry Coddington, Justice of the Peace, seated next to him, reading it over his shoulder. Coddington's eyebrows went up. The Sheriff turned the page. Without preamble he read out loud what he had written.

"PLANE MURDER FOLDERS

- How did the perp know they existed? He had seen them before? In the house? Ergo, he knew KP? Or the husband? Or both? When?
- How did he know they had been found? A Guess? On learning of the murder? Overheard?
- How did he know where they were? Prior - KP or the husband told him?
- Post - Familiar with police procedure?
- How did he obtain his disguise?
- How did he leave the Courthouse?
- He must have come from somewhere before and must have gone somewhere after heisting the folders.
- Could this be the murderer?
- Or someone else?"

The Sheriff frowned down on what he had written. "I can't help feeling we're missing something simple," he said. "The disguise, how he left and his whereabouts will only be answered by making the usual enquiries, which will take manpower and time."

"Get on that," the DA said to Assistant District Attorney Easton.

"There are only three ways he could have known about those folders," the Sheriff continued. "He saw them, he was told about them or - "

"He put them there himself!" Sermon Hazard said.

"Which would beg a further set of questions: How? When? Why? Why put something so valuable in...no, I don't buy that. The logical person with the means to buy bearer shares of such value would be Plane. He gives them to his wife. She puts them in the trunk..."

"No way," the DA said. "Can you see Plane watching something so valuable being put into a tin trunk under her bed, I mean, their bed? Come on, man, Plane's a millionaire. Millionaires have safes, in the wall, under the floor, in the bank, you name it. That's where they put cash, jewels, anything of value. Not under the bed."

"Which means?"

Silence.

Which was when Police Constable Thomas Brady, like the proverbial fly on the wall, there to watch and listen, not to voice an opinion, now cleared his throat, leant forward, and, uninvited, blurted out, "Excuse me, maybe he did give them to her!"

Every eye turned on him. He felt himself turning pink.

"Go on," said the Sheriff.

"I don't mean the husband, Mr. Plane, but this other man. A man was seen going into her house. He brings her the folders. Maybe he is the same man who has taken the folders? They belong to him."

"Rubbish," Coddington said. "How are we to believe an unknown man turns up with shares worth millions to give to Mrs. Plane? There are enough millionaires in this affair already not to add another."

"Maybe he wasn't giving them to her?" Brady's face was now red.

"What d'you mean?"

"Maybe she was hiding them for him?"

"Poppycock," Coddington said.

"Actually no, not poppycock," the Sheriff said. "The lad's on to something. It would explain how, when and why. Go on, Brady. Spell it out."

Brady hesitated. He suddenly felt trapped by his own impetuosity. He stammered, "I...m.m.maybe, I..."

"Take a deep breath, son," Chief Hazard said. "When you're ready..."

Brady swallowed. Looked at his Chief. Who nodded encouragement. Bright red, Brady said, "Maybe you are right, Mr. Coddington. The man is not a millionaire. He has taken or stolen the shares from where he works. He needs to hide them. Somehow, he knows Mrs. Plane. Knows her well enough to think she will agree to his scheme. They meet that Saturday. He gives her the shares for safe keeping. Since she keeps some cash and jewels in her trunk, she puts the folders in there. He leaves…"

"Reads about the murder," the DA said, "knows all about police procedure, dresses himself up as a cop, comes up here and helps himself. Come on, Sheriff, you couldn't write a better yarn. Don't tell me you think this is what happened?"

The Sheriff was about to answer when he caught Chief Hazard's eye. The Chief minutely shook his head, no. "Thank you, Brady," he said. "We'll follow up. There are a lot of leads. Let's get to work."

+   +   +   +

Afterwards the Chief invited the Sheriff and Brady into his office on the ground floor. Settled behind his desk, he pulled a cheroot out of his pocket, lit up, inhaled, blew a puff of smoke up to the ceiling, and said, "You want to smoke, be my guest." Neither man did, so they watched the Chief puffing away while he thought. The Sheriff, calm. Brady, apprehensive.

The Chief finally said, "Those guys upstairs depend on votes to stay in office. We work for the State. They worry about headlines on the front page; we deal with all the crap inside. None of them are going to go down a dark alley to stop a fight; we do it every day. I am not advocating we ignore them. No, sir. I like to think of them as a bump in the road of duty, there to be negotiated, but for guys like us on the payroll, never forget, the road goes on forever." Taking another long drag on his smoke, he looked directly at Brady, and said "I'm sure I speak for the Sheriff, Mr. Brady, by saying how encouraged I am seeing young men like yourself in the Force, capable of thinking independently and unafraid of expressing their thoughts. You realise you're the only person born this century on this case? In a world going down the toilet we need men like you. Keep at it. Sheriff?"

"You have put your finger on something, Brady," the Sheriff said. "Could you expand on what you said up there? Take us through your thinking?"

Brady swallowed, his Adam's apple visibly going up and down. "Well, you told me to try and put myself in Mrs. Plane's shoes. I thought if I was her, alone in the house, it would be extremely unlikely I would let in somebody who had sent me a threat. Then I thought why would I give the servants a half day off? It could only be to receive a private visit. I even thought it might be a visit I welcomed and therefore I wanted the house to myself to receive my visitor."

"Damn!" the Sheriff said. "Go on."

"Maybe the visitor called ahead, which would presuppose he had my, I mean, her number. My thought was that he must have mentioned he was carrying something, and it was urgent. I dismissed the theory that her husband could have given her the shares. The man had been dead for three years. He was a wealthy businessman, used to the world of big business, of bankers, accountants, brokers. It would have taken him years to accumulate that many shares. If I was him, they would be in a vault somewhere, not kept in a tin trunk. And it just seems highly unlikely that he would entrust a new wife with such a fortune. Witness the cash she had on hand, only $7 in an envelope and $28 in the trunk."

"What about the jewellery?" the Chief said.

"That I can understand. I imagine if you are rich, you may very well give your wife jewellery to wear. Sticking it in a tin box may be slightly eccentric, but at least she had them to hand if she felt like dressing up. As we speak, I find it difficult to imagine a scenario where he says 'Honey, here's a few million dollars in bearer shares. Why don't you keep them safe in that tin trunk of yours?' In that respect the DA's right. On the other hand, I can see her visitor as a fugitive, or a thief, who says something along the lines of 'Here, hold these for me till I come by to pick them up' and gives her a couple of folders which she puts in the trunk. She probably had no clue what was in the folders."

"But he does," the Sheriff said. "That implies a considerable trust. What you're saying is that they knew each other well enough for him to trust her with millions."

'Why then kill her?" the Chief said.

"He didn't!" the Sheriff and Brady said in tandem.

"Explain."

"Logically, why go through the exercise if your intention is to kill her and then leave without the shares?" the Sheriff said. "Who would do that?"

Brady nodded agreement. "He leaves. We don't know when? Or how? Nobody sees him go. Someone else enters unseen. The man who wrote the note. There is a fracas. She is raped, shot, and bludgeoned to death. The assailant tears the house apart looking for something, then unseen, also leaves, taking all his weapons with him."

"An unknown intruder?" the Chief said. "What would be his motivation?"

"Whatever it was he was looking for," the Sheriff said. "You've nailed it, Chief, the crux of this thing."

"It implies the murderer knew her and knew she was on her own," Brady said. "He must have been watching. Otherwise, how did he know the coast would be clear with all the staff and her visitor gone?"

"He must have seen the visitor come and go. Where could he be to do that?" the Chief said.

"That abandoned place at the end of the street?" the Sheriff said.

"Or inside the house?" Brady said.

For a moment time stood still, the implications of his words spiralling out in the thoughts of each man.

Then the Sheriff said, "Jesus!"

And the Chief said, "Remember, you thought it may be someone on the inside?"

"I was thinking of one of the staff. But maybe it's the man Jimmy saw. What if he came back and was there the whole time?"

"If he was, how did he get in?" Brady said. "All the doors were locked. None of the windows were broken. We have no reports from our patrolmen."

"He has a key, and he comes through the woods," the Sheriff said. "And if the guy has a key, at night he can come and go as he pleases. With the staff in the Carriage House there's no one to hear him. Brady, I want you to pick a bedroom and move into the Mansion."

"Yes, sir," Brady said.

"My gut tells me he hasn't found what he's looking for. Maybe he'll come back?"

"Yes, sir."

+ + + +

He had been tempted to throw away the key and wondered why he'd kept it. Now he knew. There was one place he had not looked. Once he found it, he'd be safe. Free. Never again rejected. Rich enough to have any woman he fancied.

+ + + +

JACOB IN THE VICEROY, 59th & PARK

Jacob, at his usual table, having finished lunch, was trying to decide whether he wanted a cognac to go with his cigar, when a familiar figure came across the room to greet him.

"Jacob!"

"Jacob?"

"Not disturbing you, am I?"

"When have you ever disturbed me, Mr. Baxter?

"Mind if I sit down?"

"Please do. Drink?"

Drinks in hand, the two bankers who shared first names, did what wealthy bankers do after a satisfying lunch, settled back into their comfortable chairs to gaze out through the window at the scurrying herd of those less fortunate souls caught in the melting slush of an early snowfall.

"You think this thing's bottomed out?" Jacob Baxter said.

"The market? At half what it was worth back in September? Yes. We've been trading sideways since November 13. It's the knock on that bothers me. London, Paris, the Far East don't look too good. I can see the dominos falling with all the bad news from here. You guys are okay though, right?"

"More by luck than anything else. We've not had the kind of run those poor bastards in the south are going through."

Jacob nodded. Every newspaper carried pictures of mobs of desperate people queued up, hoping to withdraw their savings from single unit banks, whose shuttered doors and windows told the tale of abject failure. "It's going to get worse. In the Middle West too. You saw what Menken wrote about the Republic proceeding to hell at a rapidly accelerating tempo? He's right. Batten down the hatches."

For a while they drank and smoked in contemplative silence.

Then Jacob Baxter said, "Are you going up to your place for Christmas?"

"My wife, Helen, insists. Family. You know how it is. Pain in the ass for me, I'd rather be here in the city."

"You still got your manservant?"

"You mean Jason, the butler? Of course. What an extraordinary question. Why do you ask?"

"Are you aware he is a petitioner to the probate court in Newport?"

"Jason? How's that possible?"

"Let me explain. As you know I am the executor of the estate of your one-time neighbour, Sir Kobe Plane…"

"I didn't know. But Plane's been dead for years…"

"I know. It's complicated. In fact, I shouldn't be telling you any of this. He made a will on the death of his first wife in which his butler was to receive half his estate–"

"Good Heavens!"

"Yes. Then when Plane remarried, he wrote to tell me he had made a new will leaving everything to his new wife, appointing me again as executor. The original signed copy of this will has not been found. In probate the Newport Court judge has ruled that unless it is found he will have to declare it *non existent* , despite the new wife having a letter from Plane telling her he had revoked the old will, made her the sole beneficiary under the new one, and to contact me, as executor, in the event anything happened to him. When he died that is what she did. The Judge has seen both my letter and hers but contends them to be insufficient evidence. To boot, the beneficiaries under the old will have come forward to claim the validity of that will which is where your butler comes in."

"I don't understand?"

"Jason, your butler, was formerly the butler of Kobe Plane."

"Good God!"

"You didn't know?"

"No. How could I? Helen took him on. Said he was perfect for Newport."

"Surely you got references?"

"She looks after that sort of thing. The house is hers, you know. I gave it to her. Gives her something to do if you want the truth. But - wait a minute, Plane's wife was murdered last month!"

"Which makes things even more complicated. No will made by her has been found. But even intestate her next-of-kin are the de facto beneficiaries of Plane's estate. There are no children, but apparently there's a mother living somewhere in the French Alps."

"And?"

"And?"

"What am I supposed to do?"

"Nothing. I thought you should know. Mum's the word." Jacob Baxter said, and drew his thumb across his lips, the old Mafia gesture for silence.

+   +   +   +

"Hello?" Helen said

"It's me," Jacob said. "I've just finished a meeting with Jacob Baxter, banker over at Brown Brothers, who told me Jason used to be the butler of Kobe Plane?"

"Yes. So?"

"You never told me?"

"Of course, I did. And even if I didn't, what difference does it make? You have never shown the slightest interest in the staff I hire. Can you believe that woman dismissed him after thirty years of service? You should compliment me for being kind and taking him on instead of complaining. He does a perfect job. What's the problem?"

Jacob was about to tell her, then remembered Baxter's last words and changed the subject. "I spoke to Patrick. He and Daisy will come, but not the kids, thank God."

145

"You always say that. Did you get the list I sent? Don't wait until the last minute to do the shopping. With the Christmas crowds there'll be nothing left if…"

Jason held the phone away from his ear while his wife rambled on, seemingly unaware of the plight of most people, more interested in where their next meal came from than the Christmas present they were no longer able to buy.

"…are you listening?" Helen said.

"Yes," Jacob said untruthfully.

"Good. You agree then. About the decorators, they'll be here Friday. Don't forget." And hung up.

Decorators?

+   +   +   +

BRIANÇON, HAUTES-ALPES, FRANCE

The delegation climbing the Chaussée from the Caserne Militaire in Ste.Catherine to the old town, perched behind the fortifications built two centuries before by the Marquis de Vauban, the military engineer of Louis XIVth, had reason to grumble. In winter, at an altitude of 4921 feet, the slope of the Chaussée in icy conditions made climbing it a dangerous exercise, added to which the old lady had no telephone so there was no way of being sure she was home. Dressed in black, led by the Mayor, M. Olagnier, and the Parish priest, Père Michel, they were six in number, a Sous-Préfet from Embrun, a Vice-Consul from the American Embassy, who had come all the way in the overnight express from Paris, the head of the Gendarmerie, and the former head of the French Resistance in the Alps, a formidable figure, Col. Gaston Duhamel. It would be his duty to bring the tragic news to this mother of France that her last child had been murdered far away in America. Tough as he was, Duhamel was almost in tears and it was only the muttered words of the priest - 'Courage, mon Colonel, courage' - which kept him going.

Arriving at last at the top of the Chaussée they passed under the Porte d'Embrun, a stone arch leading through the 20-foot thickness of the fort, to climb the even steeper Grande Gargouille, a ravine of houses four arm's length apart, the principal axis of the town, with an open drain running down the centre. Halfway up the street, at No. 36, they arrived at their destination, a small wooden door with the date, 1713, carved into a panel.

The Priest knocked.

Silence.

The Priest knocked again.

Above his head, in the narrow facade of the building, a window opened, a woman looked down at him and from him to the gathered delegation. For a moment in time, she said nothing. Then she said, "Ma fille est morte."

It was not a question.

"Donnez-moi un moment," she said. And when next she appeared she wore a shapeless black peasant smock with a black shawl covering her head as she opened the door to let them into the tiny room beyond. Here she had already put out seven glasses and a bottle of wine on a white lace cloth laid on a sewing table. In a niche in the wall, where there was the plaster figure of a Madonna, she had lit a candle. Beside the niche was a sepia photograph in a black frame, showing her family sitting on the ramparts of the fortified town. Louis, Maman, Papa, Karla, Henri.

When they had all squeezed into the room she closed the door, stood with her back to it, and said, "Je vous écoute."

+ + + +

Afterwards, in the train going back to Paris, the American Vice-Consul watches with unseeing eyes the countryside wheel past the carriage window. 'My daughter is dead.' 'Give me a moment.' 'I am listening.' The words circle and circle in his head. Three simple phrases. No histrionics.

The Priest tells her to be brave. The Mayor mutters about a death certificate and introduces the Sous-Préfet who says he is honoured to meet the mother of a heroine. The Captain of the Gendarmerie talks of sacrifice defending Liberty, Equality, and Fraternity. The Vice- Consul says something complicated about an inheritance. It is left to Col. Duhamel to show some emotion. His voice strained, with tears in his eyes, he recites, nobody is sure why, Apollinaire's poem *Le Pont Mirabeau,* stumbling badly on the last refrain *Vienne la nuit sonne l'heure / Les jours s'en vont je demeure.* When he's finished, she serves them wine.

The woman's name is Gabriella Pinard. Originally from Sestriere, across the border in Italy. Her husband was in the 2nd Regiment of the Chasseur Alpin. She met him skiing in Montgenèvre before the war. He died for our country in 1914, she says. She points him out in the sepia photograph. They all follow her finger. They stare. That one on the left is Louis, my eldest, she says. He was killed in '15. There is not a sound in the room. On the right is Henri, still a boy eighteen years old when he was shot dead in 1917. And now Karla. She adjusts the scarf on her head. I am nearly 70, she says. It is not right that a woman should bury all her children before she herself dies. She raises her glass. Let us drink to their memory. May they all rest in peace.

In the train the Vice-Consul knows he has failed in his mission. He has no idea what he will say in the report he has to make. For him the woman's stoicism is unfathomable. He had been sent to inform Madame Pinard, as sole next-of-kin, that she was the beneficiary of the estate bequeathed to her daughter. That the inheritance was enormous. That the will, if it could be found, was challenged. That she would need legal representation in various jurisdictions in America. That the matter would take many months, perhaps years, to be resolved. He shakes his head. Something comes loose; a word detaches itself - murder! No one in the delegation had dared use the word.

What had she said? *It is not right that a woman should bury all her children before she herself dies.* He makes the connection : *Vienne la nuit sonne l'heure / Les jours s'en vont je demeure.* The wheels of the train have picked up the refrain. *The days pass I remain. The days pass I remain. The days pass...*

Exhausted, the Vice-Consul falls asleep.

+   +   +   +

A BEDROOM IN THE MURDER MANSION

Thomas could not believe his luck. The bedroom was bigger than the entire ground floor of his parents' house in Jamestown; the adjoining dressing room was bigger than his own bedroom at home. Molly giggled when she saw his one change of clothes hanging in solitary isolation amidst dozens of empty hangers.

"You'll have to do better if you want to be a millionaire," she said.

She was excited as he was to have him living next door to her, on one condition. "Don't you be getting your hopes up about what's going to happen in here," she said, when she caught him lying fully dressed on the bed, propped on the pillows, hands behind his head, smiling his come hither smile as she came through the door with a vase of flowers in her hands.

Having Thomas in the house created a new dynamic. All the staff felt it. Whereas before they went about their duties with no purpose other than 'moving the dust from here to there' as Mrs. Lister complained, now it was as if there was a new Master in charge. The Sheriff noted the change the day Thomas moved in. As he was shown into the library he was asked if he would be staying for supper.

"Well Brady," he said, pulling out a chair at the table where Brady conducted interviews, "what's it feel like to be Gatsby?"

Thomas blushed. To hide his confusion he said, "Are you sure I should be here?"

"Of course. This is a crime scene. You're a policeman. We don't have to justify this to anyone. Besides, the staff must eat. Feeding one more person is neither here nor there. Now then, focus, who could have a key to this place?"

"I have been thinking about that. There are only three ways in, the front door, the pantry, and the coal bunker. There are two fire escapes from the first-floor bedroom suites, but access is only from the inside. We know there is only one key to the bunker which is kept in the key box. I checked; it's there. We know there are two keys to the pantry, one for the staff and a spare kept in the key box. The one for the staff is in the door as we speak as they leave it there until they lock up at night. The spare is also where it should be, on its hook in the box. That leaves the front door.." Brady stopped speaking as someone knocked on the library door. "Yes? Come in." he called.

It was Molly. "Cook asks which wine you would like to be served with your supper?"

The Sheriff raised an eyebrow. "Brady?"

Thomas had never ordered a bottle of wine in his life. He did what he always did when embarrassed, he turned bright red.

The Sheriff, ever game, said to Molly, "What has Cook on the menu tonight?"

"Veal chops, sir, with mashed potatoes and carrots and some salad and cheese for after."

"Then I think a claret, don't you?"

"Yes, sir. Which one?"

Put on the spot, the Sheriff said, "What do you recommend?"

"There's a lot down there. Must be thousands of bottles. Old Mr. Plane loved his wine. He'd have one of the lighter Bordeaux with veal, like the Angelus, I think. We have a 1921 which would suit."

"Splendid!" the Sheriff said. "If I may ask, Molly, how is it you know about wine?"

"Over fourteen years you learn if you listen. He was a very kind man, was Mr Plane. When he saw I was interested he would take me down the cellars with him to explain about vintages, corkage, humidity, fining, how to turn the older bottles, and which wines had to be drunk before they turned sour. It got so it would annoy Mr. Jason, who thought the cellars were his territory."

"Jason?" The Sheriff was suddenly alert.

"The butler, sir. Mr. Jason."

"You don't mean the man who works for Roberts?"

"The same, sir. When he was dismissed here after Mr. Plane died, he got a job there. Lucky for him, way things are."

The Sheriff exchanged a look with Thomas, then said, "Thank you, Molly."

Molly hesitated.

'Yes?" the Sheriff said.

"With the dining room locked, sir, where would you like me to set up?"

"The Sheriff looked at Brady.

Brady said, "I gave orders to keep it locked until the case was closed."

"Good man," the Sheriff said, and to Molly he added, "Please tell Cook we'll dine in the kitchen."

The maid left, closing the library door behind her. For a moment the two men were frozen, each trying to resolve the implications of what they had just heard.

Then the Sheriff said, "You're thinking what I'm thinking."

Brady nodded. "He kept a house key."

+ + + +

A FIRST MEETING

The funeral of Sir Kobe Plane was conducted in the Old North Church, Boston, and he was buried in the family plot beside his parents and brother in Forest Hills Cemetery, Jamaica Plain, on a fine autumnal afternoon, Saturday, October 2, 1926. Sir Kobe had been a popular figure and the church was packed with those wishing to say adieu, but, at the request of his wife, only a few intimates were invited to be at the graveside. With trees shedding their Fall leaves in a gorgeous palette running from burnt umber to magenta to marigold yellow, it was a befitting send-off to a colourful life, contrasted sharply by the tall, stark, slim exclamation point of the widow in black.

From where he stood in the shadows cast by a tree fifty metres away, the uninvited butler removed his bowler hat to honour the man he had served for thirty years, His eyes were fixed on Karla as she followed the coffin, face pale, to the edge of the freshly dug grave. As if to give her space, the officiating priest, the gravediggers, and the few onlookers had all stepped back a half-dozen paces, forming a circle, as Karla, tearless, standing alone by the grave after the coffin had been lowered, bowed her head and took a small shovel to sprinkle dirt down onto the lacquered mahogany box containing her husband's remains.

Which is when a man stepped out of the circle.

"Mrs. Plane," he said, "I am deeply sorry for your loss. I am Jacob Baxter, your late husband's executor. When you feel up to it, we should talk."

Unspeaking, Klara looked at this man in astonishment. "Demain," she eventually said in French.

"Tomorrow." She translated for him.

+ + + +

He came to Newport the following day, Sunday, to be admitted to Planetree House by a maid, who led him through the Great Hall, through two reception rooms, to the Parlour, where a table had been set on a Persian rug with two Biedermeier chairs facing each other.

"Mrs. Plane will be down shortly, sir," the maid said. "While you are waiting, may I bring you tea, or a glass of water if you prefer?"

He declined, sat down and waited. He was nervous. It was difficult to admit to himself, but he was. It stemmed from the moment he first saw Karla in the church and then in the cemetery. He shocked himself at the thud of lust he felt flow through his loins. In his life he had never seen, never even imagined, that such a woman existed. All night he had wrestled with the images his fervid imagination conjured up of himself with her in ever more convoluted couplings. How had Plane, dumpy-as-a-wet-mattress Plane, managed to beguile this otherworldly creature into marriage? He tried to get hold of himself knowing the message he had to deliver would be compromised by the visceral undertow of his feelings. He must cool down. Twenty minutes later he was still waiting. He was about to get up to look for the maid when he heard voices, then footsteps, and then Karla, in a long black kaftan, appeared in the doorway of the Parlour. She looked troubled. "I can't find it," she said.

"Pardon, me?" he said standing up.

"The will. In your letter you said how important it was to show the will in court. I have looked nearly everywhere. I can't find it. That is why you are here, n'est-ce pas?"

"Yes. Yes, indeed," Jacob Baxter was troubled. "Look Mrs. Plane, I wish to apologise if I appeared a bit brusque yesterday during the ceremony. Perhaps we could begin again?" Still standing, he offered his hand. How could you not shake the hand so diplomatically extended? Karla shook hands.

"Please sit," she said, and when they were seated, she repeated the maid's invitation for tea or water. Again, he declined. To which she smiled and said, "Let us drink Champagne instead." And rang a handbell on the table which brought the maid back to the parlour door.

"Ah, Molly," Karla said "Be so good as to bring us Champagne and those nuts and almonds I like. Merci!"

When the champagne had been served, the maid withdrew. "Alors," Karla said, raising her glass, "a toast to new beginnings."

+ + + +

As a moth to a flame, Jacob Baxter felt himself drawn close and then closer and closer still to the beguiling enchantress he had come to instruct. He did not know where to look, his eyes going from her eyes to her mouth down to the opening in the kaftan to her incredibly long black hair, to her hands and back up to her face. At first, he had started out talking to her as one would to a foreigner, over loudly, in short declarative sentences, the kind a waitress could understand, to which she listened with grave countenance.

"First," he said, "my colleagues at the bank. And I. Extend our deepest condolences to you. In your bereavement."

Alors? Karla thought.

"Thank you for your letter," he said. "With Mr. Plane's letter inside. Unfortunately. It may not be enough. You understand?"

Il me prend pour une idiote, Karla thought.

"I also have a letter. From Mr. Plane. About the will. I have it here. To show you."

Il est con ou quoi? Karla thought.

"Please read this." Mr. Baxter drew an envelope from the inside pocket of his jacket, opened it and withdrew a single sheet of paper. His hand trembled as he handed it to her.

Karla read: '*My dear Jacob, I write to formally inform you that I have made a new will in favour of my wife, Karla, whom I recently married in France (I attach a copy of the notarised 'Livret de Famille' the official marriage certificate in France). This will revokes all previous wills. Karla will be my sole heir. You remain as executor. As such, in the event of my demise, please provide her with an inventory of all my assets, goods and chattels. The new will is dated January 2, 1926 and is signed and witnessed. I have it in safe keeping. Rest assured I am of sound mind, in good health and under no influence. Respectfully yours, Kobe Plane, Kt.'*

"You understand?" Baxter said.

"Mr. Baxter," Karla spoke quietly, with the hint of a smile in her eyes. "I may have an accent, but I speak fluent English. You probably think of me as a waitress? Yes? In fact, I have a degree in history from the Sorbonne. Be assured, I understand you very well. I wrote to you because that is what my late husband told me to do in the event of his death or incapacity. You know this because I sent you the letter he gave me confirming he had made a new will in my favour. In fact, he showed me the will when he signed it. Where he put it, I do not know." With a finger she moved a strand of hair from in front of her face. "Pardon. Please go on."

Thus corrected, Mr. Baxter relaxed into a role familiar to him, that of banker to important client. Also, that of a male confronted by a very tempting female. He squirmed, adjusted his trousers, and cleared his throat. "Very well," he said. "As the executor of the will your husband made on the death of the first Mrs. Plane ten years ago…"

"Which will has been revoked, is that the correct term, by the new will in my favour?" Karla interrupted.

"Precisely. But you do not have it and nor do I. Which is why finding the new will is so important. I must present the facts to the Probate Judge in Newport Court, and he will determine who are the rightful heirs to the property and other assets of the deceased." He smiled; eyebrows raised.

"Now I do not understand," Karla said. "Do you mean he could say that I am not the heir? How can that be?"

"In our legal system, if there is no will, a person called the administrator of the estate is appointed by the Court to administer the deceased person's estate. This includes collecting in the assets, paying tax or other liabilities, and distributing the estate to the people who the Judge determines are entitled to inherit it."

"But I am the wife. Enfin, the widow. How can they say I am not?"

"They will not say that. Of course, you are his widow. And in the normal course of events a notice will be sent to any devisee in the will and to all the heirs of the deceased. The Judge will determine what portion of the deceased person's estate is yours."

"But we have the letters to say it is all mine!"

"For the judge the letters only demonstrate intent. He must have the original ink-signed will, properly witnessed, as proof of intent. I misspeak, even if it's not witnessed it is legal if it's signed."

"But why? It is so unfair!" Karla was no longer speaking quietly

"Not from the perspective of a probate judge. Please be calm, Mrs. Plane." Baxter's words came smooth as oil. "If the deceased was capable of revoking one will, he could revoke another. Wherein lies an additional problem. Currently, the only extant will is the will from 10 years ago and the original of that will has been filed with the Probate Court in Newport. I am charged by the beneficiaries of that will to protect their interests." Baxter paused to take a sip of Champagne. "Let me explain so that the matter is clear in your mind. As executor I do not represent anyone. My role is solely to carry out the intent of the deceased as expressed in the will pursuant to which I have been appointed. Only a lawyer can represent the interests of a party. If there are two wills that specify different heirs, it is up to the court to determine which will is the operative one, and it is that will which the executor is bound to carry out. As you know this is a very large estate. The parties to a big probate proceeding do not operate through an executor. Rather their attorneys petition the court for whatever relief they seek and the executor simply carries out the instructions of the court. Out of consideration for the late Mr. Plane, a man whom I held in high respect, I would advise you to appoint a lawyer to represent you."

"Je vois. I see." Karla said, and she in turn sipped champagne. "Tell me, Monsieur Baxter, by the ring on your finger you are a married man, n'est-ce pas?"

"Yes," Baxter said, fingering his ring, surprised by this abrupt change in direction.

"Children?"

"Four."

"You have made a will in their favour?"

"Of course."

"Of course, you have! It is only natural that if you were to die your wife and children would inherit your estate. But let us suppose you have been unfaithful to your wife…"

"What!"

"Have I struck a nerve?"

"This is outrageous!"

"Be calm, Monsieur. I merely present a hypothesis." Leaning forward to pour more champagne into her visitor's glass she was well aware he was looking down her kaftan at the curves so subtly concealed. "If this hypothetical lover said you had to divorce your wife, marry her, revoke your *extant will for a new will in her favour,* what do you think your wife would do?"

Baxter was speechless.

"I will tell you what she would do. She would fight tooth and nail for what is rightfully hers. Precisely, you will say. But tell me this, Monsieur Baxter, if you could not give up your lover, but divorced and remarried and made a new will leaving everything to her and then unfortunately you died, who would inherit your estate? How would your probate judge *determine the matter?*"

Mute, Baxter could only stare at her.

Karla put down her glass on the table, stood up and said, "Venez avec moi. Come with me." And led him out of the Parlour, through the two reception rooms, across the Great Hall, through the Music Room, into the library, where in the company of 14,000 leather-bound books, she came to rest in front of her portrait. Of equal height, she and her image looked at each other eye-to-eye, the one dressed, the other naked.

Baxter gaped.

"As an intelligent man," Karla said, 'I am sure you can see the difference between a hypothesis and reality" - with the slightest wave of her hand between the picture and herself - "Need I add the first Mrs. Plane died childless ten years ago. In marrying me, my husband thought it right to make me his heir. Who are you or anyone to say otherwise, n'est-ce pas, Monsieur Baxter? Tooth and nail, remember that, tooth and nail."

+ + + +

ON BELLEVUE AVENUE

"Good morning, Jimmy!"

"Morning, Mr. Jason. How's my buddy, Sam?" Jimmy bent down to pet the neck of a Dalmatian on a leash. The dog licked his hand, then tried to lick his face, nearly knocking Jimmy down in the process. The butler laughed, giving the boy the leash to hold as they strolled down the avenue together in bright early morning sunshine, a gentle breeze carrying the scent of salt from the Atlantic across the town.

"Have you thought what to give your mother for Christmas?" the butler said.

"It's a secret," Jimmy said.

"I can keep a secret."

"Don't tell anyone, ok? I'm knitting her some warm booties to wear when it's cold."

"You know how to knit?"

"Cook is teaching me. It's not that difficult once you get the knack. She's got a big basket of wool and let me pick a colour. I picked red."

Sam stopped to smell the bottom of a lamppost.

"Give Cook my regards," the butler said. "She must be pleased to have you to teach; keep her busy with nothing else to do."

"Says who?" Jimmy said. "We've a guest now. A policeman sleeps in the house. Our Molly's soft on him, makes sure Cook treats him royally. Since he eats in the kitchen with the rest of us, guess what, we eat royally too."

Sam yanked on his leash. Jimmy patted the dog's head. "Bye, Sam," he said. "I've gotta scoot. See ya soon, Mr. Jason."

The butler, leash in hand, watched the boy skip off down Bellevue Court on the corner of Bellevue Avenue to the mansion three doors away.

+ + + +

THE PLEASURE OF GETTING LOST

B eyond my ken
A spacious place
A backward glimpse to where I've been
And forward to where
I'll be going

A patio of surprises
Round each corner
Behind each wall
Curiosity arises

Unpredictable, unforeseeable
Seeking, what?
Pleasure discovered in
Anonymous design
Made by a hand unmeasurable

A patio of surprises
Behind each wall
Around each corner
Curiosity arises

A staircase up
A staircase down

To spaces above and below
A matter of connecting curiosity
To all that does not show

A patio of surprises
Around the corner
Behind that door
Curiosity arises

A mystery of place
A joy that revelation brings
In jungle, town or mountain round
The light I seek and follow
Shows a way to burrow

Around that corner
Behind that door
Curiosity arises
A patio of surprises

Of a sudden, lost, without
Direction, scale or location
Beyond my sight
I see myself
Standing in isolation

Behind that door
Around the corner
Curiosity arises
A patio of surprises

What charm is there
To at once discover
The changing nature of beauty?

Little by little is better by far
It provokes the truth in a needle

A patio of surprises
Around each corner
Behind that wall
Curiosity arises

The happiness of mystery
Of living in imagination
Not given to us all at once
A woman clothed, unsheathed,
In shadow, naked

Behind the wall
A patio of surprises
Around each corner
Curiosity arises

Alas, more often than I like,
I find I've lost my way,
God's guide is wrong
But I see a dog
Who seems to know the way

Around the corner
Behind that wall
Curiosity arises
A patio of surprises

What binds the world?
'Tis colour. In life. On earth.
It colours the path through the maze
Of life's happiness

And sorrows

Around the corner beyond the wall in the space
'Neath the ground
Surely mine, alone
Tomorrow.

Brenton

+ + + +

"I must tell you, Sheriff," the Secretary said, "some members are complaining about the amount of room your missives occupy on our bulletin board. They will go wild with this latest effort, a masterpiece, if I may be so bold. Rest assured; it will not be touched."

"Thank you," the Sheriff said.

"In committee, if you see no objection, I propose we gather your writings and publish them in a private edition for the edification of a select group of our more enlightened members. At no cost to yourself, rest assured. We have a small budget for the arts, so a slim volume of, say, 35 pages? Bound in calfskin? An imprint of 50 copies? I'll start a subscription right away if you're favourable. Yes?"

"Do you think that's a good idea? Who'll buy such a thing?"

"My problem, Sheriff. You worry about the writing."

+ + + +

As if he didn't have enough to worry about, the Sheriff thought. Focus. If the guy has a key and he hasn't found what he's looking for it was logical to suppose he'd be back. If it was the butler, what could be his motivation? Hatred of Karla for dismissing him? Motive for murder? It seemed scarcely credible. Half the estate? Did he even know the contents of the old will?

As was his wont when lost in thought, the Sheriff moved absently about his suite, touching this, touching that, unaware the telephone was ringing. It rang for some time then stopped. Time. Time was against him. With the newspapers filled with the despair of the growing numbers out of work, house foreclosures, bank failures, what was the importance of another

165

murder two months after it happened? The note? '*Wait till I get you!*' It was hard to imagine the butler sitting down to write it. Why? If you had a key and were already in the house, why threaten her? Why put her on guard? Which is when he heard someone knocking on his door.

It was the Secretary.

"Sorry to bother you, Sheriff. Your phone was ringing but the operator said you were not picking up. There's a message for you from a Mr. Jason. He's butler to the Roberts. He'd like a meeting with you at your convenience."

+   +   +   +

LATER THAT MORNING IN NEWPORT

From the top of the stairs Karla heard the pantry door close and the key turn in the lock as the last of the staff left. A clock struck eleven. Just to be sure she was alone she went down the steps, through the kitchen into the pantry. No one. By reflex she tried the door. It was locked.

Back upstairs, at a loss how to kill the time, she wandered from room to room suddenly aware of how empty she felt, as empty as the house. On impulse she went up to the first floor. To the left was her suite, to the right that of her late husband. In the three years since his death, she had hardly ever been in his suite. Now she went in. The main bedroom, vast, the herringbone-pattern oak floor, polished, the tall sandalwood built-in cupboards, immaculate, the view via French windows onto a little private terrace... Empty. The attached secondary bedroom he used as an office. Equally immaculate. As empty. The bathroom, with fresh towels and his bathrobe. Empty. What did she expect? She continued her inspection up to the second floor, opening all the doors to all six bedrooms. Every bed made. Immaculate. Empty. It wasn't the note. It was the phone call. Deep in the night. Wine-soused, she'd struggled awake. A voice she hadn't heard in years.

"Karla? It's me."

"Markus!"

"Yes. I must see you. Alone. I can be there at 11.30."

"What -"

"Can't explain now. You must help me. 11.30."

167

Pacing the rooms of the empty house Karla felt her heart accelerate. She catches a reflection of herself in a mirror, pale, wearing a silver chemise dress by Worth, sleeveless, bloused, with a fashionably dropped waist and a peach satin underslip. She wrinkles her nose, looks at her watch. 11.22. Quickly she goes back down two floors, walks through the billiard room to the enclosed glass verandah which overlooks the gardens and the path to the front gate. Nobody.

Which is when the bell rang.

Despite expecting it, the sound made Karla's nerves jump as she retraced her steps. Eleven years, she thought as she crossed the Great Hall to open the front door. Hand outstretched, she hesitated. Which is when the bell rang again. So close and loud, she was literally startled. She opened the door.

+ + + +

She opened the door.

"Thank God," Markus said, walking in. He dropped the bundle he was carrying on the floor, swept Karla into his arms and the eleven years since they had last embraced vanished. Minutes passed entwined. A tactile memory of lips and tongues and hands and an unearthed ache and yearning. With the 5-metre-high front door still ajar.

Coming up for air, all Markus could say was, "Du!"

"Du," he said, "Denn Gott ist mein Zeuge, du bist schöner als vorher!"

"Salaud," Karla said, "de me faire attendre tant d'années!"

"How can you be more beautiful than before?" Markus said.

"How could you keep me waiting for so long?" Karla said. And, with her foot, closed the front door.

Thunk.

A solid sound shutting out the world.

In the pungent privacy of that moment, just the two of them in the vast silence of the Great Hall, each taking measure of the other, time remembered stood still. Paris. The piano. Her virginity. The war. Danger shared. Death. Survival. Until Markus broke the spell, grinned, and waved a hand.

"So," he said, "it is as I imagined, the Princess in her magic castle."

His gesture encompassed the frescoed ceiling 15 metres overhead, the floor paved with stone inlaid with black and white marble, the wainscoting and wrought cornices, the monumental stone fireplace lined with high panelling inlaid in red and black, the two pairs of giant mullioned windows either side of the entrance through which daylight flooded onto the marble staircase down which she had just come.

"Schnell," he said, "Quick, where can we hide that?"

The bundle lay where he had dropped it.

"Not now," Karla said. "Come."

"But -," Markus said.

"Come." Karla took his hand and walked him to the Music Room. As soon as she opened the door he knew why. The room, 50-feet square, with soaring ceilings and enormous French Doors out to the terrace, was dominated by a Bösendorfer Imperial Grand piano, nearly 3 metres long, with a full 8 octaves in tonal range, in all its elegant black-polished-ebony lacquered glory.

He flexed his fingers.

"I haven't played in a long, long time," he said. "And never on an instrument like this."

Sitting on the piano bench he smiled as the memory of his shabby crib and the small upright antique piano glided in and out of his mind. He opened the lid; gazed down in wonder at the 97 keys. Again, he stretched and flexed his fingers, looked up at Karla standing, smiling down at him, closed his eyes and allowed himself to gently caress the keys, run his fingertips up and down the keyboard, noting how perfectly the piano was tuned, before straightening his posture, poise his hands as his fingers moved to play. Beethoven. *'Für Elise.'* Alternating E and D-sharp, the first five notes repeat. Karla can feel the goosebumps on her arms.

And then, as he had done so long ago, he stops. Gestures with his left hand. "Sit here next to me," he says.

The years fall away. Just as he did then he did now. With his right hand he played the melody. His left hand played the accompanying arpeggio on her thigh. Slowly, slowly drawing up her skirt. Then on her bare skin. The fingers probe. Part her legs. Reach their target. Languorously, Karla closes her eyes. The warmth she now feels is what she then felt. She hadn't stopped him then, why stop him now? She leans her head to rest on his shoulder. Markus plays on…

Inevitably they end up in Karla's bed in Karla's bedroom, the bundle on the floor, no time to draw the curtains across the French windows out to her private terrace. What must take place, takes place. When they're done, content in giving and taking, they fall into a naked embrace on the pillows and Karla says, "You took advantage of me."

Markus chuckles. "You couldn't wait for it to happen."

"I'm talking about then. I was hardly out of school."

"You were a university student bored out of her mind with mediaeval history, wondering why nobody would seduce you?"

"I see what those girls meant."

"What girls?"

'Those two, that first day in the bar, the day war was declared. They said you were a musician and to be careful."

"How can you remember that?"

"I remember a lot of things about you." Karla sat up. "I especially remember you after the war returning to Paris. Come for me, I thought. How could I be so stupid? Behind my back you continued to screw anything in a skirt."

"So? You think the leopard changes his spots?"

"How did you know where to find me?"

With his forefinger Markus tapped the side of his nose. "I smelled you out."

She pointed at the bundle on the floor. "So? What's in there that I must hide?"

"Some papers. Best you don't know."

"Have you stolen something?"

"Not really."

"What does that mean?" Karla frowned. "After all we lived through, you don't trust me?"

"It's for your own safety, Karla. If you don't know you can't tell."

"Tell whom? What's going on Markus? You could hide papers anytime like we did in the war. You taught me how, remember?"

+   +   +   +

PARIS. GARE DE L'EST

Thursday, 10.22pm, November 5, 1914

Standing in the shadow of a kiosk closed for the night, his small suitcase packed, his student beard shaved off, hair neatly trimmed, shoes polished, grey trilby tipped forward, the brim just hiding the granny glasses disguising his face, Markus, anonymous as all the other grey-suited clerks waiting to board the train, was ready to go.

From behind him Karla said "You've got your ticket?"

"Nein, dumme. I intend to attract attention by telling the guard I don't have one. Stop being so nervous."

"Sorry."

"Okay. Tell me what you must do."

"Once a week go on my bicycle to the poste restante in Pigalle to ask if there is mail for me. The envelope with my name will contain a second which I am to deliver to whomever it is addressed. I am to follow the instructions I receive only if there is a handwritten note from you signed by you in the first envelope. if there is no mail, come back a week later. If there is no letter after one month go to the Poste Restante at Vincennes. After Vincennes, then Batignolles, Porte d'Orléans, Raspail, Rue du Louvre, Monceau, Neuilly, shall I tell them all?"

"No. Just remember, never go back after a month. Never. Never give anyone a reason to remember you. Look no one in the eye. Don't chat with strangers. If asked, you are waiting for news from the front. If there is no handwritten note signed by me, run. I fear this war may last; God knows how long. You will not know where I am nor if we will meet again."

"What if I must send you a message?"

"If you receive a letter giving you a Poste Restante in Switzerland or Luxembourg, send it there." Markus looked at his watch.

"Time to go." He bent, picked up his suitcase, and joined the flow of passengers headed for the overnight express to Strasbourg. He didn't look back. Karla tried to follow him with her eyes. Two minutes later he was gone.

+   +   +   +

"That's too important to put in the post." Markus now said. "It will only be for a short while, I promise. If you don't hear from me in a month, what's in there is yours." In the distance a clock chimed 3. "Time to go."

"You always say that when you're going to disappear. What if I'm not here when you want to come back?"

"What do you mean? This is yours, isn't it?" Markus swept his arm through the air, encompassing the room, the house, the gardens, Newport.

"I'm going to sell it," Karla said, "once the estate is settled. I'm going to go back to live in France."

"And be a waitress again? Remember - "

He stopped.

Listened.

Suddenly alert, he said, "Is there someone in the house?"

"No." Karla said.

"I distinctly heard something?"

"What?"

"There!"

They strain to listen. Silence. They both stand up.

"Who's there?" Karla yells as loud as she can. Naked, she stalks to the bedroom door, throws it open and again shouts, "Who's there!"

Silence.

"There's nobody," she says, coming back into the room. "Must be your imagination."

"I can't be seen." Markus is already dressing. "Can I get out that way?" He points at the French windows. She nods.

"There's a spiral staircase from the terrace down. It's an old fire escape. Be careful. It's very slippery with this drizzle," she says.

"Hide that." Markus gives her the bundle. He's about to leave. Hesitates. "Will you be safe?" he says.

"Nein, dumme," she says, smiling.

"I'll be in touch," he says.

"Wait!" she says. And bends to pull out from under her bed an old, japanned tin trunk, its hinged lid screeching as she opens it. "This is where I keep my jewellery. Your papers will be safe here. Better you know."

The bundle goes in the trunk, the trunk goes under the bed, the naked woman hugs the man dressed to leave. When he's gone, she gets back in bed, drained.

Markus!

His reappearance in her life...incomprehensible. There was so much she wanted to tell him. And she remembers - the will. Hiding in plain sight amid the kitchen receipts where she found it when doing the accounts. Markus would have laughed. On an impulse she gets out of bed, drags out her tin trunk again to open the bundle of fat files he left in her care. Uncomprehending, she stares. Share certificates? She looks at the French windows through which he'd left for an answer. Then, from where it lies under her jewellery, takes the envelope with the will, and puts it in with the shares. She shivers, shoves the trunk back, and shivering hops under the bed covers, not sure what she's done. The unspoken bond between them... and her mind goes back to another envelope...

+ + + +

PARIS, PIGALLE

Wednesday, September 2, 1914

As she had done for the previous three weeks, Karla cycled across town, up the Rue Blanche to the Boulevard de Clichy, turned right, until she reached the steps of the Pigalle post office at Number 43, and, after propping her bike against the metal screen of the pissoir on the pavement directly opposite the entrance, she went into the bureaucratic gloom of all French public institutions. She was dressed in her oldest, most unfashionable clothes, a long-sleeved, high-waisted, belted pale grey dress, the skirt reaching to her ankles, covering cotton pantaloons and gaiters as protection from the cold, with a black woollen tunic covering everything, which made her look like a sausage she thought. Her long black hair was caught up in a Breton fisherman's beret. There was nothing she could do to hide her height other than walk with her head cast down.

She joined the queue of people in front of the Poste Restante window and gave her name when it was her turn. Having received nothing previously, she was almost startled when the postman behind the guichet handed her a large buff envelope with a postmark from Luxembourg and pointed at where she should sign for its receipt in his ledger.

Once outside, she put the envelope in the wicker basket attached to the handlebar of her bicycle, mounted up and made her way back downhill across Paris to the Left Bank, Montparnasse and to her tiny room in the Passage d'Enfer. It was only with the door shut that she felt she could safely open the envelope. True to his word, the envelope contained a second one, with no address, and a note in pencil on what she should do.

K - You will not believe my incredible luck. I am seconded to the office of the Prussian Minister for War as his interpreter. The enclosed document comes from there. You must get this to a senior French officer in the Grand Quartier General in Vitry-le-François on the Place Royer-Collard. How you do this I leave to you but do not delay. Once you have read this note, burn it. - M.

Post scriptum - burn the envelope as well.

For the longest time Karla stared at the note. Bloody Markus. Not a word of encouragement or inquiry as to her health, safety, well-being…and nothing about himself other than his luck. She had so much to tell him. He was right, the Sorbonne did close. Without a bourse she did what he had suggested and in no time was modelling at the Grand Chaumière where every painter and sculptor from Bourdelle to Zadkine tried to seduce her. But no, she was faithful. Every night as she fell asleep, she relived the magic of their love-making. She ached for him. Why couldn't he at least write Love, M? Instead of a series of instructions? Then, despite herself, she took the matchbox next to the candleholder, struck a match and did as instructed, flushing the ashes down the toilet.

She resisted the temptation to open the second envelope. There was no way for her to get to the front at Vitry-le-François, and even if she could, what then? She could not imagine approaching a soldier and asking for the name of a high-ranking officer. Que faire? And when the answer came to her it was simplicity itself. She addressed the anonymous envelope in capital letters to:

LE COMMANDANT-EN-CHEF, LE GÉNÉRALE JOFFRE
GRAND QUARTIER GÉNÉRALE
PLACE ROYER-COLLARD
VITRY-LE- FRANÇOIS
MARNE

And that same evening, in the downcast gloom of wartime Paris, with the lampposts and the headlights of cars dimmed, she walked past the shop windows with their anti-bomb tape, down the Boulevard Raspail to where it met Boulevard Montparnasse, and the post-box opposite La Rotonde to post the letter.

+ + + +

The French Deuxième Bureau, temporarily located in classrooms on the second floor of a school building in Vitry, was tasked with counter-intelligence. The content of the envelope, a dossier stamped *Aufmarsch II West,* was forwarded to them from GQG to ascertain its origin and authenticity. It ended up on the desk of Colonel Charles Joseph Dupont. He could not believe what he had in his hands, a draft modifying Schlieffen's Plan of Invasion and signed by von Moltke himself. He immediately called on his superior, General Henri Berthelot, aide-major of the 2ème Bureau.

"When did GQG get this?" Berthelot said.

"By this morning's mail," Dupont said. 'It was posted in Paris three days ago."

'Nothing else? No indication of who sent it?"

"No, nothing."

"Have you checked the signature?"

"Yes. It appears to be authentic. We've called for a graphologist to be sure."

"Mon Dieu! Right out of the lion's mouth. Whoever stole it has balls of iron."

"Makes you think."

"What?"

"If it could happen over there, maybe it could also happen here?"

"A traitor? Here?"

Before Dupont could answer an orderly knocked on the door, opened it, saluted, and said "We are ready to move, mon General."

"About bloody time!" General Berthelot said.

Little did he realise that GQG and all its dependents, after the defeat and retreat from Mons, would have to hastily relocate its headquarters progressively westwards before the German onslaught. It moved to Bar-sur-

Aube on 31 August, Châtillon-sur-Seine on 6 September, Romilly-sur-Seine on 28 September and, on 29 November, 1914 to Chantilly,

And it was in Chantilly that a second envelope arrived.

+ + + +

GERMAN ARMY GHQ, Esch-sur-Alzette, Grand Duchy of Luxembourg

Geneneral Erich Georg Anton von Falkenhayn, Prussian Minister of War and Chief of the German General Staff, looked at the young recruit standing at attention across the war-room.

"This is the man I mentioned in my report," his Aide-de-Camp said.

"I understand you are an historian, educated at the Sorbonne, speaking fluent French?" von Falkenhayn said to the recruit.

"Yes, Sir," Markus said. "However, I did not graduate…"

"Because the war started, I know. I also know you are insubordinate, outspoken, with little regard for authority" - he glanced again at the report he held in his hands - "particularly military authority. Sit over there. We will speak in a moment."

Markus sat where directed and von Falkenhayn turned with his aide to study three giant maps stretching across an entire wall, one of Europe, one of the Eastern Front and one of the West. Broad red arrows marked the thrust of the German advance through Luxembourg into Belgium and Northern France. Even straining an ear, Markus could not hear all that was being said until abruptly von Falkenhayn's tone changed and he raised his voice in anger.

"Ermattungskreig, am I clear? A war of exhaustion," the General said. With a long thin baton, he tapped each location on the map. "They've lost 180,000 men on the Mons retreat alone, here." Tap. "And last month 70,000 in Lorraine - Tap - 25,000 in Mulhouse - Tap - 89,000 in the

Ardennes - Tap - and 15,000 in Charleroi." Double tap. "How long can they keep this up?"

"But surely Schlieffen and von Moltke are correct and a quick success against France is of the utmost importance so as to have the troops available for deployment on the eastern front against the Russians?"

"At what cost? We always boast of the enemy dead and ignore our own. They are retreating, yes, but I wager they will counter-attack when the British get up to full strength. Enough. You have your orders. Go."

His Aide out of the room, von Falkenhayn continued to study the maps. Without turning his head, he said, "You, the historian, come here."

Markus got up and came to stand at the shoulder of the General.

"What do you see?" the General said.

"May I be frank?"

"Of course. It's why you are here. I have enough arse-lickers not to add another."

"I see a problem."

"Which is?"

"Logistics. Your supplies." Taking the baton from the General's hands, Markus tapped Berlin and then Marne. "They're approximately 1000 kilometres apart, with just two main railway lines, and advancing only through Belgium means that you must squeeze the 600,000 men of your 1st and 2nd armies through a gap 19 kilometres wide, which makes it vital that the Belgian railways captured remain intact for you to have any realistic chance of an offensive strategy against France. Worse, if our attrition rate is anything like theirs, the front lines of your reserves would arrive here while the tail would still be in Berlin."

"They teach you this in the university?" von Falkenhayn tried to hide his astonishment. "How old are you?"

"Nineteen - nearly twenty."

"And from sitting over there," the General waved at the chair vacated by Markus, "all this was evident to you?"

"No, sir. From reading Caesar's commentaries on the Gallic Wars. He had the same problems you have, overlong supply lines from Rome to Gaul, the need to feed his armies, lack of reserves, an enemy ever ready to hit him in the flanks. It's just reverse engineering." Markus shrugged modestly.

"Unglaublich. Why don't I have ten of you? Beginning today, right now, you are assigned to this office. You will start by translating this."

'This' was a copy of the supposedly ultra-secret **Plan XVII** issued to French army commanders on 7 February 1914 as modified in a final draft on 1 May. The document was not a campaign plan, but it contained a statement that the Germans were expected to concentrate the bulk of their army on the Franco-German border and might cross before French operations could begin. The instruction of their Commander in Chief was significant: 'Whatever the circumstances, it is the Commander in Chief's intention to advance with all forces united to the attack of the German armies. The action of the French armies will be developed in two main operations: one, on the right in the country between the wooded district of the Vosges and the Moselle below Toul; the other, on the left, north of a line Verdun–Metz. The two operations will be closely connected by forces operating on the Hauts de Meuse and in the Woëvre.'

It was signed, *JOFFRE*

It was Markus's turn to be astonished at what he held in his hands. The General, pleased by the effect, tapped the side of his nose with his forefinger, a strange gesture coming from such a stern, bald-headed, Prussian Junker. "We have our sources in Paris, nicht war?" he said, with an emphatic twirl on the ends of his walrus moustache.

+   +   +   +

It was the end of October when Karla picked up the second envelope at the poste restante in the post office at the Porte d'Orléans. It was stamped and franked in Brussels. The note inside from Markus was alarming:

> **K - There is a spy (maybe more than one) operating in the French military HQ. I do not have a name but the material I am given to translate is very sensitive and suggests a high-ranking official is sending it. Conversely, this person may know or suspect there is a leak here in the German HQ and**

will start counter-measures. Beware of strangers trying to talk to you. Do not be brave, just be very, very careful. - M.

As before, the envelope contained a second, and as before Karla simply addressed it to General Joffre and sent it off. She was perplexed. What did he mean by 'do not be brave'? Cycling from one post office to another scarcely merited the term. It was so frustrating not being able to communicate with him. She had been following newspaper reports of the Battle of Ypres since it started on the 19th of October in western Flanders and the trench warfare that ensued. The reported German casualty figures were incredible. She couldn't imagine where Markus might be but feared for his safety…as she fell asleep in the cosy warmth of her bed in Newport and failed to hear a floorboard squeak.

+ + + +

He freezes. Stands stock still, listens. Silence. Very gently he shifts the weight of his foot. Waits. The sound of her shouting 'Who's there?' still an echo in his ears. He is acutely aware of time flowing. Soon the servants would be back. He reaches for the doorknob. The floorboard squeaks again.

+ + + +

That sound again.

From sleep to open-eyed awareness.

There is someone in the house!

Karla wakes in panic. Wildly, she looks around. Hesitates. Lock the door to her bedroom? Her heart pounding, barely breathing, she leaps out of bed. Still naked, runs across the room, presses her ear to her bedroom door. Silence. For a long moment she remains listening. Then she straightens her spine. It's her house. Why should she be afraid? She reaches for the doorknob. Throws open the door…

"YOU!"

Her scream is cut off by a hand on her throat.

+ + + +

AN INTERVIEW IN THE READING ROOM

"**B**efore we start, Mr. Jason, please confirm that this interview is at your own request."

"It is."

"I am the Sheriff, and this is my colleague, Thomas Brady. He will record what is said here. You will be given a transcript which you will sign. Do you understand?"

"Yes."

"Please state your name."

"Fleet."

"Excuse me?"

"My surname is Fleet."

"And Jason?"

"My Christian name."

"I see. How should we proceed? Fleet or Jason?"

"I am known as Jason at work."

"Very well. Occupation?"

"Butler."

"Address?"

"2, Bellevue Court."

"Is that where you work or where you live?"

"Both."

"How long have you been employed there?"

"3 years."

"Where were you employed before that?"

"At Number 6, Bellevue Court."

"For how long were you employed there?"

"All told, 30 years."

"All told?"

"I entered service with Mr. Plane when I was 25, in 1896. During the war he enlisted with the British forces well before the United States entered the conflict. I was his batman. Technically not a butler, as that is not a rank in the military. After we were demobbed, I reverted to being his butler, until…"

"Yes?"

"Until his death when I was dismissed."

"By whom?"

"Karla. I mean, Mrs. Plane."

"Date?"

"October 1926."

"For what reason were you dismissed?"

Silence.

"Mr. Jason, silence is not an answer. In your view, for what reason were you dismissed?"

"Mr. Plane had a heart attack. He died. She –"

"Yes?"

"She said she could no longer afford my services. In lieu of notice, she.."

"Let me interrupt you, Mr. Jason. Off the record."

The Sheriff leaned across the table the better to close the distance between himself and the butler.

"I am investigating the murder of Mrs. Karla Plane. Murder, Mr. Jason. The foul slaughter of a young woman. I am not here to adjudicate the rights or wrongs of a domestic dispute. Please restrict your answers to the questions I ask. I should remind you that you came forward of your own volition to ask for this interview. You may terminate it whenever you wish. If I choose to do so I can officially recall you for an interrogation under oath when your testimony could be used against you in the event you were charged with a crime. Are we clear?"

If the Sheriff thought to intimidate the butler, he was wrong. Jason sat straighter in his chair, adjusted his spectacles and in his turn leaned forward. "I am not a child, Sheriff. I am nearly 60 years old. I have come forward because I think what has been done to her is an abomination and I would do anything to apprehend the culprit. What I have to tell you may help you solve the crime. As Sir Kobe's manservant I think I knew him better than anyone else, including his two wives. There are things that are said in the intimacy of helping a man dress and undress everyday which are close to being confessional. Would you believe he wanted me to inherit half his estate?"

"You knew that?" the Sheriff said.

"Of course. He told me when he put it in his will. I told him it would not be appropriate, but he insisted. I told him I would give it all to charity. What would I do with a fortune? I explained to him that I was well off with all he had paid me over the years, but he just laughed at me. I don't think he understood my pride in being a man of service."

"Did you know he kept a handgun here?"

"His Webley? He kept it in the mudroom," the butler nodded. "It was my task to keep it clean and in good working order. He kept it as a memento. It was standard issue for every officer in the British Army. A Mark 5, .455 calibre. He kept it loaded for target practice in the woods behind the house. Why?"

"Was he afraid of something?"

"Sir Kobe? Afraid? I have no idea who could be telling you such rubbish because they most certainly didn't know the man. He fought behind the lines for most of the war, was nearly captured several times and was rewarded for his heroism by both France and England. The idea of him being afraid is preposterous. Anyway, what has this to do with Karla's murder?"

"She was shot. The gun is missing."

"Are you implying…?"

"I am not implying," the Sheriff said. "I am stating facts."

In his usual fly-on-the-wall observation post, Brady admired the Sheriff's strategy, but couldn't fail to see that it had no effect whatsoever on the butler.

"Let us now return to this will, giving you half the estate," the Sheriff said.

"Why?" Jason said. "It is moot since I was witness to the will he made in favour of Karla. Whenever he travelled abroad, I went with him. He would ask my opinion about everything that interested him, from art to wine, and particularly regarding the people he met. Nobody here knew the late Mrs. Plane better than I did. During the year Sir Kobe spent wooing her, I was there beside him the entire time. On those occasions, first in Paris, then after they married, when we chanced to be alone, I became her confidante. She insisted I call her Karla. She was very unsure why Sir Kobe was so intent on marrying her and asked my advice about older men, given the 40-year age gap between them." Jason smiled wryly. "I take it, you've seen her portrait in the library?"

"I have," the Sheriff said.

Jason nodded. "What more is there to say? It is not my place to comment on her physical beauty, but I doubt a more beguiling woman existed. She was totally innocent of the effect she had on men…no, not innocent, more like unaware. As a waitress - did you know she was a waitress?"

"Yes," the Sheriff said.

"She worked in the same restaurant for over 10 years. She ran her network from there."

"Network?" the Sheriff said.

"Yes. Didn't you know? She was a spy. She supplied the French military with secrets of what the German command intended to do before the Germans themselves knew. Her source in Germany was never detected and how they communicated is still a secret. Old Monsieur Aubert, who owned the restaurant, must have known; at least that is what he hinted to Sir Kobe. I don't think it surprised him. Little did."

Jason paused and now it was the Sheriff's turn to say, "How is any of this germane to her getting killed?"

"I looked out for her, Sheriff," Jason said. "Even working for the Roberts, I looked out for her. She got me my job with them, you know. When Sir Kobe passed away, she was living on whatever the executor of his estate thought appropriate, certainly not enough to afford a butler. She knew the Roberts were looking for someone since the retirement of Old Carruthers, their man. We did a little song and dance about getting dismissed to solicit the sympathy of Mrs. Roberts. It worked and I even got a raise. Karla got a few knives in the back for supposedly firing me. Not that she cared. She had few friends here in America and she liked it that I lived around the corner. She gave me a key to her place so I could pop in for a chat in my free time. Perhaps she was afraid all alone here? Perhaps she knew too much from the war?"

"She mentioned this?"

"Not in so many words. It was more what she didn't say. Something made her uneasy. But I can tell you this, somebody was in that house who should not have been there."

"What? How do you -"

"That Saturday, after you people had trampled all over the place, late in the night I let myself in. When you've lived in a house for over 30 years you know every little detail, right down to which door cannot be opened without the hinge squeaking and the stair runner that is always out of whack. Just by walking into a room you can tell if someone has been there. Even in the dark. Imagine my surprise then, when I found the toilet on the second floor had been recently used."

"How -?"

"A lingering smell, Sheriff. Just the faintest whiff. The toilet had been flushed but you could still see traces of faeces under the waterline."

Which is when someone knocked on the door.

It was the Secretary.

"Sorry to bother you again, Sheriff. Phone call from the Plane mansion. You are wanted there urgently."

+   +   +   +

IN THE BACK BAR OF THE PEARL

Two days to Christmas and Kale was half drunk. He was worried. His brother's boat was late. MacFarland's boat to be precise, on which his brother was crew, out fishing in the North Atlantic in bad weather. No radio contact in the past two days. The bar was crowded with fishermen, grizzle-bearded veterans, and youngsters, all glad to be safe in port, a pint in hand, with a gale blowing up outside. Somebody nudged his drinking arm.

"Move over, sunshine," Buck said. "Christ in heaven, you do look miserable."

"Lake's out there." With his thumb Kale pointed out to the ocean.

"Why in fuck's sake?"

"We needed some money. MacFarland was short-handed." Kale shrugged.

"Well, you needn't worry then. Nothing will sink MacFarland. You seen today's paper?"

"No. It's all the same shit."

"Not this," Buck took a folded copy of the Newport Reporter from his donkey jacket. "Here," he tapped the front page, "right up your street."

Beneath the headline, '*SLASHED MASTERPIECE*', was a picture occupying one quarter of the front page. It showed the life-sized portrait of a semi-naked woman wearing a pearl necklace, lacerated by multiple gashes running right to left, some canvas strips hanging down over the frame.

Stunned, Kale fished out his spectacles, settled them on his nose and read:

'Newport, Sunday, December 22, 1929 - District Attorney William Clarke, reported a sensational development in the stalled murder case of Mrs. Karla Plane, who was shot and beaten to death on October 26 in her home at No. 6, Bellevue Court, adjacent to The Elms.

The portrait of his wife, by the French Academician, P.A.Belanopek, was commissioned by her late husband, Sir Kobe Plane. It was found shredded where it hung in the library of Planetree House. Staff called the police on discovering the outrage Saturday afternoon. "We are moving forward on the assumption that this was the work of a madman, her slayer," DA Clarke said. "Any person who may have seen someone enter the Mansion is asked to report it to the police. All information will be held in the strictest confidence." When asked if there was any specific suspect, DA Clarke said, "No comment." When asked if the Mansion was adequately protected, he answered, "No comment." When asked if such a priceless work of art could be restored, he replied, "Expert, informed opinion will be sought. It will take time. Finding the perpetrator of such a senseless act is our priority." '

Which is when Lake, still in his oilskins and Sou'wester, water dripping from the brim, came in, shouldered his way to the bar next to his brother, and triumphantly slammed down a copy of the Reporter. "Bet you haven't seen this!" he said.

The two newspapers lay side by side open to the same front page. Kale and Buck looked at him. For a moment he looked from them to the papers and back to them. 'Fuck you too," he said.

+   +   +   +

FURY IN THE COURTHOUSE

A normally calm man, Clarke was incandescent. Forgetting his Quaker upbringing, shaking with rage, he pounded his desk on which copies of the Sunday National press lay open.

"This is a fucking scandal! We have the place patrolled, with a man living on the premises, and this shit happens!" The District Attorney glared at his assembled colleagues. "See this?" He grabbed some newspapers. "I hold each one of you personally responsible, each one, am I clear? Starting with you, Chief, and you, Sheriff! How can a man in broad daylight penetrate a guarded building and commit such barbarity without being seen or heard? What in tarnation have you been doing, apart from sleeping on the job? Do you remotely understand the damage this has done to our reputation? The Governor himself tore a strip off me, going as far as suggesting I consider resignation! Me! Resign? Before that happens, I'll have each one of you fired."

He closed his eyes in the vain hope his problems would vanish. When this didn't work, he returned to glaring. "Well? Don't just sit there." He stabbed a finger at the Chief. "Say something!"

Thus fingered, the Chief did what he did best, pass the buck.

"Sheriff?" he said.

Sheriff Brenton had been sitting quietly watching the fireworks. He took his time. It never ceased to amaze him how senior officials were capable of heaping blame on those lower down the food chain. A thought crossed his mind, maybe the Secretary was right, he should become a writer? From an inside pocket he took out his notebook, slowly thumbed the pages with an almost insolent deliberation before finding a blank page which he carefully flattened out. From his breast pocket he took a black Parker pen, carefully unscrewed the cap, inspected the nib, and wrote as he intoned:

"On Saturday, December 21, 1929, at 10 AM,

having worked continuously for the previous 56 days

with no time off in our investigation of the murder of Mrs. Karla Plane,

I, and my assistant, Police Constable Thomas Brady,

in my suite of rooms in the Reading Room, Newport,

were conducting the interview of Mr. Jason Fleet,

former butler to Sir Kobe Plane, who informed us

that on that fatal Saturday, October 26, when Mrs. Plane was

assassinated, he entered the premises with a key she had given him -"

"What!"

"What?"

One an exclamation, the other an astonished question, both words said simultaneously by the District Attorney and the Chief of Police.

"- late that night," the Sheriff continued over the interruption without breaking the flow and tone of his voice or the precision of his writing,

"To discover evidence in the toilet on the second floor

that someone unknown had been in the Mansion

which is when the Secretary of the Reading Room interrupted our

interview to say we were urgently needed at Planetree House

to where we promptly adjourned to discover the place in uproar,

the staff terrified and the mutilated portrait in the library -"

The Sheriff paused, turned to a fresh page in his notebook, and continued on.

"- We immediately instigated a search of the premises to no avail.

Staff were questioned. Meg, the undermaid, saw the picture intact

when she was dusting in the library at 10.45am approximately.

Subsequently no one went in there.

Staff were either in their rooms in the Carriage House.

Or helping Cook prepare Saturday lunch.
And it was on her way to lunch
That Molly, seeing the library doors closed
Which doors normally stood open
Investigated and screamed when she saw
What had been done -"

"Alright, Sheriff, enough!" The District Attorney threw his hands up in mock surrender. "Do you believe this fellow, the butler?"

"Unfortunately, yes. We had him down as a prime suspect. Then he ups and volunteers for an interview, tells us he has a key, and what he saw. The implication is that the murderer was still in the Mansion when the alarm was given that Saturday and was still there when we arrived. Pretty cool customer if true. Imagine butchering that woman and then staying put. Covered in blood more than likely. Which poses the question, where did he hide? Because we made a very thorough search of the whole building and found nothing."

"Not forgetting he shot and raped her," the Chief said.

"Then comes back to mutilate her picture? I don't get it," the DA said. "Why?"

"Because he still hasn't found what he's looking for," Brady said.

For a moment they all stared at him, the forgotten man in the room. Brady turned pink.

"Go on, son," the Sheriff said. "Lay it out for us."

"I asked myself the same question, why? He's already turned the house upside down weeks ago and not found whatever it is he's looking for. But then it occurs to him, there is one place he has not looked, Behind the picture. Unfortunately for him, the picture is huge and is hung in a niche in the bookcases which makes it impossible for one man to take down, quite apart from the noise such a move would make. So, he does the obvious; he cuts through the canvas. Whether he found anything we don't know, but we now know it was small enough to be hidden in a picture frame."

"Good man," the Sheriff said. "But to do that in the middle of the day with staff in the house, how the hell did he get into the library without being seen?"

"By hiding in plain sight," Brady said, taking from his briefcase a plan. "Remember you asked me to make a floorplan for the mansion?"

Brady stood up from where he sat, crossed to the District Attorney's desk, and spread his plan across the newspapers lying there. "See how all the public rooms are interconnected?"

All the men stood to gather around the desk to examine the plan.

"Since we searched everywhere, by a process of elimination there is only one place he could have been. Here." Brady tapped the plan. "In the dining room, which communicates through these doors to the library."

"And we didn't look in there because we ordered those doors locked since it was there her body was found," the Sheriff said.

"By God!" District Attorney Clarke said. "He's got a key!"

"You think he's been in there the whole time?" Assistant District Attorney Easton said. And then voiced the unthinkable, "Could he still be there?"

+   +   +   +

After calling the Mansion to alert the staff, they raced across town to Bellevue Court, the Sheriff glancing occasionally at Brady striding, stoic and silent, next to him. Halfway there he said, "Alright. Out with it. What's on your mind?"

"He won't be there, you know that. This guy's too smart. And since he is, he's figured out we'll think of the dining room. What we must do is figure what he'll do next and be there to catch him."

"Unless he found what he was looking for and is long gone."

"I don't think he has. If you picture the way he slashed the picture, he's right-handed, he started at the top, and cut across at a downward angle right to left. If he found what he was looking for he would not have continued slashing the picture. The second cut is parallel but lower and the canvas is pulled away for him to see down the inside of the picture because he is still looking. The third cut opens up the entire bottom of the canvas which hangs out and down over the picture frame. Why would he do that if not to be certain nothing was there? So, he's still looking. The question is, what for?"

+   +   +   +

THREE YEARS BEFORE
IN LOS ANGELES

"Mr. Giannini will see you now, sir."

The secretary ushered the administrator into the palatial office of Amadeo Pietro Giannini, managing partner of the Bank of Italy, on the corner of 7th and Olive.

"Welcome to our city, Mr. Baxter," the banker stood to shake hands. "What brings you to the West Coast, business or pleasure?"

"A little of both, I hope," Jacob Baxter shook hands. "It's an honour to meet you, Mr. Giannini."

It was not often that one met one of the titans of the industry. AP, as he was popularly known, had successfully survived both the 1906 earthquake and fire in San Francisco, and then the panic of 1907 when many banks went under, while Bank of Italy, its gold and currency reserves intact, went on a buying spree acquiring banks throughout California and then nationwide to become the first branch-banking system in America.

"How are things in the Big Apple?" Mr. Giannini said, when both men were seated.

"Fine, until you look under the rug," Mr. Baxter said. "The popular press touts the boom in industry, trumpets the growth figures being played up by the government, scarcely mentions the overproduction and underconsumption of consumer goods. Too much speculation going into overvalued shares; people who cannot afford it gambling on margin; banks lending to these people. It makes me very uncomfortable."

195

"I share your view. We have made it a policy not to lend on margin. Our typical customer is a small businessman who needs money to grow his business. We also back women who have an entrepreneurial spirit and those in new and exciting industries, like the motion picture business out here. What concerns me is access to easy credit, with everyone and his aunt borrowing to buy things they don't necessarily need. People have short memories. They've forgotten what happens when there is a bank run and liquidity dries up. I fear a repetition of 1907."

"Thank God we've got the Fed now as lender of last resort."

"Which makes me even more fearful. Trust is undermined and risk increased by unscrupulous reliance on the Fed being there to bail you out. Therein lies complacency. Never forget, Mr. Baxter, our industry is built on trust. Morgan famously said, 'a man I do not trust could not get money from me on all the bonds in Christendom.'" Mr. Giannini took a gold pocket watch from his vest to check the time. "Enough philosophising. How can I help you?"

"I am here as the Court appointed administrator of the estate of the late Sir Kobe Plane. You are aware he passed away?"

"Yes. It saddened me greatly. He was a most unusual man, probably the only customer we've ever had who never asked after his account balance or how much we had made for him. He used to come and see me in San Francisco to enquire how he could contribute to the well-being of our employees. When asked why he was concerned, you know what he said? 'Look at me, I'm fat. No point getting fatter. Times are difficult. I'd rather see others eat.' Mr. Giannini nodded. "He insisted on contributing to our employees' pension fund. Anonymously, mark you. For all his outward jollity he was a modest man who had no need for applause, content in his own generous nature."

"You knew a side of him I did not," Jacob Baxter said. "He banked with us and appointed me executor under his will, the original of which has been filed with the Probate Court in Newport, Rhode Island. My task is to make an inventory of all his assets." Baxter opened his briefcase and extracted a sheaf of documents.

"I have here letters testamentary from the Court, a list of all the property he owned in California, pass keys to the various buildings, bank accounts related to each, keys to safe deposit boxes and the like. As far as our records show, all the accounts and deposits are with you, here, at the Bank of Italy. What would be the most convenient way for us to proceed?"

"Knowing you were coming, I have arranged to have a conference room set aside for you. I do not know all the details of Sir Kobe's holdings, only that they were substantial. One of our directors will assist you. He is the manager in charge of Plane's account -" at a knock on the door - "and, as expected, here he is."

A small, middle aged, bald man, wearing horn-rimmed spectacles, came in.

"Harrison," Mr. Giannini said, "this is Jacob Baxter, the executor for the Plane estate. I have told him you will give him every assistance in his enquiries."

Harrison sniffed, seemingly unimpressed with the task. "The Boss told you this is going to take days?" he said, shaking hands with Baxter.

"Days? Really?"

"You better believe. Wait till you see the stuff I've lined up for you in the conference room. Where you staying?"

"I've a room in the Beverly Hills Hotel."

"Shoot. You'll spend all day commuting back and forth. Better check into the Biltmore, right here downtown. Don't worry, we'll handle it."

+   +   +   +

TEMPTATION IN THE CONFERENCE ROOM

They did. To his pleasant surprise, Jacob Baxter found his suitcases switched from one hotel to the other and instead of a room he had a suite on the seventh floor of the Biltmore, overlooking Pershing Square. Every morning in bright sunshine, he enjoyed the stroll down Olive for two blocks to the bank, a distinct change from the misery of winter in New York. What he had not anticipated was the complexity of his task. Harrison's warning had not prepared him for his first view into the conference room and the mountains of files awaiting his inspection stretching down the length of the conference table.

"Where do you want to start?" Harrison said. "These are the statements for 12 major buildings he owned here in the city and for the Ice House in Beverly Hills. I've teed up the property managers and told them you will want to tour the buildings, and to have available the current leases, reports on vacancies, ongoing repairs and maintenance, up to date accounts, and future budgets. Then there's the land in Palm Springs, which'll take a day going there and back, and the two buildings in San Diego, which'll take another two days. Call it two weeks."

Baxter had to call the bank in New York to give them the news and then he had to call his wife, Edith, to tell her.

"And after Los Angeles, there's Chicago, then Houston and Dallas, and then Boston and Newport," he said.

"Does that mean you won't be home for Christmas? What will I tell the kids?"

"Tell them I'm with Father Christmas helping with the presents."

"Don't joke, Jacob. They will be very, very disappointed."

"Have I ever joked about business, Edith? You think I like being on the road, living out of a suitcase? This is an opportunity for us -" he had nearly said 'me' - "a once-in-a-lifetime opportunity. If I do good, maybe the bank will offer me a partnership? Think how that will change our lives."

'That's all you care about, money! What about our family?' Now it was she who nearly said 'me'.

"Please, Edith. Not on the telephone. How many times do we have to have the same argument? Of course, I care about money. That's what bankers do. Don't worry. I'll be back in time. Give the kids my love."

The kids. Not her. Edith hung up.

Jacob looked at the silent receiver in his hand. He was a religious man, who faithfully said his prayers every night, asking for the Lord's protection of his family and of those he held dearest. Since his meeting with her at the funeral, for reasons that tortured him, he included Karla in his prayers. He could neither get her out of his mind nor devise a way to change their relationship. His imagination led to sleepless nights in which he played the most improbable roles to seduce her. 'Lead us not into temptation.' The very ambiguity in the sentence tortured him. It was ironic that it should be Harrison who delivered the epiphany when he said, "Perhaps we should start with the safe deposit boxes?" and led the way to the bank vaults in the basement of Bank of Italy, where, past the five-foot-thick steel doors, were row upon row of black steel boxes with their double keyholes.

"Those four and that big one are Sir Kobe Plane's," Harrison said. "You insert your key and I mine, to open the door to each box. Inside are containers which can only be opened with your key. There is a private room" - he pointed outside the vault - "for you to examine the contents. When you have finished, please use this bell to call me and I will return for us to lock up. But first you must sign the registry."

Jacob did as instructed, and after he had signed and when all the keys had been inserted and the doors to each box opened and after Harrison had withdrawn, he removed the first container. For something smaller than a shoebox it was curiously heavy. Painted jet-black, with the monogram of the bank on the lid. In the privacy of the private room with its door closed, on the table provided there, he opened the container with his key and stared.

GOLD! It was packed with gold coins. American Eagles. 100% pure gold.

His mouth ajar, he fetched and opened the second container. GOLD INGOTS! Stamped, Suisse, 1 once. Fine gold. Or pur 999.9.

His hands shaking, he returned to fetch and open the third container. GOLD DUCATS! GOLD KRUGERRANDS! GOLD SOVEREIGNS! Minted in Austria, South Africa, Great Britain.

Sweat jumping off his brow, he went back for the fourth time, returned, glanced at the door of the private room to be sure it was closed, then opened the container. GOLD KRONER! In four, tightly-packed rows, 248 20-crown gold coins from Norway, weighing a total of four kilograms of pure gold.

Almost panicked, Jacob locked each container. He eyed them where they lay lined up. Who knew about this? They were too heavy to carry comfortably. Ergo, they must have been carried down to the vaults for Plane. What was he thinking? His mind jumped. Of course not. Plane must have bought the coins and ingots over the years as he acquired property and rented more deposit boxes as he needed them. Nothing unusual in that. Wealthy men regularly carried gold pieces. Had he himself not given each of his children at birth a commemorative 20-dollar gold Eagle? He knew of men who would give the carver at Locke-Ober in Boston a Mexican gold 5-pesos as a tip for slicing their beef exactly to their liking. Plane must also have signed the register each time he came down to the vaults. He would ask Harrison. Which is when it dawned on him that he had not opened the largest box.

Breathing deeply to slow his heart, he returned to the vault. In size, the box was like a small Frigidaire. There was no way he could carry it to the private room. A strange fear gripped him. What if he were seen? It took an effort on his part to remind himself that his mission was perfectly legitimate. He inserted his key. Opened the door. And nearly fainted.

From top to bottom, like a layered cake, perfectly wrapped packets of money. $100, $500, $1000. $5000. Respectively adorned with the features of Presidents Calvin Coolidge, William McKinley, Grover Cleveland and James Madison. Each denomination on a different shelf. Four crammed shelves. He slammed and locked the door. His heart thumping, he looked around. No one. He pressed his forehead against the cold steel. Steadied himself. Then walked backwards and forwards to fetch the four containers and deposit them back in their respective boxes. The effort calmed him. Then he pressed the bell to summon Harrison.

It wasn't until two weeks later, his tour of inspection complete, while saying goodbye to Mr. Harrison, who had come to Union Station to see him off to Chicago, that he casually said, "One last thing, apart from Sir Kobe, did anyone else have access to the safe deposit boxes?"

"No!" Harrison said, surprised. "No one. There are just the two keys. Yours and mine."

"Good." Jacob Baxter held out his hand to shake. "Thank you for your time, Mr. Harrison, and for your help. Please give my regards to Mr. Giannini. I will be coming out this way on a regular basis until probate is wound up, so I expect to see you again."

As the train pulled out of the station to start its long journey across the continent, Jacob Baxter, in the privacy of his first-class sleeping compartment, took out his wallet to look at the faces of four presidents fanned out in monetary rank. He knew he had crossed a line. But if no one else knew...? Statistics were his strong suit; it was why the bank employed him. He knew better than most what it cost to live in America, where the average weekly wage was $36, per year, $1872, before tax. He made ten times that. And the four bills spread in front of him were a third of his yearly salary. Printed paper. Three times what the average man earned working 8-hour days for 365 days every year. Dusk came on with the countryside wheeling past the window. The banker sat with his thoughts, the rhythm of the wheels making him drowsy. Before falling to sleep, as was his wont, he recited the Lord's Prayer to himself. Our Father...forgive us our trespasses...lead us not into temptation...for ever and ever...never once thinking that perhaps Sir Kobe had not been on his own in California.

+ + + +

201

IN WHICH KARLA BECOMES A BRIDE

(and learns what her husband wants)

High in the French Alps, the butler cut an unlikely figure trying to keep erect in the slippery snow. Clad in dark grey pepper-and-salt trousers, a high-buttoned black waistcoat and a black round-tailed coat, immaculate white linen with a black tie, a dark grey silk scarf wrapped several times around his neck, with a dark grey tweed deerstalker hat, its flaps tied over his ears to protect him from the chill of a cold wind blowing down from the Col de Montgenèvre, he entered the offices of the Mairie de Briançon with a briefcase bulging with the requisite documents for a foreigner to marry a French citizen.

He was received in the narrow confines of a badly lit *salle d'attente* by the secretary of the mayor, a sparrow-like creature of indeterminate age, her hair pulled back in a severe bun, suspicion written all over her face. What good could come from an antique American marrying a young French woman? The mayor had warned her, it was a union of the first importance; she was not to upset the applecart. What is afoot? She would get to the bottom of this affair, believe it. And for the principles not to come in person, but instead send their manservant? Quel scandale. She picked up her pen, stabbed it into the inkwell, ready to strike out every non-conforming entry in the proffered papers on her desk. If they thought getting a *Cértificat de Marriage* was easy, they could think again.

Jason smiled at her.

"You have the birth certificates?"

"Yes." Jason handed them over.

"They are less than three months old?"

"Yes. As you can see."

"And the apostille?"

"Yes." Jason handed over the certificate that authenticated the signatures of the public officials who certified the authenticity of the birth certificates.

"And the official translations?"

"Here."

"And the verification of the authenticity of the documents and the correctness of the translation?"

"Here."

"And the apostille of the Foreign Office?"

"Here."

"*Le Certificat de Célibat?*

"Here."

"*Le Certificat de Coutume?*"

"Here."

The secretary spied an opportunity.

"The man is a widow?" she said.

"Yes. His wife died ten years ago."

"You have the death certificate?"

"Yes." Jason handed it over.

"It has been officially translated?"

"Yes." Jason handed over the translation.

"And the verification of the authenticity of this document and the correctness of the translation?"

"Here."

"You understand, Monsieur, polygamy is strictly prohibited in France."

"Yes."

"A new marriage cannot take place until a prior marriage has been entirely dissolved."

"The former Mrs. Plane has been dead for ten years," Jason said, trying to keep a straight face, "I am sure she is entirely dissolved."

The secretary gave him a sharp look. "This is a serious matter, Monsieur. It is not for the making of jokes."

"Of course."

"Now, the *Contrat de Mariage*?"

"There is none."

"The parties understand the consequences?"

"Yes."

"If their primary residence is in France, she gets everything if he dies and there are no children."

"They will live in America."

The secretary sniffed. "I wish her good fortune with that. You have the *Déclaration*?"

"Here."

She read:

'We, the undersigned, declare out intention to marry
Name - PLANE,
First Name(s) - Kobe
Profession - Retired
Address - Planetree House, 6 Bellevue Court
Newport, Rhode Island,
U.S.A.
And
Name - Pinard
First Name(s) - Karla
Profession - Serveuse
Address - 18 Rue de Montpensier
Paris, 75001
FRANCE
As witnessed by
Name - Aubert
First Name(s) - Bertrand & Phuong (Mariée)

Profession - Restaurateurs
Address - No.I, Galerie Vero-Dodat,
Paris, 75001
FRANCE

Properly dated, with four signatures, duly witnessed. The secretary was perplexed. Everything seemed in order. Except? She pounced.

"*'Preuve de Résidence'?"* They have to prove they have resided in our commune for the past 30 days!"

"No problem," Jason said. "Here."

He gave her a copy of the purchase and sale agreement of a sumptuous Art Nouveau house on the Avenue du Lautaret.

"But that was the house of Docteur Fey!"

"And now it is the house of Karla Pinard."

"How is it possible if she is a waitress?"

"Everything is possible if you are as rich as Monsieur Plane."

+ + + +

Over tea, in the comfort of their new home looking out over the snow-covered Alps, the yet-to-be married couple were entertained by their butler's account of his meeting in the Mairie. After slicing and serving the baba-au-rhum and a second round of tea, the butler withdrew.

"Remarkable fellow, our Jason," Sir Kobe said, "I don't know how I'd manage without him. You've no idea what a chore it's been getting all those papers stamped and witnessed. If I'd known how complicated your French bureaucracy was -"

"You can still change your mind," Karla interrupted.

"And so can you?" he smiled. "Tempted?"

Karla tried to scowl. "You should really marry my mother," she said.

"It is not your mother hanging on the wall in my library back home." Sir Kobe chuckled at the idea. Karla's scowl deepened. "But what if we asked Belanopek to do a twin picture? You think she'd look good in your veil?"

Despite herself, Karla had to laugh. "Don't you dare suggest it! She already thinks you're a dirty old man."

"That I am for sure. I have also been called eccentric, irascible, odd, out of line, and bizarre. In a word, nuts. But it has served me well. That and a belief that lawyers are the devil incarnate. Beware of ever becoming embroiled with them. Now, about the future - our future. After posting the banns, in ten days we will be officially married by the mayor. Then a week later we have the church wedding. You will be, both in the eyes of the State and the Church, legally my spouse. As such, I want you to read this."

Sir Kobe gave Karla an envelope on the cover of which was written in black copperplate

'The Last Will and Testament of Sir Kobe Plane, Kt.'

She hesitated to open it.

"Go on," he said.

Inside she read:

'The Last Will and Testament of Kobe Plane.'

'I, Kobe Plane, a childless widower and resident of Newport, Rhode Island, being of sound mind and body, declare this to be my Last Will and Testament. I hereby revoke any and all other wills and codicils that I have made at any time in the past.'

Perplexed, Karla stopped reading. She had never read a will and she had never given any consideration to writing one herself. It was almost a superstition. The orderly disposal of your earthly goods when you were no longer here. Almost sacrilegious to read while the person who wrote it was sitting across the room in a comfortable leather armchair eating cake.

"Go on," Sir Kobe said.

'I appoint Jacob Baxter, of 502, Park Avenue, New York City, as my Executor. I direct that he should not have to post any bond or other security in connection with his acting as my Executor.'

Again, Karla stopped reading. "I do not understand some of the legal language," she said.

"Go on," Sir Kobe said. "I'll explain afterwards."

For some atavistic reason, Karla shivered.

'I direct that all of the assets of my estate, both real and personal, be given to my sole heir and future spouse, Karla Pinard, currently of 18, Rue du Montpensier, Paris 75001, France.

I further direct that if anyone other than Karla Pinard contests this Will and claims that he, she or anyone else is entitled to any part of my estate, then I give to that person the sum of $1.00 only, and direct that such person is otherwise to be completely and entirely disinherited.

I signed this Last Will and Testament on the 2nd day of January 1926, in Paris, France.

Kobe Plane

First Witness - Signature J. Fleet, 6, Bellevue Court, Newport, R.I.

Second Witness - Signature Aubert, Bertrand, No.1 Galerie Vero-Dodat, Paris 75001'

For the longest time after she had finished reading, Karla sat with her head bowed and her hands folded in her lap. When at last she looked up at Sir Kobe, she said, "Why are you doing this?"

"If you are to be my wife," Sir Kobe said, "it is only proper I safeguard your future; particularly living in a strange country to which you are not familiar. That document is a will, entirely legal both here and in America. I do not want any future claimant, if there is one, to challenge my authority. When we go home it is my intention for us to go on a tour of my properties across the country so that you have some appreciation of what you will inherit one day. I also want you to meet the various bankers with whom I do business, my trustees, and my personal accountant. There should be no secrets between us. I have sent you a registered letter to your address in Paris giving you details on how to contact Baxter in the event of my demise…you're not going to cry, are you?"

"No."

"You should see the look on your face."

"I have not bargained for this."

"What?"

"Losing you."

Sir Kobe laughed. "Not right away, God willing."

+ + + +

Eight months later he was dead.

Karla was stunned. The fairy-tale had come to an end. Molly told Jason this when she saw him come in the front door.

"I just heard. How is she?" Jason said.

"She won't come down. She's just sitting up there staring at nothing."

"I'll go talk to her."

As he walked up the stairs to the first floor, he had no idea what he was going to say and paused before knocking on Karla's door, reviewing all the usual platitudes people trotted out when sharing the unshareable grief of death. Then, through the door, he heard her say, "Is that you, Jason? Come in."

What then happened was unexpected. Karla, still in the dressing gown she was wearing when she got the call from New York, stood, and went to the butler as he came in. She hugged him.

"My poor Jason," she said. "It is so, so sad. You have lost your friend and I, my husband. C'est pas juste. It's not fair."

No tears. Clear eyed. She was consoling him!

"I am so sorry," he said. "I came as soon as I heard."

"The Beekman doorman?"

"Yes. He said he'd already called you. The housemaid –"

"I know. He told me she found Kobe dead in bed when she went in with his breakfast. At least he died in his sleep." Karla sat down on the bedroom bench at the foot of her bed.

"I feel so useless. I don't know what to do, Jason."

And just like that, the butler took charge.

"First things first. Get dressed. You'll have to go to New York. I'll arrange that with Mrs. Lister. Have you eaten?"

"I'm not hungry."

"You will be, so you better eat something."

"Shouldn't I call a doctor?"

"Already done. The people at Beekman are very efficient. There'll be an autopsy. You may be asked to identify Sir Kobe. It will not be easy. Perhaps I should go with you?"

"Thank you, Jason. I'll be fine. There's one thing though. Do you know a man called Baxter?"

"Yes. His executor. Why?"

"Kobe told me to get in touch with him in the event of his, his…" she couldn't say the word, and now it was the butler's turn to console the widow as her eyes filled with tears.

+ + + +

THE SECOND MEETING

On the first anniversary of the death of her husband, Karla was in Manhattan to meet, at his request, Jacob Baxter, at the Bank's headquarters on Wall Street. The meeting was scheduled for 10 o'clock in the morning, which meant she had to come to New York by train the previous day. Despite it being closed for a year, she had decided to spend the night in her late husband's 4-bedroom apartment on Beekman Place overlooking the East River and she brought Molly with her to help put things in order. This meant drawing open the curtains, washing the filthy windows, removing the dust sheets covering the furniture, making the beds with fresh linen, vacuuming the rugs, getting ice for the ice box, cleaning the bathrooms, and polishing the floors. She insisted on helping and the two women did the work in less than four hours.

Finished, with her hands on her hips, Karla surveyed her domain. "The only thing missing are some flowers. We can pick some up when we go to dinner. Where shall we go, Molly?" she said.

Molly giggled. She was a maid. She had only been in the city once before as a small child with her parents one New Year's Eve, a treat she could hardly remember. The very idea of eating out in a restaurant with her mistress never occurred to her. "I don't know," she said. "You go. I have nothing to wear that would suit."

"Nonsense. We'll ask the doorman the best place that's nearby," Karla said, taking off her apron. "Better have a bath first. Off you go."

In her room in the Carriage House in Newport, Molly's notion of a bath was a basin of cold water and a flannel cloth to swipe across her face, under her arms and between her legs. Here, filling a tub with hot water just for herself, felt sinful. Washing her hair with shampoo and rinsing it under a cascade of water from a showerhead as big as a colander was almost orgasmic. Drying herself in front of a steamed-up floor-to-ceiling mirror, she saw a clean, pink, red-haired woman smelling of lavender soap and for a fraction wondered who it could be? If a man could see me now, she thought. And blushed. She was drying her hair when Karla came in after a rap on the bathroom door.

"Here are a couple of skirts and blouses for you to try on...Mon Dieu, si un homme te voyait comme ça..."she said, and immediately translated, "if a man saw you like that - you would be ravaged on the spot."

They dined at L'Aiglon on East 55th Street like two friends out for a quiet evening together. The menu was in French and so was the food and wine. Tiny tarte à l'oignon with a delicate salad to begin, followed by Cuisses de Grenouille Sauté Grenobloise, Brochet Sauté Belle Meunière accompanied with Pointe d'Asperge Hollandaise, Poire Belle Hélène for dessert, and a selection of cheeses for a savoury finish. They had a Coupe de Champagne to start, a Pouilly Fuissé with the fish, and a half-bottle of Margaux with the cheese.

"I'm going to burst," Molly said.

"As good as Paris," Karla said. "Remind me to tip the doorman for his recommendation."

Since the weather was fine, they walked home. On the way Karla said, "I would like to ask a favour. I have a meeting tomorrow and I would like you to come with me. The meeting is with the executor of my husband's estate. I don't know why he wants to meet me, but I don't want to meet him alone. You're a level-headed woman. I'll tell him you're my *conseillère*, that's what we say in French, my counsellor. Do you mind?"

Falling asleep that night in a bigger bed and a bigger bedroom than she had ever slept in before, Molly smiled. What a day! From maid to counsellor.

They were dressed to kill when they walked into the bank. Karla in a pale grey strictly tailored pants suit, her long black hair framing not just her face but the perfection of a man's Chauvet shirt in grey silk with black pearl studs in the shirt front and securing the standing collar and cuffs. By way of contrast, to set off her red hair, Molly was in fuchsia pink, from pleated skirt to ruched-sleeved blouse, with a slim silk black ribbon tied in a bow at her throat. Thus accosted, and for all his training, Jacob Baxter was discombobulated, his plans out the window.

His office, on the eighth floor, with its oak panelled walls, outsized desk, Persian carpet, adjacent conference room and reception area, had been professionally designed to impress his importance and that of the Bank on all who came in. It was a requisite of the management of wealth. That and the view down Wall Street.

While his secretary saw his visitors to their seats at the conference table, Molly caught a flash of recognition in Baxter's glance before introductions had been made.

"Thank you for coming," the banker said to Karla. "I apologise for the inconvenience."

"Pas de problèmes," Karla said. "My counsellor, Miss Malone, and I have business in the city. You are well?'

"I am, thank you," Baxter said. Counsellor, my eye, he thought, she looks like the Madame in charge of a bordello. I know I've seen her before. Why was she here? The whole reason for the meeting was to get Karla to himself, to show her just who he was in his princely realm. He was angry, but hid it well

"You look more prosperous since I saw you last year," Karla said. "Fleecing the rich or lending to the poor?"

Baxter laughed. "Some of us have been lucky, or perhaps I should say prudent," he said with false modesty.

"So? We are here. Why has it taken you so long to resolve this probate? I do not appreciate having to wait for you to pay the bills on my house and give me my allowance."

"I am only following instructions. Your late husband left a very large estate, as you know. Complicated by the matter of the will. Have you found it?"

"No. I thought you said the Probate Judge would adjudicate after he saw the letters we submitted?"

"He has generously given us more time to find the will." Baxter paused. "If it exists."

As soon as he said the last three words, he regretted it. Too late.

"Did I hear you correctly?" Karla said. "You doubt my word? Are you suggesting my husband did not write a will? Even if he said he did in his letter to you?" The ice in Karla's voice would have frozen the Northwest Passage. "Are you not his executor? There to see that what he has willed is done?"

"I have an obligation under the old will…"

"I will speak to the Judge myself."

"As I've told you, for that you will need a lawyer to petition the court."

"It is why we are in the city." Karla stood up.

"And if you challenge the will, you may well find yourself disinherited."

"Challenge? Who said anything about challenging. Remember what I said? Tooth and nail. Come, Molly, we have finished here."

It was only after they had swept out that a synapse closed in Jacob Baxter's brain.

The maid! Of course. She had come with her maid. What an insult! Damn the woman! But in his heart, he could not help but admire the sheer brazenness of someone who could do that.

+ + + +

Out in the street, Karla said, "Well, what do you make of him?"

Molly said, "It's obvious. He's trying to seduce you."

"He's married, with four kids."

"When did that ever stop a man's prick?"

"Molly!"

"I am your counsellor. I am from Providence, home of the mob. In the mafia a consigliere always warns his capo of danger. There's something not right with this guy. Be careful."

+ + + +

213

IN WHICH KARLA APPOINTS A LAWYER

Karla found a lawyer the way she found the restaurant. She asked the doorman.

"I need a lawyer," she said. "Do you know a good lawyer?"

"Good?" the doorman said. "I don't think they come 'good'. I know some with smarts; guys who're cunning, tricky, sly, sharp, calculating. But good? No, I don't know any like that."

"My husband said they are all crooks."

"He's right. We have one of those," the doorman grinned. "In our family we have one of everything, a dentist, a musician, a doctor, a grocer, even a crooked lawyer who is honest. We come from the Bronx. You know the Bronx?"

"No. Where is this place?"

"Well, it ain't the upper Eastside. We're the poorest borough in the city, but we've got Yankee Stadium. You fancy a lawyer from there? He's my cousin. The guy'll work for peanuts."

Which is how Karla and Molly found themselves a long way from Wall Street, down in the Hub, the retail heart of the South Bronx. They got off the subway looking for an address on Simpson Street where they had an appointment with the cousin, Steven Masry, a one-man law firm, located in a dingy room on the third floor of a soot-covered redbrick office building. On the frosted glass of the door to his office, below his name, was a notice: **'Bell out of order. Knock loudly.'**

They knocked. Loudly. No answer.

215

Molly tried the doorknob. The door opened into a chaos of dusty old files piled on the floor, on the only chair they could see and all over a worn-out desk eaten by termites. Through the pale light of the one window in the room it was obvious Mr. Masry was not there. Which is when the door to the office next door opened, a bald head popped out, and said, "You lookin' for Stevie? He's drinkin' bullshots in the bar across the street. That's where he does his business."

Mid-afternoon, that's where he was, in the semi-darkness of the bar across the street. "I drink this," he said by way of introduction, pouring more vodka into a tankard of warm beef broth, "to keep the bugs out and my dreams in."

He raised the tankard in salute. "Here's to you pretty ladies." Drank. Burped. Smiled.

"How can I help?"

Karla explained.

"Just to be clear," the lawyer said when she had finished, "on the recommendation of my dumb cousin, your doorman, you want me to represent you before the Probate Judge in Newport to petition a hearing for your rights to the multi-million-dollar estate of your late husband whose will bequeathing this fortune to you cannot be found?"

"Yes," Karla said.

"Who are you kidding? Look around you, lady. We're in the Bronx. I've done a little of this and a little of that in terms of legal work, even some probate litigation in the past, but it's not really in my wheelhouse. I look like a lawyer that handles that sort of business? Get a life."

"Get a brain, dickhead," Molly cut in. "We've come to this slum because your cousin said you're honest."

"He said that?"

"Well, he said 'crooked' but honest."

"Okay. That sounds like Louis. He tell you I'm not cheap?"

"No. He said you work for peanuts."

"Looks like you know all my secrets," Steven Masry said. "You guys want a drink?"

+   +   +   +

216

THE PETITION

The first time Masry came to Newport he immediately knew he had been right. He was out of his depth. If Planetree House was an eyeopener, the size of the deceased's estate, with assets all over the country, was mind-boggling. You'd need an army of accountants to properly value everything and battalions of lawyers to verify the facts. Honesty being his calling card, he said to Karla, "You better find somebody else. It's way over my head. You need a lawyer who specialises in probates."

"That's why we chose you, Shylock," Molly said, still in her role as consigliere. "We don't want some guy who plays the game, compromising, stalling, racking up billing time."

They were in the library, the magnificence of which Masry never imagined belonging to a private individual, leave alone one whose nude portrait hung on the wall behind where she sat fully clothed in front of him.

"You any idea how long this could take?" he said. "The Probate Court meets just two times a month up here. They've got a pretty full calendar and we would be way down the pecking order. I'm a guy from the Bronx; I don't fit in. I don't even dress right. You need an attorney with some regional clout - get the Judge's ear."

"Ça va," Karla said. "Enough complaining. We will go shopping to buy what you need. You can stay here when the Court's in session. We will cover your travel expenses. How do you say it in English, the longest journey begins with one step? Eh bien, step by step. Begin, Monsieur Masry."

"Right. Just so you have an idea of what's involved, probate petitions need to be fully documented and filed with the clerk of the Probate Court to be heard by the court on a motion brought by the party seeking the relief asked for in the petition. There are countless different probate statutes. All are not applicable to your situation…"

"Step by step," Karla interrupted. "Molly will show you to your room. Make yourself comfortable. It is a year since my husband died and I have seen no progress from the executor -"

"What do you mean? No accounts? Nothing?"

"Nothing."

"That's not right. He has an obligation to report to the Court. The probate code provides for annual accounts and for you as beneficiary to petition the court to compel an annual account. Once a year, at the very least. Is this guy honest?"

"Honest?" Karla almost spat the word. "He said if I challenge the will I may well find myself disinherited."

"Rubbish. Just because he's in charge doesn't mean he gets to decide whether your conduct constitutes a challenge or not; that's simply not true. The Judge will rule. The only time you can possibly be disinherited from a will is if the will expressly states that a contest will result in disinheritance and if you actually file a will contest. That means that you must file a petition that challenges the terms of the will.

"Well, I am, aren't I?"

"No. Our contention is that under the terms of the will your husband made just before he married you, he revoked any and all prior wills, and made you his sole heir. The will hasn't been found, but that is what your letter says, and the Court has that letter. Keeping the executor honest by making sure he is complying with the terms of the will for you to receive the inheritance you're supposed to is a legitimate reason to petition the Court. Before doing that I have to write to him. You, the widow, have an absolute right to know, financially speaking, what's going on inside the probate estate. This guy, Baxter, must know that. Why's he threatening you?"

"I've no idea." Karla said. Then she added, "For somebody over his head you seem remarkably well informed."

"I've been doing my homework. We'll have to petition Baxter to produce the documents we need. Properly stated, a petition such as this would consume 10 pages or more. It would go into detail to recite what the executor did and did not do. It would state that the petitioner has first-hand knowledge of the existence of all the properties and of the safe deposit boxes and recite every bank in every state where they existed and the circumstances of how she has such first-hand knowledge." Masry raised his eyebrows. "Yes?"

"Yes? Of course, yes!" Karla said.

"It would state why the proposed accounting was inadequate and it would ask the court to remove Baxter because he has either negligently or wilfully omitted material assets of the estate." Masry paused. "Shall I go on?"

"No. Do it."

+   +   +   +

A WALK

Towards way off
_____
Ego, borrowed and in patches
A Freudian assimilation
Shredded bits of others
Joined, pre-programmed, in
The womb.
Ex nihilo, out of nothing
I am
Me

The Sheriff headed north, to walk his thoughts home to the cottage he owned on the waterfront in Portsmouth, on the eastern shore of Narragansett Bay, 10 miles from Newport. Whenever he had the time, he walked. He crossed a marsh and a forest, with dramatic views of the Atlantic Ocean and the Sakonnet Passage on his right and the Bay on his left. He carried his notebook and pen and would stop on impulse to make notes. He had always shown his wife what he had written and valued her judgement, given with a wry humour, both critical and encouraging.

'Keep it up, Homer,' she would say. Or 'You and your poems, the Trojan Horse in the jailhouse.' She cooked for him, did the shopping, cleaned the cottage, never complained about the weird hours his job imposed, and always - always - said he was the most handsome man she had ever met. She had been a schoolteacher until cancer carried her off. What had been a welcome homecoming while she was alive was now a hollow emptiness when he pushed the front door open. The cottage even smelled disused. Three vacant bedrooms destined for the children they never had. He knew he should sell it and find something smaller and more convenient. But knowing it and doing it were two different things.

Taking off his boots and socks, barefooted he walked into the kitchen to put the kettle on. He was partial to tea which he took black, with three teaspoons of sugar.

With a mug in his hand, he went out the back door for the simple pleasure of grass in his toes as he followed the lawn down to the strand to watch the setting sun reflect rays off the water into his eyes.

There was a bench there on which he sat. He closed his eyes.

Peace. Twilight set in.

Life should be this simple, he thought. He was sixty years old, born in Boston, where his father had been a dentist. His mother had taught him to read, and he still had the book she gave him on his sixth birthday, *The Adventures of Tom Sawyer*, by Mark Twain, published that very year, 1876, the same year Lt. Colonel George Custer lost his life battling the Sioux and Cheyenne Indians on the bluffs above the Little Big Horn River, and Colorado became the 38th state. The book, dogeared now, has been on his bedside table for fifty-four years, the pages so familiar they put him to sleep every night, Tom's voice in his head:

'Right is right, and wrong is wrong, and a body ain't got no business doing wrong when he ain't ignorant and knows better.'

Who knows the imprint words make on a young mind? Who knows?

You walk, you write, make tea, watch the sun go down. And remember. Aged eleven, an erstwhile cowboy in the backyard up against cousin Marty, with a cap pistol replaying Wyatt Earp and Doc Holliday, October 26, 1881, shooting down the Clanton gang in the O.K. Corral in Tombstone, Arizona, and aged fifteen, going with your parents as a treat to see the newly arrived Statue of Liberty in New York Harbour, a gift from France in 1885, and enrolling at the Police Station on Boylston Street to start his apprenticeship as a cop when he was nineteen, the same year, 1889, that 50,000 settlers charged across the country to claim what they could stake in the Oklahoma Land Rush that robbed 1.92 million acres of land previously given to the American Indian tribes. Two years later, September 6, 1901, President McKinley, shot dead, the same year his father died, and he and his mother moved to Newport, and he had to begin again as a rookie on the force. Two more years later, Orville and Wilbur Wright, for the first time in human history, flew their aeroplane a distance of just 120 feet, December 17, 1903. And only twenty-five years after that, May 21, 1927, Lindbergh flew the Atlantic. He wonders whether he chose the wrong profession. Had to be dumb to be a lawman. He knew the statistics. Across the nation, fifty-four homicides per day. Every day. 365 days in the year. 20,000 people gunned down per annum. Unsolved crimes? 90%! 1300 gangs in Chicago alone. 900 in Boston. Providence, a Mafia town. What was one murder? Why bother?

One word. Duty.

That's why.

Like a pit bull with its jaws locked on a bone, a murder committed on his watch, in his town, would be prosecuted through hell and high water. And in his mind's eye he sees again the woman's bloodied body, the battered face. What demons possess a man to use an ice-pick and crowbar to bludgeon another human being to death?

He only opened his eyes when he felt the neighbour's dog sniffing his bare feet. Mr. and Mrs. Smyth, an Irish couple, immigrants, who moved to New England at the turn of the century, and bred pedigree terriers, taking one of their dogs for a stroll.

"Lulu," Mrs. Smyth said. "Stop that! Leave the Sheriff's feet alone."

Lulu ignored her mistress and licked the Sheriff's toes.

"Sorry," Mr. Smyth said, yanking Lulu away on her leash.

"No worries." The Sheriff smiled.

When the Irish couple and their dog were dots in the distance he stood up to go back into his cottage. Maybe I should get a dog, he thought. And remembered the gunshot.

+   +   +   +

IN WHICH KARLA RETURNS HOME

"Your lawyer guy said it was important you call him as soon as you got back." Molly said, the day Karla came home from the Olympics.

"I don't want to talk to him on the telephone," Karla said. "You call him, please. Ask him to come up here as soon as it is convenient."

Two days later Stephen Masry was shown into the library, where he was offered coffee and the morning newspaper while waiting for his appointment with Karla. It was springtime in America with the country preoccupied with the upcoming presidential election between the Republican, Herbert Hoover, and Alfred Smith, a Democrat. Ten years on from the end of the bloodbath that was the Great War, both parties laid claim to the prevailing climate of peace and prosperity. Both made promises to improve the lot of the working man, with Hoover extolling the 'American system of rugged individualism'. Ironically, between Hoover's boosterism and a piece on the invention of a new machine to slice bread, was an article about a serial killer who confessed to having murdered twenty-one people, committed thousands of burglaries, robberies, larcenies, arsons and, finally, "I have committed sodomy on more than 1000 male human beings." Adding, "For all these things I am not in the least bit sorry."

Masry was so engrossed in the story he did not realise Karla had come into the room and was now standing behind him. "Talk about rugged individualism," she said.

Masry jumped. "Only in America," he said. "Welcome home."

"Thank you."

"How were the Olympics?"

"Freezing cold. I'm glad to be back."

Standard pleasantries, until Karla took her seat, gestured at the lawyer's bulging briefcase, and said, "Any surprises?"

"Oddly, no. Baxter has been very forthcoming. He has produced the documents I requested on your behalf; all the business records, bank statements, cancelled cheques, deposit slips and other transactions for all the properties going back five years before your husband passed. As you can see, there is a lot of stuff, worth a fortune. I hired a couple of accountants to reconcile the accounts and I have here -" Masry fished in a folder, "their certificate that they, I quote, 'have mailed this day by U.S.Mail, postage prepaid, a true and correct copy of the above reconciliation.' It all adds up. Look."

Page after page of accounts. It took Karla two hours to read to the end and when she finished, she had one question.

"I see no mention of the contents of the safety deposit boxes."

"Exactly."

"You asked me if I would testify that in every bank, in every city where he did business, Kobe had deposit boxes in the vaults where he kept his cash and gold. I told you yes. He showed them to me. One day on our tour he said this will all be yours. Some of the gold coins were quite rare and worth more than their gold content. He was proud of his collection. I told you, get on with it."

"Are you sure of this?"

"What an extraordinary question. I just told you I saw them with my own eyes."

Masry sat back. "You do realise what this means?"

"He's been stealing from me."

"Easy to say; hard to prove."

"What do you mean?"

"In the eyes of the Judge, if Baxter contests what you say, without any proof, it will boil down to 'she said, he said'.

"Oh, but I have the proof. An eyewitness."

"In that case, sign this."

+ + + +

PETITION TO THE PROBATE COURT OF NEWPORT COUNTY, RHODE ISLAND

IN THE MATTER OF THE ESTATE OF KOBE PLANE, DECEASED

Comes now **KARLA PLANE**, herein called **Contestant,** and files this contest to the Petition for Approval of First and Final Accounting and for Authority to Distribute the Remaining Assets of the Estate and Discharge Executor, filed by **Jacob Baxter**, as Executor of the Estate of **KOBE PLANE,** on October,1926, covering the period to June 1928.

1. KARLA PLANE, is the sole beneficiary named in the last Will of Decedent, **KOBE PLANE,** in the above-entitled proceeding.

2. It is not clear from the said Petition and Final Accounting filed by **Jacob Baxter** that the contents of those certain safety deposit boxes in the listed banks (see attached) where the deceased had accounts, have been received and when the same occurred. The Account appears to be confused and incomplete on its face.

Wherefore, Contestant requests an Order that:

1. The Account of **Jacob Baxter** regarding the **Estate of Kobe Plane**, not be settled and allowed as filed.

2. That **Jacob Baxter**, as Executor of the Estate of Decedent be ordered immediately to render a true, correct and legally sufficient and verified account of the contents of the said safety deposit boxes.

3. A referee be appointed to examine the account and to report on the account, subject to confirmation by the Court.

Respectfully submitted,

Karla Plane, Contestant

By:

Steven Masry, Attorney

N.Y.State Bar No. 328/2028

+

OF COUNSEL

Steven Masry, Attorney,

10,Simpson Street,

South Bronx,

New York, N.Y. June 6, 1928

Certificate of Service

This is to certify that, I, STEVEN MASRY, attorney for KARLA PLANE, have this day served a true and correct copy of the above and foregoing Contest of Final Account by U.S.Mail, postage fully prepaid, to the following counsel of record for the Executor:

JACOB BAXTER,

Brown Brothers & Company

63 Wall Street

New York, N.Y.

+ + + +

TWO DAYS TO CHRISTMAS

1929

In the Reading Room the Sheriff looked over the list he was making. Two months after the fact. All the unknowns:

- Blood? Impossible to kill her like that and not get splashed?
- A gunshot. That nobody hears?
  - Weapons that have not been found?
  - Bearer shares stolen? Recovered? By whom?
  - What was hidden in the slashed painting?
  - The missing will? Motivation?
  - The message. Who wrote it? Why?
  - Every known male suspect - the gardener, Buck; the butler, Fleet?
  - Every unknown suspect - the thief; the man with the key; the man in the woods with claw marks on his face; the person who used the toilet…?
  - Timeline???
  - Maybe he should get a dog?

With the back of his pen the Sheriff scratched his scalp pondering a trail gone cold when Brady came in.

"What if it was consensual?" he said.

"What?" the Sheriff said.

"What if it was not rape, but consensual?"

"You've lost me?"

"The man who visits Mrs. Plane, the guy who leaves the shares? He knows her. They get it on. Chronologically it makes more sense. She's killed afterwards."

"By him?"

"No. By the guy who used the toilet. He's in the house. He hears them."

"Go on."

"The way I see it, after they've finished…" Brady searched for an appropriate word.

"Fucking," the Sheriff supplied.

"Yes. This guy leaves and she is confronted by the murderer who assaults her. She puts up a terrific fight and is finally killed in the dining room. All the blood we find is in the rooms downstairs. There's none in her bedroom. My guess is she had it off in her bedroom. Maybe we should ask those two pathologists, if…"

"Naked," the Sheriff said.

"What?"

"I knew we were missing something simple. She was found naked in the dining room! Under the rug. Naked! No clothes anywhere. We never thought to ask ourselves why she was naked. All we could see was the dead body. But I think you're right. For some reason she comes downstairs naked. In that house? Why?"

"She's trying to escape!"

"To get to the gun?"

The two men stare at each other.

"By Christ," the Sheriff finally said. "That's it! The killer beats her to it. She's shot but is not dead. Then he stabs and smashes her head in to make sure…"

Which is when the Secretary chose to knock on the door.

"Not disturbing anything, I hope," he said. "Package came for you over the weekend. Hand delivered. Skinny fella. Didn't want a receipt."

"How did he know I was here?" the Sheriff said.

"Didn't say."

It was a slim folder. Sealed with wax. Inside, an unsigned, typewritten note.

'ENCLOSED DOCUMENTS FOUND WITH THE BEARER SHARES. IF YOU CAN'T CATCH HIM, I WILL. AND WHEN I DO, I WILL KILL HIM FOR KARLA.'

"Jesus Christ!" the Sheriff said.

Attached to the note was the sender's copy of a Western Union Telegram addressed to Mr. Jacob Baxter, of Brown Brothers, Bankers, 63 Wall Street, New York City, New York dated October 24, 1929.

Three words and a signature:

'I'VE FOUND IT!' STOP. KARLA PLANE. STOP.

And an envelope, across which was written in black copperplate, *The Last Will and Testament of Sir Kobe Plane, Kt.'*

Total silence as the implications resonated like a door slammed in an empty room.

"Jesus Christ!" the Sheriff said again. "Baxter?"

+   +   +   +

"Baxter?" the DA said.

Two days to Christmas, he had been on the point of leaving for a planned vacation in sunny Miami, when the Sheriff called.

"You can't be serious?"

"I am," the Sheriff said. "We've checked the writing and the signature. The will's authentic."

"You know what this means? Have you informed the City Attorney?"

"Not yet. I wanted you to know first."

"Get him. And the Chief. My office, in 30 minutes."

They convened around the DA's desk. The City Attorney, Charles H. Moore, an austere man in his 60s, with a reputation for sticking strictly to the book, did not appreciate being ordered to attend a meeting about a criminal case. He handled civil cases, advising the city on legal matters and representing it in court.

"Why am I here?" he said.

Ever the diplomat, the DA said, "We need your advice, Charles."

"What's so urgent that it can't wait until the new year?"

"What you are about to hear is strictly confidential. In the context of a murder case currently under investigation, we have received, anonymously, a document, the original of a will. It could affect a probate before the Court here in Newport. Sheriff?"

The Sheriff said, "Just before noon today, the Secretary of the Reading Room brought me a package delivered to him by hand by an unknown person over the weekend. It contained this." On the desk he laid out the note, the copy of the telegram and the envelope with the will.

The City Attorney took spectacles from the breast pocket of his jacket to read what was in front of him. Finished, he nodded. "Explain," he said.

"Baxter is the executor of an estate before the Court.," the Sheriff said. "The telegram he received is dated October 24; two months ago. This is a copy of that telegram." With a forefinger, the Sheriff tapped the Western Union copy. "The person who sent the telegram was murdered on October 26. She was the sole beneficiary under the terms of the will her deceased husband wrote at the time of their marriage three years ago. This is the will."

Tap.

It took a moment for the City Attorney to digest the implications of this statement.

Tap. Tap. Tap.

"Please stop doing that," he said. "Let me understand… there was a previous will of which Baxter was the executor?"

"Yes."

"She was not a beneficiary of that will?"

"No."

"Her will, the one she finds, it had been lost?"

"For three years. Yes."

"She finds it, sends the telegram, and 2 days later is murdered?"

"Yes."

"And this note?"

"It's a long story," the District Attorney said. "Suffice it to say we are investigating. Our problem is Baxter being in New York."

The City Attorney surveyed his colleague. Nodded again. "You suspect Baxter? If I am to take up the matter with the Probate Court, I will need a statement from you, Sheriff Brenton, concerning the will. Provenance is everything. In effect Baxter has already submitted to the jurisdiction of the Rhode Island court by agreeing to be appointed as the executor of the first will. If the Newport probate judge wanted to question Baxter, he would notice a hearing that required Baxter's presence. The notice would simply state that the judge would like to share with the parties some new information that is relevant to the probate proceeding. Hearings are normally noticed by the parties and not by a judge, but a judge certainly has the authority to notice a hearing *sua sponte -*"

"Sua sponte?" Brady said, blushing. He couldn't help but show his ignorance.

"It's alright, Brady," the Sheriff said. "It's Latin, for the legal term when a judge does something on his own that is normally done by one of the parties."

"Thank you, Sheriff," Mr. Moore said. "Notice of such a hearing would be given to all parties in the case and everyone would be expected to convene for that hearing. If Baxter refused to attend, then the judge would not try to compel him to do so, but rather would probably issue an OSC"

"Order to show cause," the Sheriff translated before Brady made matters worse.

"Thank you, Sheriff," Moore said again. "The order to show cause would ask why Baxter should not be removed as executor of the first will. That order would be sent to Baxter and a subsequent hearing would be noticed on that OSC. If he then failed to appear at that hearing the judge could remove Baxter as the executor. That's probably as far as the probate judge would go. Any more efforts to get him to come to Rhode Island, by a grand jury subpoena, etc., would be up to you as the DA and not to the probate judge. Short of filing a criminal case against Baxter and having the NY marshal arrest him and transport him to Rhode Island, there is nothing anyone can do to force him to come to Rhode Island."

"Any attempt to force Baxter to come to Newport would probably be futile," the DA said." I don't think there is sufficient evidence now to file a murder case against him and issue an arrest warrant."

"Yes. But is there a real reason why Baxter would not attend the hearing issued by the judge *sua sponte*?" Chief Hazard said. "He does not know that we have the second will, the note, or the telegram. Let him find out at the hearing."

"Excellent," the City Attorney said. "Can I go home now?"

+ + + +

It was only after he had left that the DA said, "Okay. He's on board. Now, it's taken two months for this guy, the thief, to find the will and the telegram -"

"Not necessarily," the Sheriff said. "He could have found them earlier but only sent them back now. Let's say that sometime in the past two months he finds them amongst the bearer shares he took from the police station."

"Whatever," the DA said. "His note is a threat. We can't have some guy running around threatening to kill somebody. What are we going to do?"

Brady, the fly on the wall, spoke up.

"With respect, he's not 'some guy'. He's her lover. He was in the house at the same time as the murderer. He's not a thief if he has reclaimed what was his. Because of the telegram he knows that two months ago Baxter knew she had found the will. Why does he not inform the probate court? What can he hope to gain by not doing so? But Baxter does not know our guy has found the will and the telegram. Our guy not only knows, but he also knows where to find Baxter. At the bank in New York. Does he go after him? No. He informs us he will only if we don't. If you think about it, this 'guy' is quite brave."

Silence.

"Thank you, Mr. Brady," the Sheriff said. "Why are we all tiptoeing around? Avoiding saying the obvious? Mr. Jacob Baxter is now the prime suspect for the murder of Karla Plane."

"Right," the DA said. "String him up. Come on, Sheriff. This man is a director of Brown Brothers. He's also executor of Plane's estate. For all we know he might have a perfectly legitimate reason for his conduct. We haven't got a shred of evidence he was even in Newport the day she was murdered."

For a moment the Sheriff was taken aback. "You're not suggesting...?"

"Anything," the DA said. 'What I am saying is tread lightly, Sheriff. Think it through. I would have to convene a grand jury and have the grand jury issue a subpoena to Baxter to testify in Newport on a given time and day. The subpoena would then get sent to the Sheriff of New York City for service. If Baxter refuses to appear, a proceeding could then be brought in Newport for contempt, notice of which is again served by the Sheriff of NYC. Once held in contempt, a warrant could be issued by our court for Baxter's arrest and the Marshall of NYC would be dispatched to take him into custody and transport him to Newport. Of course, once he is dragged into the grand jury room here for questioning, he could always take the 5th and refuse to answer any questions. Most likely, if I did serve a grand jury subpoena on Baxter, he will have his attorney contact me and ask if he is a suspect. I will be obliged to say yes. The attorney will then tell me that the entire process will be futile because Baxter will just plead the 5th and not answer any questions. At which point the investigation would have to proceed without any cooperation from Baxter. Clear?"

"But -" the Chief of Police started to say.

"There are no buts," the DA said. "Without a smoking gun we have nothing."

+   +   +   +

Two days to Christmas, the tree up, decorated, colourful, bow-tied presents on the floor peeking out below the lowest branches, a constant temptation to the sniffing Dalmatian, ever looking out for something to eat or something to pee on.

Jacob watched the dog from where he was sitting in his armchair by the fireside, a brandy on the side table at his elbow. Helen was out doing last minute shopping; Jason was at the station in Providence to pick up the McCarthys. He was at peace, with the house to himself. And his thoughts.

Damn strange to have Christmas midweek. Freezing outside. Monday, two feet of snow dumped on Texas in 24-hours. 650 bank failures so far and more on the way. For all his millions, Hoover was useless, always too little, too late. American individualism, my ass. What did he say? 'We shall soon with the help of God be in sight of the day when poverty will be banished from this nation forever." Asinine, with the Dow down 50% and still sliding. Talk about bailing Niagara Falls with a bucket. If he couldn't inspire confidence in financial institutions, it was not surprising people were clamouring for their money - if they still had any left. Even the Fed can't stop the rot. Thank God we're out. Must remember to talk to Jason about Baxter's remark.

+ + + +

Two days to Christmas. The man, Herbert Clark Hoover, born on August 10, 1874, in a tiny town of just 265 people called West Branch, Iowa, in a two-room, whitewashed cottage built by his father, glanced up from his desk to look out over the East Lawn of the White House and remembered he did not cross east of the Mississippi until he was 22 years old, never dreaming he would one day be the 31st President of the United States. And yet here he was, 55 years old, in the middle of an economic crisis he inherited the day he won the election. He was working on a speech he had to give in the New Year to the press corps, a body not given to cooperation with the White House, whoever the incumbent.

He wrote 'The Nation has passed through a trying period this past month' - (months would be more accurate, he thought) - 'with fear, alarm, pessimism and hesitation sweeping the country' - (too strong? Strike hesitation, they might blame him) - 'which, unchecked, might well have precipitated a panic throughout the business world with untold misery in its wake. These acute dangers, now happily passed, were far greater than we can disclose at the present time. But you, the Washington correspondents and the press as a whole, not only sensed that danger, but gave us your whole-hearted cooperation which contributed in large degree to smothering the conflagration' - (bit of flattery never hurt) - It pleases me to say that when the national interest requires it, the press does not fail to shift from combat to cooperation' - (say it with a wry grin) - 'We shall undoubtedly feel some aftereffects' - (strike undoubtedly) - 'but with definite signs that business and industry have turned the corner, any lack of confidence in the economic future and basic strength of business in the United States is foolish.'

Tell a lie boldly enough and it becomes the truth, he thought.

+ + + +

Two days to Christmas. As senior director, Jacob Baxter found himself in charge of the bank, the partners having left the previous Friday as the bell struck 4 o'clock in the Exchange. It was a traditional perk. Come what may - war, pestilence, the economy down the toilet - in a stressful profession, the partners bearing the responsibility of endless make-or-break decisions that governed their world, packed up and left on vacation. A small bonus for being boss.

One day the bonus will be mine, Baxter thought - if…if, like an anchor grabbing at the muddy bottom of a stream, his thoughts snagged on the fateful day two months previously when his secretary came into his office saying, "Telegram for you, Mr. Baxter!"

Which is when his secretary came into the office saying, "You have a visitor."

+ + + +

"My name is Blake," the visitor said, handing the banker his engraved business card. "Thank you for finding the time to see me this close to the holidays."

"Baxter," the banker said, shaking hands, glancing at the card. Peon Blake. Strange first name. He had no idea who his visitor was or how he had made an appointment. "Please be seated. How may I assist you?"

Almost as if he could read his mind, Mr. Blake said, "I bribed your girl." And smiled, a twinkle in his eye. "Wonderful what a Franklin can do in these hard times." He sat where he was invited to sit, in a black leather buttoned armchair facing its twin across the broad expanse of Baxter's desk. The chair swivelled. Turning from side to side afforded a view of the Street eight floors down.

"Upon my word, you have a splendid view!" Mr. Blake said.

"Thank you." Baxter took his time to study his guest. Small. Trim. Well-dressed. Despite his perfect English, a foreigner. Self-confident, to the point of being…impertinent. "But I am sure it is not for the view that you came to see me?"

"You are correct. I am in the property business. I am particularly attracted to New England. The Boston area and Newport. For the sailing. An acquaintance told me you represent an estate in probate, including a mansion on Bellevue Avenue. Am I correct?"

Baxter nodded. "Bellevue Court actually, but close enough. What is your interest?"

"I am told it may be for sale?"

"Told by whom?"

"An attorney here in the city."

"He is well informed. A trifle premature perhaps. Until probate is granted nothing can be done and then it will be up to the heirs of the deceased."

"A woman I'm told. Recently murdered. Is that true?"

"What a curious question from someone in the property business? I think you will agree it is scarcely relevant to your inquiry, Mr. Blake. Whoever your informant is does you no favour with reported gossip. Which makes me wonder if you are really interested in purchasing the mansion?"

"If it's large enough, yes."

"It is a substantial property on three acres with ten bedrooms."

"Value?"

"That is not for me to say. Time and the market will determine the price. But if you are looking for a bargain you will not find it here. We are talking millions of dollars."

"Good. It will keep out the hoi polloi. Can I visit the place?"

"No."

"No?"

"The property is out of bounds at the moment."

"Why?"

"Why, Mr. Blake, is none of your business." Jacob Baxter stood up. "This interview is over. Good day to you, Mr. Blake. My 'girl' will show you out. You do not have to tip her as you leave."

+ + + +

From his window Baxter watched Blake trying to flag a taxi on the street far below. When a cab finally stopped, just before he got in, Blake turned, looked up as if he knew he was being watched, and waved. When the cab door slammed shut and the taxi took off, Baxter was left to wonder. What was the real motive for Blake's visit? He went back to his desk, took up the man's card to read the address. The Chelsea Hotel? He called and asked to speak to Mr. Blake.

"I am sorry, sir. We have no one with that name registered at the hotel," the receptionist said.

+ + + +

ON LEESIDE

At last the sea
(until then never seen)
Stretched
        A great real sweep of curved steel green-blue nothing
Revealing more distance than I'd ever imagined.

Swept (away)
The familiar furniture of home
And,
Closed that part of my life
Forever.
(A total extravagance before the accounts came in.)

The sea
A floating frogskin of flitting drowsy antship flies.
Inland, small, hired men push prams around the park.
Butterflies and thistles carelessly left
Behind fermenting families' slack-coloured curtains...
pearl-chokered invalids.
Honey crumbled eyes, flecked pupils

Watching, watched
The sixteen-year-old girl who burned my clothes
(Heartstoppingly voluptuous)
lead me proudly by the hand
up the eroded staircase of my mind

to the temporary sanctity of a room without a roof and it was in this
fragment that I knew I was in luck and took it easy in the scruffy
world of conspiratorial garrets.

Her lips on loan to my impoverished tale
A soft breathing heap of love.
Blood, thicker than theory,
a reasonable compromise between thought and horsewhip
In shut streets on rainy Sundays with no trains to come
The breath of pointless hours expiring…

Padded cats,
The sleek black-backed priests
(beggars, nursed to a peak of malformation)
horrors let out one by one
day and night
covered with sores
dragging their bodies, sacks without feet, imploring the empty air.

Mute concentrations of martyrdom.
Young and old, emanations of a stifling medievalism,
The pock-marked blasphemous effigies of scorch-marked churches.
Stamping sermons
On
unresisting limbs.

Thinks:
Old man
Why such sombre thoughts?
Snuggled down
In the soft-budding comfort of a
Teenaged bosom?

Brenton

+   +   +   +

"Splendid stuff, Sheriff," the Secretary said. "Quite splendid. Each time you outdo yourself. I love 'the budding comfort of a teenaged bosom.' What an echo to the past. Not many here would admit to such feelings."

"Thank you," the Sheriff said.

"Where is Leeside? Ireland?"

"No. I made it up. To honour a young poet from Gloucestershire."

"Goodness. What must go on in your mind? How does catching criminals square with poetry?"

"It's a daily reminder that there are more important things in life."

"Here, here!" The Secretary said. "Doff the uniform, Sheriff. Follow your muse. Writer's write!"

"Yeah? In times like these a cheque at the end of the month pays the bills. No money in poems, sad to say."

"I see you have signed up for our charity Christmas Dinner tomorrow. Perhaps I could persuade you to read one of your missives to our members?"

"I don't think so. It would only spoil their dinner."

"You are too modest, Sheriff. I will put you down. Father Christmas will introduce you after my wife's piano solo."

+ + + +

As obligation and habit would have it, it was at the same Christmas dinner in the Reading Room that the City Attorney and the Probate Judge found themselves seated at the same table. Habit also dictated that their wives should both decide to go to the Ladies Room at the same time. In mutual incomprehension, both men raised their eyebrows in synchronous sympathy and bafflement at this female ritual. Leaning across to his learned companion, City Attorney Moore said, "A word if I may? We have a problem. You may have to bend the rules."

Probate Judge Robert Burke raised his eyebrows, nodded. "I'm listening," he said.

Succinctly Moore related the essence of his meeting with the District Attorney.

"Baxter?" Burke said. "Curious you should mention him. Middle of last year, this woman who was murdered, Plane's widow, had her attorney

241

file a petition to challenge the accounting filed by Baxter as executor of Plane's estate. Something to do with the missing contents of certain safety deposit boxes. She even had an eyewitness, an employee from one of the banks, who testified to having seen gold coins in one of the boxes. Baxter was very forthright. He readily admitted opening the boxes only to find them empty. He assumed that whatever had been there was taken by Plane without telling his wife. I was put in the position of ruling on a challenge based on a hypothetical will that had not been found. I had no choice but to reject it and allow Baxter to file under an old will already admitted to probate. And now you say this new will exists?"

"Yes."

"Jesus!"

A popular reaction, which is when the two wives returned to their husbands and the dinner continued. It was only after the event, while waiting to get their coats from the cloakroom, that Burke found the opportunity to say to Moore, "Bring me the will. I know what to do."

+   +   +   +

NEWPORT COUNTY SUPERIOR COURT
45 WASHINGTON SQUARE
NEWPORT, RHODE ISLAND
December 27, 1929

NOTICE IS HEREBY GIVEN that a hearing before the Honourable Robert Burke, in the Matter of the Estate of Sir Kobe Plane, Deceased, Case No.1151126, has been calendared by the Court, sua sponte, for the First Session of the Court, at 10 am on January 15, 1930, in Courtroom No.3, when new information in the possession of the Court and pertaining to this case will be presented to all parties.
Amanda Higgins,
Clerk of the Newport County Superior Court

Jason received his copy of the notice on New Year's Eve. It came by ordinary post in a buff envelope. Normally, as butler, he sorted and distributed the mail after he fetched it from the mailbox, but this morning he was down in the wine cellar selecting what would be drunk that evening, and it was Jacob Roberts who went down to the mailbox at the front gate and brought back a small stack of belated Christmas cards, assorted bills and letters and the envelope for Jason.

"Something for you," he told the butler, and watched his reaction when he saw the embossed crest of the Superior Court stamped on the cover.

"Problem?" Mr. Roberts said.

Without a word, in front of his employer, Jason opened the envelope, read the contents, and handed the notice for Roberts to read.

Having done so, Mr. Roberts said, "I meant to ask you, I believe you know Jacob Baxter, Plane's executor?"

"I do," Jason said.

"He tells me you were formerly butler to Mr. Plane?"

"I was."

"And that under the terms of a will he made you inherit half his estate?"

"That was the old will. He revoked it when he remarried and made his wife his sole heir."

"Baxter says you and the other beneficiaries have come forward to assert the validity of the old will."

"That is untrue. Why would he say that?"

"Perhaps it was something you said when you met him?"

"But I have never met him."

"Never? How extraordinary. How do you know him then?"

"Only by mail. When Sir Kobe died three years ago, he sent a letter to the beneficiaries saying he had been appointed executor. Six months later he sent another letter detailing what he was doing relative to the size of the estate, that assessing its value was complicated and that it could take months if not years before any distributions could be made."

"That's all?"

"To me, yes. Karla, I mean, Mrs. Plane, before her death, had sent him a letter left to her by her husband…"

"I know. Baxter told me about the will that has not been found. He gave me the impression you were contesting the validity of that will even if it was found."

"With respect, that's rubbish. As I told the Sheriff at my interview, I witnessed Sir Kobe signing the will to his wife. She hired a lawyer to protect her interests."

"Why on earth were you being interviewed by the Sheriff?"

"I volunteered."

"For what?"

"Information I had to help catch her murderer."

+ + + +

With all the house staff off duty, Jacob Roberts could not help himself. Normally the soul of discretion, a carafe of Cheval Blanc during dinner, and a large cognac with a cigar while waiting for midnight to ring in the new year, undid his caution. He unburdened himself and told his wife, Helen, and his two houseguests, Daisy and Patrick McCarthy, of his conversation with his butler.

"Can you imagine Plane leaving half his wealth to his butler?" Helen was outraged. "He'd be richer than us!"

"Really, Helen, what's that got to do with anything?" Jacob said. "Jason may help solve this foul murder. I must say I can't fathom Baxter's motive."

"Listening to your description it almost sounds like Baxter is trying to throw suspicion on Jason?" Patrick said.

"It does, doesn't it?" Daisy said. "Isn't it a gross indiscretion on his part to even suggest such a thing?"

"It's all speculation," Jacob said. He already regretted his outburst. Too much wine. "What I have told you must be treated in the strictest confidence." He looked at his wife. "Which includes you, darling." Jacob smiled to take the sting out of his remark as he sized up his wife over the rim of his glass.

"That's so unfair," Helen predictably said. "Why pick on me?" She was the picture of innocence. "You know I only talk to Daisy."

Daisy was about to contradict her but thought better of it. "Curious, isn't it?" she said. "Here we sit in cosy comfort having a drink and down the street someone is murdered, while across the country people lose all they possess and end up in a bread line. Is that fair?"

"Worse," Patrick said. "It's iniquitous."

+   +   +   +

MIDNIGHT ON E 37TH ST,
MURRAY HILL, NEW YORK CITY

Tuesday, December 31, 1929

The Baxters lived in a four-storey brownstone a block away from the Morgan Library. The house was a wedding present from Edith's father, a successful stockbroker, now dead. For all the prestige of the address, the gift was something of a white elephant, with eye-watering maintenance bills and property taxes. Added to staff wages, tuition, and clothing for the four children, veterinary fees for the two dogs, food and - she was about to add 'entertainment' but silently scratched that item in her mind while seated patiently waiting for the chimes of midnight on the sofa in front of the cheerful flames of a log fire in the hearth of the library on the first floor. In the distance she could hear the chimes of the church bells in the twin spires of St. Patrick's Cathedral. She glanced at her husband reading the Wall Street Journal in his armchair to the left of the fireplace. On New Year's Eve. Typical. While thousands gathered to watch the ball drop on Times Square and make whoopee, he was frowning at the disastrous glidepath down of the Dow Jones Index. Without raising his eyes from the paper her husband said, "I know what you're thinking. You're thinking it's Tuesday, December the 31st, and we should be out celebrating with the mob in Times Square."

Despite herself, she nodded. A movement he did not see.

"What's there to celebrate?" he looked up at her. "See what it says here - 'Angry mob storms jobless job office'. Even Hoover has the sense to stay home in The White House with his wife. I am still not sure you understand the gravity of the crisis this country faces. Have you the remotest idea of what has transpired?" Warming to his subject, he flicked the paper with his forefinger. "Allow me to quote this headline - 'Culmination and Collapse of the Greatest of Stock Exchange Speculations' - and this - 'A Stock Exchange panic of unexampled violence'. At this rate we'll be lucky to afford this house."

There it was again. Her fault her wise father had put the house in a trust for her and the children. A trust he couldn't break or the house would have been sold long ago. She was about to say something but held her peace. There was a certain wisdom in remaining silent. Why had he grown so bitter? She knew he resented not making partner in the bank. What was it he said? I'm just a suit in a fancy office with no real authority. Which recalled the three new, tailored suits he had hanging in his closet. He must have got a year-end bonus…

"I thought things were getting better?" she said.

With great deliberation her husband took off his reading spectacles to study his wife. "For Christ's sake, Edith, you're not an idiot." He said it quietly. "Think before you speak. How many times do I have to say it? You know as well as I do, we are only just keeping our heads above water." He paused to let that sink in. "You know I do my best, but times are hard."

Meek, sweet, affectionate.

But Edith was not an idiot. They'd drifted apart. Come to the point. She wondered if they had ever been together. Their marriage was loveless. She felt like a piece of furniture, to be used when convenient. Wham-bam-thank-you-Ma'am! Result, four kids. Thank God for separate bedrooms. And, in truth, the children. They were a blessing. She was still thrilled when they called her Mummy. Instead of her name, which she hated. Edith. Why wasn't she called Penelope or Hermione? Or even Laura?

"You're not listening to me, are you, Edith?" her husband said, as in the hallway their grandfather clock struck midnight.

No, I'm not listening, Edith thought. I only wish I had the courage to ask where you got the two gold coins in the waistcoat of one of your new suits?

"Anyway, happy New Year," her husband said, putting on his spectacles and returning to the Journal. "I'll be off on tour to California on the 3rd and I'll finish up at a court hearing in Newport on the 15th. That's a Wednesday, so I'll be home for the weekend after that. Okay?"

Edith shrugged. Ok.

+ + + +

PLANETREE HOUSE, NEW YEAR'S DAY

1930

Without knocking, Molly came into Thomas' bedroom with breakfast on a tray: coffee, two poached eggs, rashers of bacon, fried tomatoes, toast, freshly squeezed orange juice.

"Happy New Year!" She sang out. "Up you get, lazy bones. Look what Cook's made you."

Thomas groaned.

"Come on. You're taking me for a walk, remember?" She threw open the curtains to a pale day dawning with the thermometer hovering near zero.

They had been to his home in Jamestown the previous evening, where Thomas, apprehensive about their reaction, presented Molly to his parents. Blushing, he said, "Dad, Mother, this is my fiancée, Molly."

The first thing his father said was "She has freckles!"

It made Molly laugh. "And not just on my face," she said.

"You'll start him thinking," Mrs. Brady said.

Easily as that, the ice was broken. Mrs. Brady had prepared a rack of lamb with black-eyed peas and lentils and thick slices of cornbread, and they had drunk champagne well past midnight. When it was time to leave, she said, "It's very late. Why don't you sleep here?"

Thomas blushed.

"Would you look at your son," Molly said.

The Bradys nudged each other, smiling.

"Can't leave the House unprotected," Thomas said to hide his embarrassment.

"Aren't you frightened to live there?" Mrs. Brady said to Molly.

"Not with Thomas to protect us."

"Joy," Mr. Brady said, kissing Molly on both cheeks. "You're a lucky lad, Thomas."

Riding pillion home on Thomas' motorbike, hugging the back of her man, Molly had never felt happier. When they drove down Bellevue Court she had very nearly allowed herself to be dragged into his bedroom but remained true to herself with the flimsy excuse of having to pee and rushing off to the chaste harbour of her bedroom in the Carriage House.

Now she said, "You know what Cook and I just heard on the radio in the kitchen? Tonight, the Moon will make its closest approach to Earth this century. Just 220,000 miles away. The next time it comes this close will be January 1, 2257."

Propping himself up on his pillow Thomas said, "And guess where we'll be then?"

"Don't you be laughing, Thomas Brady," Molly said. "You'll be with me in heaven, and you know it."

More like down the other place, Thomas thought, not for the first time. Just looking at Molly he wanted to tear her clothes off. Was it a sin?

"Don't you be looking at me like that," Molly said, reading his mind. "Come on, eat your breakfast before it gets cold." She sat on the end of his bed. "You're lucky, you know, to have parents that don't hide their love for you."

And added, "I hope they liked me."

+   +   +   +

IN WHICH THE SHERIFF CRAWLS
UNDER A FENCE

SATURDAY, JANUARY 4, 1930

Jimmy, carrying a birthday cake his mother made, shoved open the front gate of Planetree House with his shoulder and kicked it shut with his foot. Whistling his way to the front door of the mansion, he was surprised to see the Sheriff come out.

"Good morning, Jimmy," the Sheriff said. "What have you got there?"

"'Morning, Sheriff," Jimmy said. "It's a cake for Molly's birthday my Ma made."

"Molly's birthday?"

"Yeah. She's 34 today. We don't have any candles, but Ma said to ask Cook. It's a secret, so don't say anything until the party this evening."

Unsure if he would be invited, the Sheriff could only nod at the lad. "Good man. When you've finished with Cook, I want you to give me a hand. I'll be over by the fence next door."

Next door was the grounds of the derelict Van Hals mansion. Jimmy found the Sheriff trying to peer through the thick overgrowth which totally covered the fence separating the two properties.

"Is there a way through this?" the Sheriff said.

"Not standing," Jimmy said. "You've got to get down on your hands and knees." He eyed the Sheriff sceptically. "You want me to show you?"

The boy showed the Sheriff how to crawl under the bushes to a place where time had rotted part of the fence and it was possible to wriggle

251

through a gap. Once in, standing up, brushing off his trousers and dusting his hands, the Sheriff found himself in a gloomy overgrown wilderness, with giant trees hundreds of years old, a carpet of dead leaves at their feet. Wherever he looked was a thicket of interlocked branches and vines in a landscape untended for decades.

"Christ," the Sheriff said, "How do you get to the house?"

"Follow the animals," Jimmy said and pointed to an almost invisible track which went off zigzagging through the dense bushes. It took the best part of ten minutes for them to finally fetch up next to the ruined mansion.

"It's easier when you come in off the road if the front gates are not locked." Jimmy said.

Turning back to view the path they had taken, the Sheriff thought how easy it would be to hide the murder weapons in such a jungle, the pick, stiletto, knife or gun, even the iron bar if that's what was used to bash her head in. You'd need an army to search the place properly. He said, "You can't even see Planetree from here."

"Only from upstairs," Jimmy said.

"You've been up there?"

Jimmy nodded.

"Could you find your way here at night?"

Jimmy shook his head. "Too spooky," he said.

They walked the perimeter of the ruin when it began to rain. An ice-cold drizzle at first, turning into a downpour. Sheltering in what had once been the porte-cochère of the mansion as the skies darkened and thunder boomed out over the Atlantic, the Sheriff tried to picture the murderer. Getting out unseen in broad daylight when the staff came back early from their half-day break? Covered in blood? Carrying his weapons? If indeed it was the man Jimmy saw from the coal cellar? Wearing pinstripe tailored trousers? In Newport?

"Jimmy," the Sheriff said, "in your interview with Mr. Brady, you said you saw a man wearing pinstripe trousers when you chanced to look out of the coal cellar? You remember?"

"Yes."

"Did you ever see him again?"

"You mean the trousers? Cause I never really saw who was wearing them."

"Yes, the trousers. Who would wear pinstripes around here?"

"Well, all the butlers, it's part of their uniform, and even some of the footmen, depending who they work for. Then also some of the lawyers and bankers. Even that Secretary in your club."

Yes, the Sheriff thought, part of the uniform, ubiquitous. But would you crawl under a fence wearing them? Make a note. Check the dry cleaners. Then he saw Jimmy sniffing the air.

"What?" he said.

"The rain's putting out a bonfire. Look." Jimmy pointed way down the overgrown driveway to where a thin wisp of smoke was rising from the centre of what appeared to be a large pile of ashes. Like in Autumn when the gardeners burnt the piles of raked up leaves and the fragrant smell of wood smoke was carried on the breeze. Could be a new poem.

AUTUMN
Raked piles of leaves
Burn
A breeze carries the
Woodsmoke
To a gardener's nose.

The Sheriff chuckled to himself. Almost a haiku.

"In the middle of winter, in a dump like this, why bother?" Jimmy said.

+   +   +   +

CIMETIÈRE VAUBAN, BRIANÇON

FRIDAY, JANUARY 10, 1930

Surrounded by snow covered mountains, outside the city walls, the elderly guardian slowly brushed a path through the snow to the freshly dug plot along the north boundary of the austere cemetery where there was still room for a grave. In the distance he could see the hearse drawn by a black horse with black plumes in a headband on its forehead come through the Porte de Pignerol, the main gateway into the immense fortress that Vauban had rebuilt in 1692. The hearse was followed by a small contingent of the town's dignitaries led by the mayor, supporting on his arm the mother of the deceased, a tiny figure dressed in black mourning. At the back was a delegation from Paris sent to escort the coffin since its arrival in Le Havre on a steamship from America. At the very tail end could be seen a distinguished couple, the man walking slowly with a cane, assisted by a beautiful Vietnamese woman.

In the cold, the ceremony they attended was as brief as the attending priest could decently make it and finished when he intoned, "Eternal rest grant unto her, O Lord, and may thy perpetual light shine upon her. May her soul, and the souls of all the faithful departed, through the mercy of God, rest in peace. Amen"

The journalist from La Provence sent to cover the event wrote, "As the coffin was lowered into the frozen ground, a detachment from the Chasseur Alpin addressed arms and fired a volley to honour the memory of a fallen heroine, saluted by Col. Gaston Duhamel and the General de Brigade of the Gendarmerie National, Alphonse Picard.'

The following Monday morning a simple granite gravestone engraved with 'Si git Karla Plane (née Pinard) 1896 - 1929' was laid by the local undertaker before the kneeling figure of Karla's mother come to put fresh flowers on her daughter's tomb.

That same afternoon neither the inscription nor the flowers were visible under the freshly fallen snow.

+   +   +   +

NEWPORT COUNTY SUPERIOR COURT 45 WASHINGTON SQUARE, NEWPORT, RHODE ISLAND

WEDNESDAY, JANUARY 15, 1930

Courtroom 3, on the second floor of the building, was bright with morning sunshine coming through the windows after bouncing off a sprinkling of snow on the nearby trees.

The room was modest in size, tastefully panelled in pale oak patinated by time. At 10AM precisely the doors were opened and those invited to the probate hearing filed in to take their seats. Right at the back Molly sat next to Thomas Brady. She had not been officially invited but, at the Sheriff's insistence, given that she was one of the few people in Newport with intimate knowledge of Karla, was there as an observer. And the first thing she noted was the arrival of Stephen Masry. And then she saw Jason, the butler, taking his seat. What was he doing here?

"All rise," the bailiff said, as Judge Robert Burke entered from his chambers to take his place on the bench to which he had been appointed for nearly a quarter century. Thus elevated, he viewed the assembled company as they stood in greeting.

"Courtroom 3 of the Newport County Superior Court is now in session," the bailiff intoned, "the Honourable Robert Burke presiding. You may be seated,"

Burke nodded to acknowledge the presence of District Attorney William Clarke, and the City Attorney Charles Moore, sitting side by side, directly in front of him. To their left sat the executor, Jacob Baxter, with a bulging briefcase at his hip. Behind them were members of the press and various people he did not immediately recognise, beneficiaries or claimants no doubt. He noted the Chief of Police and the Sheriff sitting somewhat apart, where they could observe the company without it being too obvious.

"Good morning," he said. "Before we begin, for the record, let me state the obvious. The role of the probate court during the probate process is to ensure that the wishes of the decedent are met to the letter of the law."

He paused.

Then added, "If there is a will. A will needs to be probated in order for it to be deemed a valid will. The word probate comes from the Latin, probare, to prove."

Again, he paused.

"In the event there is a will, the Court must make sure that the directives of the will are followed exactly. A nominated Executor is not authorised by law to act in accordance with the will until the will is proven to the Court to be the last will and testament of the deceased individual. The last will alone determines who receives property and what property they receive."

Get on with it, the Sheriff thought, and made a mental bet that Jacob Baxter, whom he was watching closely, had just thought the same thing. At least the bugger had come, you had to give him that. Does he suspect anything? Impossible to tell. But someone in the courtroom had blood on their hands. In the silence a fly could be heard buzzing against one of the windowpanes, anxious to get out.

But there was no hurrying the Judge.

"The Court also issues rulings on any appeals made by heirs or beneficiaries to the estate and to creditors of the estate that may claim their right to such assets as there may be. Where there is no will, the heirs are the closest living relatives of the decedent - the spouse, if living, and the living children, including adopted children and those born out of wedlock. If the decedent has neither a living spouse nor children, the decedent's mother and father are the heirs. If the decedent's mother and father are not living, the decedent's brothers and sisters, along with the children or other descendants of any deceased brothers or sisters are the heirs. But where there is a will, none of that matters because heirship is determined by what the decedent writes in his will."

Pause.

"Let us here note the difference between heirs and beneficiaries. As I have said, the heirs are the closest living relatives of the decedent. The beneficiaries are those people who inherit property by the terms of the will. If an heir or a beneficiary claim otherwise, it is within the scope of duties for the executor of the will" - a nod to Baxter - "to deny a claim, but the probate court will determine whether there is a basis for the denial or if the claim is just."

Another pause for all this to sink in, while the Judge adjusted his spectacles and consulted a note he had made, lying on top of several documents on the desk in front of him.

"I have called for this hearing, sua sponte, in the matter of the estate of Mr. Kobe Plane, Deceased, Case No.115/1126, as new information is in the possession of the Court pertaining to this case." Yet another pause while he eyed his audience.

"Before I tell you about it," the Judge said, "I think it would be useful to review some history. Mr. Plane married twice. His first wife died ten years ago at which time Plane made a will. When Mr. Plane died three years ago, in October 1926, this will was presented for probate by the named executor of the decedent, Mr. Jacob Baxter, but the Court was faced with a dilemma. His widow, the second wife, Karla Plane, had a letter from her husband in which he wrote he had made a new will in her favour. This letter was presented to the Court by the Executor, who had himself received a similar letter from Mr. Plane. I have both letters here."

The Judge held them up for all to see.

"But a letter is not a will. As this will could not be found, did it in fact exist? In fairness the Court ruled at the first Probate hearing that letters testamentary should be given to the executor named in Plane's first will," - a further nod in Baxter's direction - "with instructions to proceed to identify the heirs and beneficiaries of the estate and to establish its value. Because of the size and complexity of the estate it was estimated this would take a considerable time and again, in fairness, the Court ruled that the widow, Karla Plane, should use this time to try to find the new will she claimed her husband had made. Absent a new will, probate would be adjudged by the only will in the Court's possession, the original one from ten years ago."

The Judge took off his spectacles, cleaned and polished them on the sleeve of his robe and perched them on top of his forehead. Then he took a sip of water from a glass on his desk. The Sheriff glanced at the Chief of Police to get his reaction - raised eyebrows and a discreet shrug. Be patient.

"As part of his task the executor is required to keep the Court informed on a regular basis of his progress in valuing the estate. This he did, with an accounting every six months. In 1928, Karla Plane, through her attorney, petitioned the Court to challenge the accounts of the executor and contest his right to continue in that position. After a hearing, the Court found no merit in her petition and ordered the executor to continue his assignment."

Here the Judge took his spectacles from his forehead and placed them on his nose the better to survey his audience.

"By the perplexed look on some of you, I can see you are wondering why I am elaborating the obvious. We are a small community here in Newport, with some twenty-five thousand residents, and there cannot be a single one unaware that Mrs. Karla Plane was murdered last October. October 26, to be precise." The Judge nodded, as if accentuating the need for precision.

Then, quite dramatically, he took a small buff envelope from the papers in front of him, held it aloft, and said, "But none here could know that on October 24, two days prior to her death, Mrs. Karla Plane would send this Western Union telegram." Pause. "None, other than the recipient to whom it was addressed, Mr. Jacob Baxter, of Brown Brothers, Bankers on Wall Street in New York City, New York, her husband's executor!"

It was great theatre, the Sheriff thought.

"And what, you ask yourselves, did the telegram say?"

With a flourish, the Judge extracted the copy in the envelope and read aloud, "I've found it!"

"I've found it!" he repeated. "Three words, followed by an exclamation mark. And what had she found?"

Up went another envelope. Held high in suspense for all to see.

Now he's milking it, the Sheriff thought.

"The missing will!" The Judge said.

Gasps of astonishment, which lasted barely a second before a hubbub of comment flooded the Courtroom.

"Silence!"

The huge voice of the bailiff echoed off the ceiling.

"There will be order in this courtroom!" the bailiff bellowed, relishing the little power he had. The hubbub subsided.

"Thank you," the Judge said to the bailiff. "Now I will read the last will and testament of Mr. Kobe Plane."

He cleared his throat as he extracted a single sheet of paper from the envelope, carefully spread it out and, mindful of his role in the unfolding drama, declaimed in measured paragraphs:

'I, Kobe Plane, a childless widower and resident of Newport, Rhode Island, being of sound mind and body, declare this to be my Last Will and Testament. I hereby revoke any and all other wills and codicils that I have made at any time in the past.

'I appoint Jacob Baxter, of 502, Park Avenue, New York City, as my Executor. I direct that he should not have to post any bond or other security in connection with his acting as my Executor.

'I direct that all of the assets of my estate, both real and personal, be given to my sole heir and future spouse, Karla Pinard, currently of 18, Rue du Montpensier, Paris 75001, France.

'I further direct that if anyone other than Karla Pinard contests this Will and claims that he, she, or anyone else is entitled to any part of my estate, then I give to that person the sum of $1.00 only, and direct that such person is to be otherwise completely and entirely disinherited.

'I signed this Last Will and Testament on the 2nd day of January 1926, in Paris, France.'

The Judge stopped reading to look at his spell-bound audience.

"The will is signed by Kobe Plane," he said, "and it is witnessed by J. Fleet and Bertrand Aubert. All the signatures have been authenticated and this will is now entered in probate as being the last will and testament of Mr. Kobe Plane."

Another lengthy pause.

"It is my sad duty to acknowledge the Court's failure in doubting the existence of this will, but it is within the Court's remit to ask the executor if he did indeed receive the telegram? I would ask Mr. Baxter to please stand."

Without hesitation the banker stood up.

"Did you receive the telegram sent to you on Thursday, October 24, 1929?"

"I did."

"Why did you not inform the Court?"

"I was waiting for Mrs. Plane to tell me what she had found."

"And…?"

"I heard nothing further from her. On the following Monday I learned of her death."

"And you did not connect the two events?"

"I am a banker, sir. As a director of Brown Brothers, I have many duties. I am sure you are aware of the extraordinary circumstances with the stock market in free fall at that time. That Monday is not called Black Monday for no reason. And it was worse on the Tuesday. We were inundated with calls from our panicked customers on the telephone, by mail, by wire. Many in person. Naturally I was shocked to learn of the death of Mrs. Plane, but…"

"Murder," the Judge said. "She was murdered, Mr. Baxter!"

"A distinction without a difference, if I may be so bold, Judge. She was dead."

It was cold hearted the way Baxter said it. And it shocked the court. The man was obviously completely sure of himself, and it made the Sheriff sit up, alert - this was not the behaviour of a guilty person.

"As executor you had a duty," the Judge said. "A legal duty on which you swore an oath."

"Yes," Baxter said. "An oath to carry out my duties to identify the heirs and beneficiaries of the decedent's estate and to establish the value of that estate as you have so clearly pointed out. I have done this to the best of my ability for the past three years. I do not have to defend myself. This is not a trial. I have come here today at your invitation and along with everyone else in this courtroom I have heard you read the last will and testament of Sir Kobe Plane. I note that I am still the nominated executor in it. Is it the Court's wish that I continue in this role, or would you prefer to name another executor?"

Game, set and match, the Sheriff thought.

+   +   +   +

A post-mortem was held in the District Attorney's office immediately after the hearing.

"What bug bit Burke banging on like that?" the DA said. "I've never known him to be so pedantic."

"Banging on? I thought he was very astute, making it absolutely clear that with the new will, Plane's second wife got everything, and now she's dead, even if intestate, it all goes to her heirs," the City Attorney said.

"Thank the Lord we didn't subpoena Baxter," the DA said.

"Amen," the City Attorney said.

"We clear on this, Chief" The DA looked at the Chief of Police. "I've said it before, but I will say it again. There will be no harassment, no interrogation. Without a smoking gun there is no case against Baxter. Or anyone else for that matter. All this business about keys. I will not risk my career on flimsy circumstantial evidence or the imaginative conjecture of your staff." Here he looked at the Sheriff. "Got it?"

"What is imaginative about a woman slaughtered in her own home?" the Sheriff said. "Someone did it. That someone is walking about free, and the woman is in a hole in the ground. You're not suggesting we forget the whole thing?"

"Look, Brenton, we've known each other for a long time. Obviously, I share your feelings. I even share your anger. But this isn't some penny dreadful novel." The DA mimed reading with his hands opening an invisible book. "There's no Sherlock to tie everything in a neat package in the last chapter so we can all go home satisfied that the guilty party was caught. This is real life. We have an economy down the toilet, millions out of work, desperate people turning to crime to feed their families. You want me to go on? You've got what, two years before retirement? Don't screw up your pension. Need I remind you, we've a backlog of cases that needs the attention of everyone on the force? If there is no new, specific evidence to nail this bastard, whoever he is, I think it wise to wind up the investigation now and attend to business. Period. Case closed. End of story. Clear?"

+ + + +

A different post-mortem was conducted by Molly and her betrothed, Thomas Brady, as they walked back to Planetree House.

"Did you know Jason, the butler, would be there?" Molly said.

"No. Why?"

"I was watching him," Molly said. "He was smiling when Baxter was asked to stand up, but his face went white, and he wasn't smiling when Baxter waltzed out of there."

Which is when someone behind them said, "Excuse me", and they turned to see Stephen Masry.

"May I have a word, Miss Malone?" Masry said. "Alone?"

"Why, Mr. Masry, how nice to see you," Molly said. "What brings you here? If the matter is to do with the hearing, this is my fiancé, Thomas Brady. He can hear what you have to say. He's in charge of the investigation."

Brady blushed at this description as he shook hands with Masry.

"I was contacted by the French Embassy to represent the interests of the deceased's mother," Masry said. Off the blank look on Molly's face, he added. "The late Mrs. Plane's mother. She is next of kin."

"If you mean Karla, say Karla." Molly said. "I hate all this dancing around saying the 'deceased' and the 'late'.

"Sorry," Masry said.

"How did they know to contact you?" Brady said.

"I was surprised when they did. Apparently the late - sorry - apparently Karla had mentioned it to them that I represented her when we petitioned the Court a couple of years ago to challenge the executor's accounts. We contended there should have been gold and cash in several safety deposit boxes, and the executor said they were empty. The Court said it all boiled down to she said, he said, with no proof either way, and our petition was dismissed. You remember, Miss Malone?"

"It's Molly. Yes, I remember."

"Just now the Judge brushed it all under the rug. But I've been ferreting around. Do you have a safety deposit box?"

Spontaneously, Molly and Thomas laughed.

"Neither do I," Masry said. "The banks make it complicated, both for the depositor and to protect themselves. There's a whole song and dance you must go through to access the vaults, with duplicate keys, appointments, signatures on a registry, etcetera. So much so, that even Mr. Plane when he was alive, had to submit to these regulations. Karla had given me a list of the banks where Plane had accounts, and the French Embassy provided me with the credentials to get access to the books. It was easy enough to track who signed in. Guess what? During the seven months the Planes were married, each bank was visited just once by them as shown by Mr. Plane's signature. In each case, according to Karla, he showed her the contents of the various deposit boxes and the boxes were returned full of gold or cash to the vaults, exactly as they had come out. Plane did not come back to empty the deposit boxes as the executor contends and there are no signatures to prove otherwise." Here Masry paused. Then raised a finger to signal the importance of what he was about to say.

"But, in the three years after Plane's death, the executor makes multiple visits to each bank, ostensibly to go over the accounts of the various properties in Plane's portfolio, always ending up each visit with an obligatory signed access to the vaults. Why? If, as he states, the deposit boxes were empty, what possible reason could there be for him to go back to look at empty deposit boxes on each and every visit? On the contrary, finding the boxes empty, as a diligent executor, he should have, would have, cancelled their rental from the banks to save the estate unnecessary expenditure. No. There can only be one explanation."

"He was stealing?" Molly asked a question.

"He was stealing." For Brady it was a statement.

"Yes." Steven Masry said. "I believe he was steadily taking what he could safely carry and hide. Now we must prove it."

+ + + +

"I thought Jason took the news well," Jacob Roberts said. He and Patrick had been at the hearing to support the butler and they were having afternoon tea at home with their wives, agog for news.

"Didn't flinch. Damned if I could do that." Patrick said. "He's on track to receive millions and bingo! Out the window. Odd thing. I didn't know Baxter had a place on Park?"

"What do you mean?"

"In the will the judge read out, it gave Baxter an address on Park Avenue. I thought he lived on Murray Hill behind the Morgan."

"Maybe he's richer than you think," Helen said. "Probably that's where he stashes his mistress."

+ + + +

On the train back to New York that afternoon, Baxter had one thought. As he left the courtroom, he saw the slight figure of a man going down the stairs ahead of him. Mr. Peon Blake. What was he doing there?

+ + + +

THE READING ROOM, NEWPORT

SATURDAY, JANUARY 18, 1930

Coming into the Sheriff's suite, Chief Hazard said, "I saw your car outside and figured you'd be in here. It's the weekend, Sheriff. For Christ's sake, take a break. If you want to know, you look like shit."

"Probably." The Sheriff looked at the lists he had made, and the photographs of the ransacked rooms in the mansion the day of the murder, strewn across his desk.

"Why the glum face, Brenton?" the Chief said. "You heard the DA. We must wrap this up. You'll have to move back to the station."

"Quit?"

"Wind down."

"How long do I have?"

"End of the month. With Baxter in your sights, you pissed he walked away?"

The Sheriff shook his head. "Something's off. It doesn't add up," he said.

"What do you mean?"

"The timeline is wrong. All through the holidays it's been bothering me. No way one guy could have done all that in the time he had. Lookit. That Saturday the staff leave Planetree at 11 in the morning and are back by 4.30 in the afternoon. That's five and a half hours. In that time her visitor arrives, he gives her the shares, she gets laid, he leaves, the other guy accosts her, they have a bloody fight which ends with her dead in the dining room, and then her assailant tosses down the house looking for something as small as that envelope with the will? Look at these pictures." He waved at the photographs. "Think about it. In a house that size, even if he knew what he was looking for, where would he start? There are thousands of books just in the library. An envelope could be hidden in any one of them. And all the cupboards in all those bedrooms? Not to mention the attic and the basement, the kitchen, and the cellars and all the reception rooms. You would need an army to properly search for something as small as one envelope in that time frame." The Sheriff, as was his habit, started pacing the room. "And try this on, could it be he was not trying to steal something, but to destroy what he was looking for?"

The Chief nodded. "What sticks in my craw, I know you said it before, this guy leaves without a trace. Vanishes. Bloody clothes, weapons, gun, the lot. Poof! Gone! Just like that!"

The Chief snapped his fingers.

"Okay. Let's say it really was just Baxter," the Sheriff said. "According to the butler he must have been hiding out in one of the spare bedrooms where he uses the toilet. Which begs the question, when did he get in even if he had a key?" The Sheriff turned his hands out waiting for an answer. "That morning? The previous evening? In the night? Why, since he did not know, could not have known, the coast would be clear? We know, because in her testimony, the cook, Mrs. Bassett, said Karla only told them they were getting a half day off after breakfast around 10 that morning, so there's no way Baxter knew the house would be empty."

"What about the derelict house next door? At that meeting with Clarke, it was suggested anyone there could have surveyed the comings and goings at Planetree."

"You been? I mean inside the place, not out in the street? I have. With Jimmy. It's not like Easton said. From the second floor, through the trees, you can just see the west side of Planetree. When I say 'see' I mean at that distance you can make out there is a substantial building there, but, because of the trees, there's no way, even if you saw somebody, that you could accurately tell who was going where, leave alone when. No way. And keep in mind there are three other sides to Planetree you can't see at all. No. Forget it." The Sheriff paused, watching Chief Hazard. "Somehow this guy knew the staff were leaving. To know that you must ask yourself how did he know, from whom did he get the information? The answer must be from one of the staff or from Karla herself."

"Access?" the Chief said.

"Yes. Who had access to Karla or the staff?"

"According to the butler…" the Chief's voice trailed off as he stared at the Sheriff.

"Yes," the Sheriff said. "That's it. 'According' to the butler. We've accepted everything he's told us as gospel because he came forward and volunteered the information. But what if it's all lies? I've been back over all the interviews and not one person we've interviewed mentions seeing him in the house. No one. The only mention is Jimmy meeting him walking a dog on Bellevue. The housekeeper even said only she and Mrs. Plane had a key to the front door. And yet he says…" the Sheriff sifted the papers on his desk, "…here we are, he says, quote, 'She gave me a key to her place so I could pop in for a chat in my free time.' If he had a key from her and came and went whenever he liked, it is impossible the staff would not have seen him. In a house like that nobody just walks in."

"Unless…"

"What?"

"It was so common nobody thought it worth mentioning."

Now it was the Sheriff's turn to stare.

"Christ," he finally said. "You're right, Chief. I'll get Brady on it immediately."

"And another thing," the Chief said. "You remember when this thing started you said you thought it might be two men, a robber and a murderer? What if that was actually the case? Baxter and the butler?"

"Yes. But which is which?" the Sheriff said.

+ + + +

THE LIBRARY, PLANETREE HOUSE

MONDAY, JANUARY 20, 1930

"Thank you for coming, Mrs. Lister. I have just one follow-up question." PC Brady smiled and looked down at a note he had made. "In your interview here last November, I asked you who had keys to the house and you stated, I quote, 'To the front door? Nobody but Mrs. Plane and myself.' Do you remember that?"

"Yes."

"Nobody? You are sure?"

"Nobody on staff, yes, I'm sure."

"Other than staff?"

"Well, I can only think of old Jason. He used to be the butler here and kept a key to this house. I don't think Mrs. Plane had the nerve to ask for it back."

"Would you say they were close?"

"With the butler? Don't be foolish, Mr. Brady."

"Yes. Thank you, Mrs. Lister. That will be all."

+   +   +   +

"I am sorry to interrupt you, Cook," PC Brady said, coming into the kitchen. "I know you are busy. Just a quick question. In your interview back in November, I asked you in the days before Saturday, October 26, did you notice anything unusual in the behaviour of Mrs. Plane? Do you remember?"

"Yes. I said there was nothing unusual."

269

"And I asked if there were any unusual visitors?"

"Yes. I said there weren't any."

"What if I had said usual visitors?"

"Apart from old Jason coming and going like he owned the place, no, nobody."

+ + + +

"Now Lucy, you remember when I asked you in the days before that Saturday did you see any strangers around the house, and you said 'No.'"

"Yes. I remember."

"What about other people?"

"You mean like Mr. Jason?"

+ + + +

"When I interviewed you, Jimmy, you said you spoke to Mr. Jason when he walked the dog up on Bellevue Avenue. Remember?"

"Yes. I said we sometimes stop for a chat."

"Right. Did you ever see him here in the house?"

"Sure. But there's no time for a chat, he being Mr. Jason and me being me."

"I don't understand."

"Wouldn't do, would it? I've me work to do. Anyway, it wasn't me he came to see. He was along to see the lady."

"Mrs. Plane?"

"Yes. I used to think he was sweet on her."

"What!"

"Can't say I blame him."

+ + + +

When Thomas got to Molly, he found it difficult to be so direct. Not Molly.

"If you've got something to say, Thomas Brady, out with it," Molly said.

Thomas blushed.

"I know you've been questioning the others," Molly said. "Cats got your tongue? If it's about Karla, get on with it."

"Remember I asked you if she had many guests?" Thomas said.

"Yes," said Molly. "I said, none, apart from her lawyer. None. Ever."

"What about Jason?"

"Old Jason? He's scarcely a guest. I don't know why he thought - no, that's not it - I don't know what he thought he was doing in and out of here all the time."

"Was there something going on between them?"

"Karla and the butler? You've got to be kidding!"

+   +   +   +

"My God!" said the Sheriff.

"Yes," Thomas Brady said. "I couldn't believe it either. But it was the way Jimmy said it, very man-of-the-world, that made me go back to Cook. Of all the staff she is perhaps the most intuitive."

The Sheriff smiled. "More than Molly?"

It got Brady blushing again. "Seriously, when I broached the subject with Cook, she said something interesting. She said all women are flattered by attention. Karla was lonely. An avuncular figure like Jason, as unlikely as that may seem, could be a solace. Did it go beyond that? She didn't think so. But her point was, maybe Jason hoped it would."

"Jesus Christ," the Sheriff said. He was wrong. Not Baxter. Jason?

"Can we pull him in? Interrogate him?" Brady was like a hungry puppy who could smell a bone.

"No. Impossible. Remember what the DA said. Where's the smoking gun? Without hard evidence, Jason could just clam up and would be in his right to do so."

"What if we asked him to comment on what he said in his interview?"

"Worth a try, I guess. He'd be a dumb prick to answer." The Sheriff was morose. "I don't think he's that dumb."

"There's another thing," Brady said.

"What?"

And Brady told him of his conversation with Stephen Masry.

Like the Chief said, a robber and a murderer. No way to prove either. Less than two weeks to go. One last throw of the dice.

+ + + +

At 7am the following morning, the Sheriff and PC Brady stood outside No.2 Bellevue Court, and rang the front doorbell. After a long moment a maid opened the door. Seeing the two officers she looked puzzled but bobbed a curtsey.

"Good morning. How may I help you?" she said.

"Good morning," the Sheriff said. "We are sorry to disturb you so early, but we would like to speak to Mr. Jason, the butler."

"That will not be possible, sir," the maid said. "He's not here."

"When will he be back?"

"There's no telling, sir. The house is closed."

"Closed?"

"Yes, sir. Mrs. Roberts is in Lyford Cay in the Bahamas and Mr. Roberts is in New York on his way to their winter home in West Palm Beach, Florida. Mr. Jason is with Mr. Roberts. If they should call, shall I give them a message?"

Snake eyes.

+ + + +

That evening the Sheriff called on the Secretary of the Reading Room to tell him he would vacate his suite at the end of the month.

"We'll be sorry to see you go," the Secretary said. "Does it mean you've caught the perpetrator of this ghastly act?"

"Sadly, not."

"Oh dear. To think there is a killer in our midst. I fear for our little community. What is the world coming to?"

"Don't worry. We'll get him. They always think they're so clever they can never be caught."

"Does that mean no more missives for the bulletin board?"

"Actually, I have something for you."

"For me?"

"Well, for your daughter. You have a daughter I believe? How old is she now?"

"Six."

"Six already! She reads?"

"Avidly."

"Good. Please give her this."

The Sheriff carefully tore a sheet from his notebook. On it the Secretary read:

Hopping away down memory lane
I saw a rabbit
Wave
And disappear.

"I'm not sure I understand," the Secretary said.

"Never mind," the Sheriff said. "Your daughter will."

+ + + +

IN WHICH A YOUNG POLICE CONSTABLE DREAMS THE IMPOSSIBLE

That night, Brady fell asleep troubled and frustrated. The frustration came from knowing he would have to vacate Planetree House if the investigation was terminated, and that he would never have such a golden opportunity to get Molly into bed. His arousal at what he imagined could transpire between them had him tossing and turning. When finally he nodded off it was to fall into a vivid dream in which he was in the Jailhouse working with his sleeves rolled up when the Chief said, "What a racket! Would somebody please close the windows?"

Watched by the Sheriff, he, Brady, did as requested. They were in the Chief's office up on the second floor and closing the windows cut off the noise.

"Thank you," the Chief said. "At least I can now hear myself think. Right then, if you two are ready?"

"We are," the Sheriff said.

"Be careful, Brenton, this is all circumstantial. As the DA keeps reminding us, we have no smoking gun. Somehow this butler-fellow must incriminate himself. From what I gather, he's not dumb -"

"No."

"All the more reason I think you should lead."

"Not if I'm the bad cop," the Sheriff said. "Brady leads. Look at him. With that baby face, he's obviously the good cop."

Brady blushed. Good cop, bad cop. He felt he was in a play. It made him nervous.

"You set?" the Sheriff said to him, a rhetorical question. "Let's go."

Brady was nervous for a reason. In his young career he had interrogated plenty of petty criminals for a variety of crimes, shoplifting, car theft, barroom brawls, spousal abuse, desecrating property, trespassing, pickpocketing, public drunkenness. But nothing like this. A major offence, a felony charge of murder.

It had taken a week to get all the ducks in a row - the DA's phrase - and it wasn't until the weekend that the butler was taken into custody, arraigned, and locked up pending his interrogation. When they took him in, the Roberts and their guests having already returned to New York, the butler seemed more concerned about leaving the mansion unsupervised than his own predicament. He was in a holding cell on the ground floor of the Jailhouse, a very old, badly maintained building that served both as jail and police headquarters. Next-door, an even older, more dilapidated building, was being demolished and dust from the site sifted into the jail with the noise of pickaxes and the rumble of trucks, the very ordinariness of this a reminder that whatever the circumstances, life carried on.

The interrogation was conducted in a room in the basement that looked like an abattoir, with dirty-white, glazed tiles on all four walls and bright overhead lamps shining down onto a grey rectangular metal table with four wooden chairs drawn up in pairs at each end. It looked as uncomfortable as it was meant to be. The butler was brought down in handcuffs by a warden, who removed the manacles and told him to sit. He was kept sitting there by himself for ten long minutes with nothing more entertaining to do than follow the odd cockroach with his eyes as they came and went through cracks in the grout around the tiles. When at last the door to the room opened to admit the Sheriff and his deputy it was almost a relief. The Sheriff thanked the warden. The warden left the room. The Sheriff, expressionless, stood against one of the walls, lit a cigarette and blew smoke up at the ceiling. The deputy sat across from the butler and arranged some papers on the table. So, they were going to play good cop, bad cop. The cliché was laughable. But for one thing.

Silence.

It gnawed at him.

"Are you going to tell me why I'm here?" the butler finally said.

Silence.

The butler ran his tongue over the residue of something he had eaten stuck in the interstice between two teeth in the upper left of his mouth. Whatever it was had been bothering him since dinner on Saturday and his attempts at creating a vacuum with his tongue against the crevice had been to no avail other than to inflame the gum where the teeth were embedded. There was nothing in his cell he could use to get it out. He needed a toothpick.

"I need a toothpick," he said.

Silence.

Then abruptly, he, the deputy, Brady, looked up from the paper he was studying and said, "What did you say?"

"I said I need a toothpick," the butler said.

"No, before that?" Brady said.

"I asked you to tell me why I'm here?"

"Yes. You know, of course," Brady said. "We'll get to that in a minute. Now, do you recall voluntarily giving an interview at the end of November last year? Friday, the 29th, to be precise. In the Reading Room?"

His quiet voice inspired confidence, two buddies chatting about nothing very important. The butler found himself nodding.

"Yes," he said.

"You were told a transcript would be made of your voluntary interview, yes?"

"Yes."

"This is a transcript of what was said," he pushed a stapled document across the table. "A copy was given to you. Do you recognise it?"

"Yes."

"The transcript is signed on the last page. Please confirm that it is your signature."

The butler hesitated.

'Take your time," he said.

Silence.

"Yes or no?" he said, his voice hardening. "Is that your signature?"

"Yes," the butler said.

"During that interview you were reminded that you came forward of your own volition and that you could terminate the interview whenever you wished. But, at our choice, we could officially recall you for an interrogation under oath when your testimony could be used against you in the event you were charged with a crime. Do you recall this?"

"Yes."

"I am Thomas Brady and that is my colleague, Sheriff Brenton. He will record what is said here. Afterwards you will be given a transcript which you will sign. You are now under oath. You may remain silent. If you have an attorney, you may call for his assistance. Do you understand?

"Yes."

"Please state your name."

"Jason Fleet."

"Occupation?"

"Butler."

"Address?"

"2, Bellevue Court."

"Is that where you work or where you live?"

"Both."

"How long have you been employed there?"

"3 years. We've been through all this before."

"And we'll go through it again. Where were you employed before that?"

"At Number 6, Bellevue Court."

"For how long were you employed there?"

"For 30 years."

"For whom did you work?"

"Sir Kobe Plane."

"When did you start working for Mr. Plane?"

"I entered his service when I was 25, in 1896."

"And remained in that post until he died?"

"Yes."

"And then?"

"I was dismissed."

"By whom?"

"Karla. I mean, Mrs. Plane."

"Date?"

"October 1926."

"Why were you dismissed?"

"She said she could no longer afford my services."

"Did you leave on good terms?"

For a moment the butler hesitated.

"Yes, or no?"

"Yes," the butler said.

"You are sure?"

"Yes."

"Good enough for her to give you a key to her house, quote 'so you could pop in for a chat?'"

"Yes."

"You are sure she gave you the key?"

"Yes."

"Do you know Mrs. Sarah Lister?"

"The housekeeper? Yes, of course."

"She was employed at No.6 Bellevue Court at the same time as you?"

"Yes."

"How would you characterise Mrs. Lister?"

"'Characterise?'"

"Was she strict?"

"Yes."

"Fair?"

"Yes."

"Honest?"

"Yes."

"So, you would believe her if she said, and I quote from her testimony, 'He used to be the butler here and kept a key to this house. I don't think Mrs. Plane had the nerve to ask for it back.'"

Silence.

"Let me ask you again, did Mrs. Plane give you the key?"

Silence.

"I will take that as a 'no'. You kept the key. Why?"

Silence.

"Do you know Marjorie Bassett?"

"The cook? Yes."

"How would you characterise Mrs. Bassett?"

"Her cooking?"

"No. As a person."

"A very decent person."

"Believable?"

"Yes."

"So, if she said, and again I quote from her testimony, "Old Jason, coming and going like he owned the place', you would believe her?"

Silence.

"You kept a key and came and went as you pleased. You also stated, quote 'As Sir Kobe's manservant I think I knew him better than anyone else, including his two wives. There are things that are said in the intimacy of helping a man dress and undress everyday which are close to being confessional.' And, as an example, you said, quote 'Would you believe he wanted me to inherit half his estate?' Why did you say that was 'confessional'?"

"What someone puts in his will is scarcely public knowledge," the butler said.

"Granted. But you then added, quote 'I told him it would not be appropriate. What would I do with a fortune? I explained to him that I was well off with all he had paid me over the years' which was 'moot since you were a witness to the will he made in favour of Karla.' If it was moot, why did you mention it?"

Silence.

"You claim that whenever you travelled abroad with Mr. Plane, quote 'He would ask my opinion about everything that interested him, from art to wine, and particularly regarding the people he met.' Did he ask you for your opinion of Karla Pinard, as she was then?"

"Yes."

"And you said...?"

"I thought she was charming, but very young."

"30 is scarcely very young."

"Sir Kobe was 73, a difference of 43 years. By comparison she was young."

"Given she was born the same year you entered into Plane's employ, I grant you, she was young. And you were what, 55?"

"Yes."

"So the difference between you and Karla was only 25 years. By comparison, was she still young?"

Silence.

"You said, quote, 'I doubt a more beguiling woman existed. She was totally innocent of the effect she had on men...no, not innocent, more like unaware.' Did she have such an effect on you, Mr Fleet, of which you were aware?"

Silence.

"You claim, quote 'Nobody here knew the late Mrs. Plane better than I did' and also, quote 'I became her confidante.' If you were her confidante and if no one knew her better than you, how do you explain the reaction of the honest Mrs. Lister when asked if you and Karla were close, I quote, 'Don't be foolish, Mr.Brady.'?"

"Sour grapes. She and I did not get on. I think she resented my intimacy with Mrs. Plane."

"What about Miss Malone? Did you 'get on' with her?"

"Of course. Everyone did."

"Is she to be trusted?"

"More than anyone in that house."

"Really?"

"Yes."

"So, when she was asked, quote, 'Was there something going on between them?' she said, 'Karla and the butler? You've got to be kidding!' her answer is to be trusted?"

Silence.

"What was your reaction on learning Mrs. Plane would inherit what had been previously bequeathed to you?"

Silence.

"You say, quote, "I looked out for her' and 'she had few friends here in America.'"

"It's true."

"Yet in the same paragraph you say, quote, 'But I can tell you this, somebody was in that house who should not have been there.'"

"It's true. There was."

"And you went on to say, quote, 'I let myself in. When you've lived in a house for over 30 years you know every little detail, right down to which door cannot be opened without the hinge squeaking and the stair runner that is always out of whack.'"

"You're taking what I said out of context!"

"Am I? Quote, 'Even in the dark. Imagine my surprise then, when I found the toilet on the second floor had been recently used.' I put it to you, Mr. Fleet, it was you in the house. You who used the toilet that left, quote, "A lingering smell…Just the faintest whiff.' The whiff of you, the murderer…"

Which is when he woke up. Case solved! He'd solved it! He couldn't wait to tell Molly…as…as the dream vanished…a swirl of smoke dissipating in a breeze…disappearing where only the hippocampus could track it stored between his brain cells…there was a detail…desperately he tried to grasp it. It was important. It came and went. Damn. His mind was nearly blank when it came back to him, and he lurched out of bed to find a pencil and paper. He wrote 'butler said he was well-off - ask Molly.'

+ + + +

"Christ!" the Sheriff said when he saw him in the morning. "You look like you slept under a truck."

Brady was too embarrassed to mention his dream, so he said, "I didn't sleep very well. But I thought of something. Do you remember in his interview, Jason mentioned being well-off? Well, I asked Molly this morning if that was the case. She said 'Jason? Well-off? You must be joking. He was always skint, him and his gambling.' Apparently, he was addicted to gambling, betting on horses, football, even boxing. It was meant to be a secret, but the staff knew because the bookies from Providence would call looking for him and they had to say he was busy and couldn't be reached but would call back."

"Christ!" the Sheriff said again. "If he was in hock to that lot - what does she mean by skint?"

"She's from Ireland. It's slang for having no money. Perhaps we should check Jason's bank account?" Brady said.

"Get on it. Good work, Brady. Maybe not the smoking gun, but a hammer to crack this guy's nuts." The Sheriff grinned at him. "Way you're going, you'll have my job soon."

Brady blushed.

"Will the DA give us an extension?"

"Not a hope," the Sheriff shook his head. "His mind's made up. Case closed. We'll have to run with it in our own time when the Roberts get back with their butler. Probably when the season opens, the end of May, beginning of June. Keep it under your hat."

"You plan on interrogating him on your own?" Brady was wide-eyed.

"Who said anything about an interrogation?"

"Then-?"

"Stop dreaming, Brady. You heard the DA. No interrogation, no harassment."

"Well then, how-?"

The Sheriff winked. "There are more ways than one to catch a fish."

But what if there was no fish to catch?

+   +   +   +

On his return to Newport that summer, Jacob Roberts was given the message by the maid and promptly telephoned the Sheriff. The Sheriff asked to speak to the butler.

"He's gone," Jacob Roberts said. "Wretched man retired - handed in his resignation in Palm Beach. He said he was too old to go on and I should find someone younger. Damn nuisance, as if I didn't have enough problems."

"Did he leave a forwarding address?" the Sheriff said.

"No. He hopped off as soon as he collected his wages. Most unprofessional I must say, and something I would never have suspected Jason to do. My wife, Helen, is livid."

"Your wife-?"

"She hired him on the recommendation of that woman who was murdered last year, Plane's widow. It's a scandal no one has been arrested yet."

When he hung up with Roberts, the Sheriff nodded to himself. It was a scandal. And now the chief suspect had vanished. In Florida? He shrugged. Can't win 'em all.

+   +   +   +

A HOUSE ON THE FRINGE OF A
SWAMP, BISCAYNE BAY, FLORIDA

The worn lettering on the weathered wooden sign could just be made out - Senior Care: We Set the Standard. Rooms to Let. For some reason all the capitals had flaked off, but their ghostly shadows remained, pale negatives on the timber. Behind the sign was an equally worn building with a balding lawn littered with dog turds in front of it. The two mangy collies responsible for this desecration watched from the shade of the awning over the front steps as the elderly man walked up and rang the bell.

The caretaker, in keeping with the general decor, was a faded woman in her late fifties, Mrs. Mildred Dane. She was an alcoholic who smoked three packets of cigarettes a day, but vicariously enjoyed enforcing the sign on her desk which said in bold white letters on a red ground - NO SMOKING. NO ALCOHOL IN ROOMS. From where she sat behind her desk, she could also see the man behind the screened door.

"It's open!" she shouted, the fag end of a Marlboro dangling from her lower lip.

The man came in with one suitcase. Clean, well-dressed, shoes polished, not drunk. What was he doing in a pit like this?

"Yeah?" she said, peering at him through a cloud of smoke.

"You have a room?" he said.

"Is the Pope a Catholic?" she said. "You read the sign? No booze. No ciggys."

284

"Okay," the man said. "What's the cheapest you've got."

On a month-to-month she rented him a room at the back of the building she rarely managed to rent. "Do not open the window," she said.

At the far end of a narrow corridor, opposite an arrow painted on the wall along with the word TOILET, was the door to the room. It had a single bed and a chair. By way of decor, it had a copy of the red and white sign on her desk nailed to the wall, and a wire beneath the sign stretched between two brackets on which hung three metal hangers. Through the grime of one window facing the bay could be seen a tangle of dilapidated factories and industrial plants. Even closed, the smell of raw sewage from untreated runoff pouring into the swamp's polluted waters came freely through the cracked caulking around the window.

There was no air-conditioning. A leaflet on the threadbare pillowcase touted the personalised attention and peace of mind of residents who obeyed house rules and offered this advice: 'You'll find the Miami lifestyle you've always dreamed of, and the convenience to enjoy the best life has to offer, right here!'

"Guy must be on the lam, take a room like that," Mrs. Dane said to her husband, the janitor, over dinner that evening. She repeated this observation to the journalist from the Miami Herald who came to interview her after their lodger was found dead.

Murdered.

+ + + +

That was in 1932, the year Roosevelt beat Hoover in a landslide and became president on a platform that promised to pull America back from the brink of economic disaster. "I pledge you, I pledge myself, to a new deal for the American people" the President-Elect said, in that nasal Bostonian accent peculiar to him.

"New Deal, my ass," Mr. Dane said.

He and his wife were listening to the radio in their two-room flat on the second floor of the house that November 8th, when the gunshot interrupted the evening broadcast.

"The fuck was that?" Mrs. Dane said, ash from her cigarette spilling onto her bosom.

That was the end of their tenant in the back room on the ground floor. A man who kept to himself, had no visitors, neither smoked nor drank, did whatever small jobs he could find amid the thousands of destitute people flooding into Florida competing for those same small jobs and, somehow, always paid his rent on time for the smelly accommodation in which he'd lived for a record 691 days, longer than any tenant they had ever had.

All this she told the cops.

When the stiff was carted off to the morgue it was early the following morning, and it was three more days after that that the police tape came off the door and the janitor was finally allowed in to try and wash off the blood that had splashed on the floorboards and across one wall of the room that was so difficult to rent.

As written by the diligent journalist, the piece for the Herald was replete with these details, but a sub-editor saw fit to cut out what he thought was fancy folderol, and what the retired Sheriff read in his cottage on the Portsmouth waterfront was a short filler, circled in blue ink, at the bottom of the second last page.

MURDER ON THE LAGOON

September 11, 1932 - Miami-Dade County - A man was found murdered yesterday in a retirement home at the junction of Biscayne Bay with Dumbfoundling Bay. Police said that deep wounds to the face and body of the man had evidently been made with an ice-pick, but that the man had been bludgeoned with a heavy metal bar and died from a fractured skull. He was also shot. The man was registered as Mr. Tom Jones, but the police believe this to be an alias.

It was the 34th homicide of the year in Dade County, an improvement on the 41 of the year precedent.'

Below, a handwritten tag, in the same blue ink, said **'Für Karla!'**

The newspaper, posted from an address in Tampa, was addressed to him at the police station in Newport, from where it had been forwarded.

Six months into his retirement, a woollen scarf wrapped around his neck against a cold storm coming in from the Atlantic, the Sheriff had been in the yard talking to the Smyths about getting a dog to keep him company when the mailman saw him and gave him the newspaper package. After reading what it contained, he called his protégé.

"Got something to show you, Brady," he said. "Come by for dinner with that new wife of yours and tell her don't forget to bring some wine. She chooses. I pay."

+   +   +   +

Thomas and Molly Brady came to a warm welcome. A crackling fire in the living room and the delicious smell of Irish stew. Nothing of

287

importance was said over dinner, the Bradys coy in the bliss of newlyweds, the Sheriff mindful not to be too curious. With the last of the wine in their glasses, the trio settled into the comfort of the armchairs and sofa facing the hearth.

"How's it going at the Station?" the Sheriff said.

"Can't complain. The usual," Thomas said.

"He always says that" Molly said. "Never tells me anything. Then I read in the papers how he's caught a gang of cat burglars raiding empty houses."

Brady blushed. Shrugged. "Small stuff for the Sheriff."

Even retired, the Sheriff was the Sheriff. No way Brady could call him Mr. Brenton, leave alone by his Christian name, Harold. Harry. Harry Brenton. No, no way. He was the Sheriff. Brady had been made Deputy on the Sheriff's recommendation, the resulting promotion allowing him to move from the small station in Jamestown to Newport, with a concomitant raise in salary. Just what was needed to get married and qualify for a mortgage to purchase a tiny clapboard painted pale yellow at the far end of Thames Street on the corner with Lee, where, from the second floor, you had an uninterrupted view of Newport Harbour. It wasn't Planetree, but it was home. His blush deepened. Molly was pregnant. It didn't show yet, but she had made him promise he would not tell the Sheriff. To change the subject, he said, "You know the DA lost the election?"

"Yeah. I heard," the Sheriff said.

"New guy's very much by the book."

"They all start that way. Life grinds 'em down."

"It didn't you."

"More than you think."

"You miss the game?"

"Yeah. It all seems so long ago. Retirement sucks. I thought it would give me time to write, but I find that having all this time I don't write a word. No pressure. I wake up feeling deflated." The Sheriff shrugged. "An empty paper bag."

Silence.

Then, unexpectedly, Molly said, "I think I know exactly how you feel. I often feel the same since leaving Planetree."

In winding up the estate of the deceased, Karla Plane, the executor had dismissed the staff from Planetree House, auctioned the contents, then closed the mansion and put it on the market for sale.

"Luckily I'm pregnant," Molly said. "Soon as I'm a Mom I'll have no time to think."

Thomas stared at his wife breaking her own taboo.

"What? You think he hasn't guessed?" Molly looked down at her stomach, up at her husband, then to the Sheriff, back to her husband and back to the Sheriff. "You knew when I came in the door, right?"

The Sheriff pretended to squirm.

"It was the way you carried yourself. As if protecting something," he said.

"See?" Molly said to Thomas. "Not surprising he became Sheriff."

She smiled at her husband, then turned to his mentor. "He's too shy to ask why we are here?" she said. "But I'm not. Is it about Karla?"

"Yes," the Sheriff said, and showed them the newspaper.

They were stunned.

"Jason? Murdered?" Brady said. "Just like she was?"

The Sheriff nodded. "I think so," he said. "Exactly like she was."

"And the killer? The guy with the bonds? The lover?" Brady said.

The Sheriff nodded again.

"After all this time he tracked him down? Incredible! How did he do it?"

"Just as he said he would if we didn't."

"Why's he misspelt 'for' with a 'u'?" Molly said.

"I don't think it is misspelt. I think it's deliberately written in German; look at those dots on the 'u', that's an umlaut," the Sheriff said. He then stood up and walked about, touching things as was his habit when thinking. "You better call the deputy in charge down in Dade," he told Thomas. "Find out if there's more to the story. Have him send a picture, make sure it really is Jason."

The Sheriff paused.

"And then?" Brady said. "Go after the killer?"

"Then you think it through," the Sheriff said. "And you ask yourself this - has justice been served?"

+ + + +

Molly offered to help with the dishes before they left, but the Sheriff said no, no, he had his way of doing things, it was late, she needed to rest. When the Bradys had gone, he cleaned up, alone with his thoughts in his empty house.

Karla.

If he had been asked a minute before the postman handed him the newspaper, when had he last thought of Karla - if he was honest - what could be the point of not being honest? - he would have to say at least a year.

Karla, whom he never met but who had filled his mind every waking hour for eighteen months. Karla, butchered by a madman. Jason? Mad? What could explain such rage? Karla. The answer lay with her.

Karla.

The washing up finished; the Sheriff sits down to stare at the dying embers in the grate. In every case there are threads left dangling. If all the protagonists are dead, how do you get an answer, leave alone an explanation? Should he worry about it? Not his problem anymore. Thank the Lord. He can't sit still. Gets up again. Walks around. Touches things. Thinks.

Three years ago, she was alive. Hoover was president. Six years ago, she married. Coolidge was president. Three years after her death, FDR. And in between, the absolute destruction of American prosperity. Not to forget his retirement from the Force. Thank God for my pension. And feels ashamed. Cliché or not, time does march on. Even if it was long ago, how could he have forgotten her for over a year? Because she was dead? And there's nothing you can do about that except forget. Or nail the killer. Her killer. He catches sight of the Miami Herald which Brady forgot to take when they left. It lies open on the sofa.

Für Karla ringed in blue.

Justice? Or revenge. Did it matter? Whoever the man was the Sheriff could not help but feel something. Admiration? How in the name of sweet Jesus did he track him down in a Florida swamp? Which is when the telephone rings.

+   +   +   +

Of all people, it is the Secretary from the Reading Room calling.

"Sorry to disturb you at this hour, Sheriff. Have you a moment?" He sounds anxious.

"How may I help?" the Sheriff says.

"We have just finished dinner. One of our guests mentioned you. Mrs. Bassett? Do you recall she used to be the cook at Planetree House? She is a dear friend of my wife. They were discussing that awful murder back in '29, when Mrs. Bassett and a couple of others found that woman beaten to death in her dining room."

"I remember it well," the Sheriff says.

"The killer was never caught I believe?"

"Yes, that's right."

"Mrs. Bassett said you were at a dead end and…"

"You do know I'm no longer on the force?" the Sheriff interrupts.

"Yes," the Secretary says. "But another of our guests, a member here, is a medical man, a psychiatrist. He has some interesting insight into violence. He would like to meet you if you're up to it?"

"I've retired," the Sheriff says.

"Maybe from the police," the Secretary says. "But you are still that curious man of letters gumming up our bulletin board. If I may be so bold, *that* man would meet our medico because I am certain *that* man could not, cannot, possibly be satisfied with leaving a legacy of such an unsolved case on his watch."

Which is known as hitting the nail on the head. So, the Sheriff agreed.

+   +   +   +

291

As was his wont, the Sheriff walked the 10 miles to Newport for his meeting the following morning in the lounge of the Reading Room, where the Secretary made the introductions, ordered them some coffee, and then withdrew.

Dr. Jameson was a head taller than the Sheriff and ten years older. A man all in grey, from his hair to his beard, to his tweed suit, to his waistcoat across which depended a silver watch chain, to his grey socks and shoes. In vivid contrast, his tanned hands and face were those of a veteran sailor.

"I am a fan of yours, Sheriff Brenton," he said, shaking hands. "I bought your little book of poems, and it would give me great pleasure if you would oblige me by signing my copy."

With a flourish he produced the book and a pen, offering both to the Sheriff.

"You sure?" the Sheriff said.

"Yes," Dr. Jameson said.

The Sheriff signed, striking out his printed name on the title page and carefully appending his signature below.

"Thank you," Dr. Jameson said, recovering book and pen. "You have a most interesting way with words. I don't say it to flatter you, but as an observation."

"They have a singular importance," the Sheriff said with a smile.

"Indeed," Dr. Jameson said. "How would you distinguish between psychiatry and psychology?"

"One requires the training of a medical doctor, the other does not."

"Very succinct. Between the two, which discipline would you trust the most?"

"Psychiatry."

"Why?"

"One is objective, the other subjective."

"Can you elaborate?"

"Elaborate?" Again, the Sheriff smiled. "Is this a test, Doctor?"

"Humour me," Jameson said.

"You need a medical degree to be a psychiatrist, to diagnose illness and prescribe drugs for the treatment of complex serious mental illness. Psychologists, even if they have a PhD, basically just listen, and talk and call it psychotherapy. I don't say it to flatter you, but as an observation."

Now it was Dr. Jameson's turn to smile.

"Let us try two other words. Sociopathy and psychopathy."

"Both are antisocial," the Sheriff said, "but share many common traits. The main distinction is lack of empathy and remorse in the psychopath, with an inclination to manipulation and violence, while the sociopath cannot tell right from wrong and is indifferent to the pain and feelings of others."

"Who then would be more likely to identify these traits and differences, the psychiatrist or the psychologist?"

For a long moment the Sheriff was silent. He took the time to sip his coffee. Finally, he said, "I am out of my depth. I cannot answer you intelligently. You are better equipped than I am, so you must have the answer or you would not ask the question."

"I only ask because of what Mrs. Bassett said, that the one thing you could not understand was the extreme violence used by the murderer in the Planetree case."

Dr. Jameson fingered his watch chain like a monk with prayer beads.

"As a psychiatrist let me preface my remarks by saying there is no perfect answer. We know, as you have correctly remarked, that sometimes there is an overlay between the behaviour of a sociopath and that of a psychopath, a grey area difficult to define, so much so that in the same person you can find traits of both, weighted one way or the other dependant on multiple factors. Only a small fraction of people, probably less than 1% of the population, suffer from this condition and very few are murderers.

In broad brushstrokes you may picture a psychopath as having superficial charm, leading a semblance of normal life, adroit at pretending to feel emotions the better to conceal a lack of guilt or remorse for their actions. They tend to be socially successful, are often narcissistic, with a grandiose sense of self-worth, but have real difficulty in forming any kind of emotional attachment. Sociopaths tend to be more erratic, rage-prone, and have difficulty leading a normal life, with poor self-control. They are pathological liars, skilled at deception, often of themselves. But they may form close attachments to one person or a few individuals. Whatever their intelligence - and some are very, very intelligent - both suffer from poor judgement and a complete lack of shame."

Dr. Jameson paused.

"I know I sound pedantic. I hope I'm not boring you?" he said.

"On the contrary," the Sheriff said, "I wish I'd met you three years ago."

"I am told Mrs. Plane was very beautiful."

"I never knew her alive. But there was a painting of her in the library of that house and if she was anything like the painting, she must have been a real beauty. Sadly, it was slashed to pieces."

"The culprit?"

"Unknown, but more than likely the murderer."

"I would not be surprised," Dr. Jameson said. "It never pays to generalise, but from what I read in the newspapers and from Mrs. Bassett's description, the injuries suffered by Mrs. Plane suggest an assailant demented with rage, out of control, determined not just to kill but to extinguish the very being of his victim?"

"That is correct."

"Have you heard of Vollmer? August Vollmer?"

"Of course. Required reading when I was a recruit if you wanted to be a detective."

"Do you recall his maxim? 'In murders of extreme passion, the killer will always betray his pathology.' Envisage a man besotted by a woman. For whatever reason he cannot have her. In his mind such a thing is impossible. But if he cannot have her, then nobody can. He plots her destruction. He cannot help himself. But in killing her he also kills himself. He kills that notion of his omnipotent self. Do you see what I am suggesting?"

"Perhaps…"

"Perhaps the man is enraged, enraged at himself for what he is doing, so enraged he cannot stop himself slashing her picture even though she's dead?"

"We thought he was looking for something."

"Perhaps he was? His better self?" Dr. Jameson shrugged. "Of course, what I say does not in any way condone what was done. I only say it for you to better understand why it was done."

"So what is he? Psychopath or sociopath?"

"Both."

+   +   +   +

On the long walk back home to his cottage in Portsmouth the Sheriff walked alone. Alone with his thoughts. Thoughts of how inadequate he was. How could he not have seen it? In his head, the Sheriff runs a movie of what he imagines happened.

CLOSE UP of Karla, naked, staring at her bedroom door.

She is bent forward, straining to listen, as she approaches the door.

No sound. She puts her ear to the door. Nothing.

She reaches out her hand to turn the doorknob.

Fearfully, very slowly, she starts to open the door - No! - She freezes, she senses -

What?

Someone behind the door? She throws it open.

JASON!

Staring at her.

She screams.

He reaches out to stop her. Why is she screaming? At him? Why?

His hand closes -

On her throat!

She wrenches herself away, ducks past him, runs for the stairs screaming

Chased by the butler grabbing for her, tearing her hair out

Down the stairs

She runs desperately for her life

The gun! She remembers the gun. Must get the gun.

She nearly falls at the bottom of the stairs, scrambles up, runs

Her feet cold on the marble floor of the Great Hall, she

Runs, runs for her life through the adjoining reception rooms, the music room, the

Dining room, the stairs? Must get to the stairs

The stairs down to the kitchen with him gaining on her, grabbing at her back

Because he knows where she is headed - the gun in the mudroom!

Through the kitchen - the impossible image of Karla, naked, NAKED! - running

Through her own kitchen to the pantry beyond and she feels a flash of pain

And blood - HER BLOOD! - spurting from her shoulder as he slashes at her with

A meat cleaver snatched up from where it lay on the butcher's block next to the little

Door - the little door to the mudroom which she somehow manages to fling open

There it is - the loaded gun - she goes for it - has it in her hand - turns to shoot

BUT he's on her - they fight - he wrenches the gun away - she runs BAM!

The heavy bullet knocks her off her feet - incredibly she gets up, makes it back

Through the kitchen, blood everywhere, back up the stairs, trying to run

Into the dining room, she can hear him yelling - something - and then a tremendous

Explosion of pain as he smashes her down

Beats her to pulp with an iron bar…

The Sheriff stops walking. Closes his eyes. Tries to shut off the film running in his head.

+ + + +

Two days later Brady called.

"I spoke to the Deputy in charge down in Dade. From the photographs he sent, the victim is definitely Jason. Other than that, they don't have much. A few interviews with people who hired him for odd jobs. Nothing suspicious. Nobody saw anyone enter his room. Nothing in his room appears to have been taken, not that there was much to take. Only odd note in what the Dep called his fleapit, was his butler's uniform hanging on a metal hanger. Apparently immaculately cleaned and pressed, ready to go." Brady said. He cleared his throat. "They want to know what we intend to do?"

"Don't ask me," the Sheriff said. "I'm retired. Ask the new guy, your DA."

+ + + +

ON DIVORCE, DEMOLITION AND A VOYAGE

1933

7² years old, Jacob Roberts, is eating oysters at his usual table in what used to be The Viceroy Hotel but is now the Delmonico, on the corner of 59th and Park. Regrettably for his peace and comfort, he is accompanied by his wife, Helen. She has just come from her hairdresser on Madison, loaded with the latest gossip which she delivers with the same relish with which she is chomping through her steak.

"Guess what? Your friend Baxter's getting the chop."

"Where'd you hear that?"

"That hysterically jealous wife of his, has given evidence in their divorce…"

"Baxter? You're sure?"

"Yes. You never listen to me. I told you a week ago at dinner with the McCarthys, she caught him shacked up with some floosie in that place he has on Park. As if that wasn't bad enough, she accused him of having stacks of gold coins and she wants her share. Now the Revenue Service wants to know how he got the gold. He's been asked to resign from his bank and if he doesn't go quietly, he gets the chop."

Chomp. Chomp.

"You going to say something?"

Chomp. Chomp.

"Yes." Jacob Roberts says.

Silence.

"Well, what?" Helen says.

"You see that man sitting at that table over there with the pretty girl? That's Baxter and his floosie, Lady Nancy Allden. I'm going to invite them to our table for a drink."

Helen gapes at her husband.

"When they come, I will congratulate him on being made partner in his bank and you will invite him and his floosie to dinner. With 3000 bank failures and 15,000,000 people out of work, we are among the fortunate few who can still afford to celebrate." Jacob Roberts signals a waiter to carry his invitation across the room. "Do close your mouth before they get here, my dear. It is very unbecoming."

+ + + +

That same week, the Newport Council issued a demolition order for the Van Hals mansion on Bellevue Court, citing its dangerous structural decay. The contractors appointed to do the work clear the site and discover, concealed under the remains of an ancient bonfire in the driveway, what they describe as a burial pit. In the ashes are a badly rusted ice-pick, a crowbar, melted brass buttons and the frame of a burnt-out handgun. None of it has any value and it is all loaded into a skip headed for the city dump.

Jimmy, nearly 15 by then and big for his age, is part of the demolition crew and has taken to scavenging items to help his Ma if he chances to find something he thinks will sell in the weekly flea market on Bowen's Wharf. He thinks the ice-pick will clean up nicely and that he can make a wooden stock to fit the gun frame. He rescues both items from the skip. He makes six bucks.

+ + + +

In the late summer of 1933, it fell to Steve Masry to make the journey to France, first by boat to Le Havre, then by train to Paris and onwards to Lyon, Gap and Briançon, the terminus in the Alps on the Italian frontier. It is Masry's first voyage abroad. He does not speak a word of French and he is accompanied by a bi-lingual envoy from the French Foreign Office. At their destination they are met by the mayor who warns them that the old lady they will meet is in fragile health and must not be alarmed. Masry cannot help but wonder if inheriting a major fortune can be considered alarming. The documents he carries will make her the richest person in town - probably in the department, maybe richer than anyone living in the Alps.

"Que voulez-vous que je fasse avec tout ça?" the old lady says.

"What would you have me do with all this?" the envoy translates.

"Please tell her if she doesn't want it, she doesn't have to do anything," Stephen Masry says.

So, the old lady gives half to the Catholic Church in memory of her daughter, Karla, and her long departed sons, Henri and Louis, and half to the French Communist Party on behalf of her dear, dead husband, Gaston. The gifts should be tax free, but the State contends, on various contentious interpretations of the law, that death duties of 40% are due. The ensuing battle between Church and State will keep the law courts busy and enrich the lawyers for many years to come.

In September, on his way back to America, Masry briefly enjoys being a passenger on a ship in mid-Atlantic trapped in a Category-4 hurricane that starts as a tropical storm off the Lesser Antilles, turns north-northwest with wind speeds steadily intensifying to reach 225 km/h as it nears North Carolina, slows briefly as it turns due north on its way west of Cape Hatteras and the Outer Banks, before accelerating halfway between Cape Cod and the southern tip of Nova Scotia. It then degenerates into an extratropical storm over Labrador and finally dissipates east of Greenland. Arriving miraculously safe in New York Harbour, the Captain of the battered vessel relays radio reports received of 21 dead and millions in damages left in the wake of the storm.

Disembarking, Steven Masry wonders if he will ever again live so intensely.

+   +   +   +

AN ARTICLE IN THE NEWPORT
GAZETTE

Along with a fraternity of like-minded hobos, Kale and Lake were camped in the shuttered, overgrown grounds of Planetree House, now empty, for sale, with no buyers in sight thanks to the economy. They were squatting the Carriage House and were trying to light a fire in what used to be the staff's common room where many of the broken windows had cardboard instead of glass to keep out the drafts coming in off Narragansett Bay. There was no furniture. The bums used beer-crates and bricks straddled by termite riddled planks to sit on. As usual, Lake was working and Kale was reading.

"Listen up," Kale said. "You guys won't believe this. '50 years ago, in 1880, Newport County had a population of 15,000 and Los Angeles 11,000. Today we're at 27,612, and LA has 1,238,000.'"

"Bullshit," one of the bums said. "Where'd you get those numbers?"

"It says it here: 'The United States census of 1930, conducted by the Census Bureau for one month from April 1, 1930, determined the resident population of the United States to be 122,775,046, an increase of 13.7 percent over the 1920 census.' It's broken down by cities. Boston goes from 360,000 to 781,000. New York from 1,206,000 to 5,620,000."

"So what?"

"So what? We live in the wrong part of the country, asshole, that's what. We might have us some work, 'stead of rotting in a dump like this. Now just shut up and listen: 'August 4th. The 1934 challenger for the America's Cup, England's J-class boat, *Endeavour*, owned by T.O.M.

Sopwith, entered by the Royal Yacht Squadron, built for a reported $1.000.000, has set sail for Newport with a crew half of whom are amateurs after the professionals went on strike for more pay. Can you believe that?"

"Yeah, I can," Lake said. "Any guy who spends a million bucks to build his boat is not living in this world. If he's got that kind of bread to shell out for a lousy boat, everyone around him is going to want some. Doesn't matter what he gives 'em, they'll want more. Anyway, give me that. I need it to light the fire."

"I haven't finished reading," Kale said with some dignity.

"For fuck's sake, Kale. We're goin' to freeze in here. Give me the paper."

"You're so impatient," Kale said. "Why don't you just listen? 'After leaving Gosport, England, on July 23, they sailed for the Azores, leaving there on the 29th, and today report a fine day's run of some 284 nautical miles. They are expected to make landfall in Newport on August 8.' Wow. That's tomorrow. Fifteen days to get across the pond. Darn good going for a bunch of amateurs –"

Which is when his brother snatched the paper from out of his hands, balled it up, shoved it under the kindling he had prepared, struck a match, and set fire to it.

Without a word, Kale took another paper from the pocket of his jacket.

"You going to burn the Journal too?" he said.

"Fuck you," Lake said.

"You've got a great vocabulary. You know that, right?"

ACKNOWLEDGMENTS

My thanks to John Forbess for his legal expertise. Any mistakes in understanding and interpreting the law are mine.

To my daughter Pascale, and sons Erik and Alexander, for their support and encouragement - Merci!

To Walt (polarbear19325 @ Fiverr) for the interior design and layout, and to Angie (pro_ebookcovers @ Fiverr) for the cover design - thank you for your skill and patience in making this book.

The White Horse Tavern, the Black Pearl, and the Café de l'Époque are real. The people in them are fictitious.

The Murder at Midnight

The theory of the murder at midnight is as follows: M. DuPont, a man out for a late walk with his dog, finds a body in a field, a dagger in its back. Within a minute he rushes home to tell his wife. Within a minute this alarmed lady calls the neighbours, Monsieur and Madame Durand, to warn them.

'Did you call the cops?' Durand says.

'No,' she says.

'Don't worry, I'll do it. I know the Inspector,' he says. And in that same minute, his wife calls her ancient mother in the nursing home where they have placed her, to tell her: 'Lock the door to your bedroom.'

Within the next minute, the policeman, Inspector Petit, none too pleased at being woken up so late, nevertheless calls the station to tell the duty officer, Sergeant Dubois, to organize an investigation, and Dubois, within a minute, duly informs the gendarme on the late shift at the gendarmerie, Adjudant Leroy, who, on receiving the call, feels obliged, within the minute, to inform his superior, Adjudant-Chef Moreau, who is in bed with his mistress.

She asks why the fuss? But within the minute it takes her lover to tell her not to worry her pretty head, the old lady in the nursing home has already called the two elderly women either side of her room to tell them to lock their doors.

'There's a murderer outside.'

Within a minute, one of them, Madame Bonpoint, calls the Superintendent, Monsieur Langlois, to complain about the threat and he in turn tells his colleague, Monsieur Ségor, seated next to him at the booking desk, what a pain the old ladies are banging on about murderers next door, which conversation Ségor repeats a minute later to his mother, three times zones away in St.Barth, when he has her on the telephone.

Within a minute of hanging up with her son, this worthy calls her daughter, Mathilde, a student at USC Los Angeles, another four time zones away, to tell her to be careful with all these murderers going around, and the two girls who share a dorm in the University with Mathilde, Lucy Lee, from Singapore, and Amy Miyoko, from Osaka, overhear the conversation and, within a minute, call their families back home to say there was a murder at midnight and to be careful.

By simple multiplication, with each recipient of this information informing two others within a minute, within 20 minutes 5242 people knew, within 25 minutes 167,772 people knew, within 30 minutes 5,368,709 knew, and a minute later 10,737,418, and 3 minutes later, only 34 minutes after Dupont first saw the body, the entire population of France, all 66 million people, knew there had been a murder at midnight. By 1am all of Europe knew, and by 2am the entire world. The last to know was a tribal chief in New Guinea who heard on the bush telegraph that a man in France had eaten his wife in his own backyard.

The moral of the story is that tiny numbers become very big when multiplied by themselves. So if any one of you has enjoyed reading my novel, told two friends - go buy this book, you will enjoy it - and they in turn told two friends...etc., etc....we could be cooking up a literary storm by tomorrow morning.